Accidental GROOM

DANA MASON

Bookouture

Published by Bookouture in 2019

An imprint of StoryFire Ltd.

Carmelite House
50 Victoria Embankment
London EC4Y 0DZ

www.bookouture.com

ISBN: 978-1-78681-855-3
eBook ISBN: 978-1-78681-854-6

For Michelle. Thank you for your never-ending enthusiasm and support.

PROLOGUE

Mackensey

She's simultaneously the saddest and the most striking thing I've ever seen. With her knees up to her chest, she's perched sideways on the bench, talking on her cell phone… and absolutely crying her eyes out.

I'm waiting to order my coffee and from where I'm standing, she's hard to miss and impossible not to stare at.

What the hell could have upset her so much? Or *who* could have upset her so badly? And how is it that no one else has noticed her? The woman's eyes are the brightest green I've ever seen, and her rosy cheeks only enhance their color. The reason she's crying might be ugly, but she couldn't be called anything short of beautiful, crying or not.

It's hard to watch her, but I can't look away either. Is she waiting for the bus or did she just stop for a good cry? My stomach turns because it's killing me, yet I can't stop staring. I'm glued to the spot with a lump forming in my throat. Maybe I should go check on her, find out who did this, and kick his ass. Jesus! Could a man have hurt her? I squint to get a better look. She doesn't seem physically hurt and she doesn't seem scared… she looks sad. As if she's just lost her whole world.

When her eyes dart toward me, I turn quickly, and immediately feel guilty for staring at her. The line shifts forward and I take the chance to glance outside again. Tears are streaming down her pink cheeks and she's talking at a rapid pace. Maybe she's fighting with someone?

"What can I get you?" the barista asks, pulling my attention.

"Grande Americano, please." I scan my app to pay and turn, hoping to find a seat. I luck out and find an empty table facing the window. Sitting down, I watch as another woman approaches the girl and I'm so relieved, I whisper a *thank you*. They talk for a moment and the passer-by offers the green-eyed girl a handful of tissue then waves as she walks away.

Obviously, she's not in danger, but I still want to check on her. When the barista calls my name, I glance at the time and realize if I don't leave now, I'll miss my train. I turn toward the woman and take one last look, hoping whatever she's going through gets easier.

CHAPTER ONE

Mackensey

I rush inside Starbucks but stop abruptly. Jesus. I lean sideways to get a look at the line. Six more people are waiting ahead of me. Good thing I'm not in a hurry. I've already missed the light rail, so there's no point in rushing. What's another twenty minutes?

Scratching the stubble on my chin, I try to calculate if I can make it in time for the next train if I stay in this line. This Starbucks is always so damn crowded. And not your ordinary crowded, either. No, this is crazy.

I peek outside and I'm instantly reminded of last Friday. I stood in line for ten minutes and watched a young woman cry her eyes out at the bus stop outside. I'd thought about her more than once over the last week. The protective streak in me wanted to know what had happened to her, and if she was all right now. What had bothered her so much? Did she lose someone close to her? A broken heart?

As the line shifts forward, my eyes drift to the pick-up counter on the other side, and they land directly on the green eyes I was just thinking about. She's chatting with the hot, red-headed barista, then she nods and picks up her coffee with a smile.

Yeah, a smile.

My pulse picks up when she walks toward the exit. Then it settles when she turns and sits in the recently vacated seat in the corner. I smile, glad she was able to snatch up the desired real estate. If she sticks around, I might try to talk to her.

I take a couple steps forward, trying not to stare at her. She looks happier, or at least, she looks like she hasn't been crying. Her eyes lift to the window, and she stares out for a few seconds before setting her drink down. As she leans forward to slip a laptop out of her backpack, her long hair slides down and blocks my view of her face. She tucks it behind her ear and that's when I notice she's biting her lip, obviously distracted with her own thoughts. When she places her laptop on the table, her eyes lock on something ahead of her and she stares at it for a long moment. Before she looks back to her computer, her lip slips out from between her teeth and her beautifully plump mouth puckers into a pout.

Just like last week, I can't take my eyes off her. She's so contemplative. What's on her mind?

When it's my turn in line, I step up to the counter and order an Americano. The smell of roasted coffee relaxes me as I wait for my drink. I glance around the coffee shop again for a vacant seat and smile at a table of old scholars. They look retirement age, and they're arguing about politics, occasionally raising their voices in passion. There're also several students sitting at single tables working on laptops with earbuds in their ears.

When the barista calls my name, I pick up my Americano and turn to scan the room again. Another small, round table opens up and it's directly across from the green-eyed girl. I rush to occupy it before the couple behind beat me to it.

The green-eyed girl chuckles as I slip into the chair. "Congratulations! You're the envy of the room."

I'm pleasantly surprised when I realize she's speaking to me. I fight to act casual. "This place is crazy every time I come here."

She nods toward the window. "Too near Sacramento State. It's always crowded."

"Yes, *always*." I want to continue the conversation, but her focus drifts back to her laptop.

I stare at her long, dark hair, highlighted with mixed shades of brown. It shimmers in the sunlight as it drifts down her back. Her nose is a perfectly straight line in her profile and complements her oval face. The light-pink dusting on her high cheekbones looks like natural coloring and emphasizes her enchanting green eyes. Her eyes aren't as green as last Friday, but they still stand out against her porcelain skin.

She glances up, forcing me to duck my head. I look at my watch. Very late now. I hate being late but what am I missing, really? Another meeting with Kurt? My producer, Kurt, loves his Friday meetings. I'm not sure why we need to have a recurring meeting every week when we talk about that shit every single day already.

I understand that with the top-rated morning radio show in Sacramento, it's important to keep it fresh and funny—that's Kurt's job. As the show's host, it's my job to entertain the listeners. According to the stats man eighty-seven percent of our morning show listeners are women, and to these women, I'm just an object for them to imagine having a little side action with. Something my producer likes to exploit for ratings. My partner, Mimi, as a wife and mother, is someone the listeners can relate to. Someone they want as a BFF.

We get paid buckets of money, but it comes with a vicious stereotype that I'd usually hate. Being portrayed as a womanizing player wasn't part of my career plan, but I can't complain too much. Most of the women I meet are looking for a good time, not a long time, and that works for me. I'm not interested in playing the other role. I'll leave that to Mimi. Especially since even the short relationships I've had turned out to be disastrous.

The reminder is caustic so I try to shake it away. No. I'm not willing to walk that road again.

So… yeah, late is okay today. Especially since my work day should have already ended. That little troll, Kurt, schedules these stupid Friday meetings in the afternoon and our show ends at 9 a.m. That forces Mimi and me to either stick around for hours at the station or go back to work after we've already left for the day.

I flip open my messenger bag and lift my computer out. When I straighten, I catch someone staring at me from the corner of my eye. I reach into my back pocket for my phone and start dialing Kurt's number. I know what's coming and I need a way to excuse myself from the inevitable conversation.

A young woman, probably a Sac State student, is watching me. "You're Mac, right? From KQCC? *Mimi and Mac in the Morning*?" She's hot. A cute little blonde with a nice rack and a round ass, but I've already got my eye on someone else.

I grin at her and hold up a finger as I lift the phone to my ear. "Hey, Kurt. I'm missing your meeting this afternoon."

"Why? Just get your ass here, we'll wait for you."

"My truck's in the shop today for maintenance, so I'm riding the light rail. I need to pick it up in an hour, and I've still got shit to do this afternoon for my Reno gig tomorrow. Can't you guys meet without me?"

"Why didn't you just take the car?"

"I'm not parking my car in that garage. I told you that. Get me some decent reserved parking, and it won't be a problem."

"Fine, miss the damn meeting, but you're staying late Monday so I can catch you up."

"You got it, boss. See you then." I click the disconnect button and look up to see that Blondie is gone. Good. The phone call worked. I glance to my left to see Green Eyes still sitting next to me.

I boot up my computer and open Gmail, tapping out a message to my sister.

Good morning, Sunshine, thanks for brunch this morning. If I don't see you before next Friday, have a good week. And, no, you can't change your mind about that vacation! Start shopping for deals, you're going.

See you, Mackensey

My sister, Emily, is a complete workaholic. It's probably been three or four years since she's taken a vacation of any kind. Her husband, Tuck, died a few years ago and she's been single-minded about work ever since, throwing herself into her job. She barely has a personal life, so I try to spend as much time with her as I can. I'm pushing her to take a break. I think it'd be a great idea to tour Europe or spend a few days on a beach somewhere.

Once the email is sent, I glance up at Green Eyes again. She's looking around the room with a tight expression on her face.

"Something wrong?" I ask, unable to help myself.

"Ah, no… fine." She glances down at her laptop and closes the lid. Her eyes dart to the bathroom door and then back to the computer.

"I can keep an eye on that for you… if you need a bathroom break."

She looks at me. Hard and assessing. It almost makes me want to laugh, but I'm too fascinated. She has such a strong presence. Her stare focuses so intently, I'm afraid she can reach inside my head and pull the thoughts right out. Good thing I'm not picturing her naked.

"It's okay. Really. I won't… wait." I pull my driver's license out of my wallet. "Here. Collateral." I'm smiling and trying not to sound condescending, especially since she doesn't seem to know who I am, which is rare around here.

Her expression softens as she snatches the license from between my fingers. "Thank you," she whispers and skirts around her table toward the ladies' room. She didn't even look at the ID. That's fine. I don't care if she doesn't recognize me. That's why they call it radio.

My gaze follows her, and I'm taken with how gracefully she moves. Her jeans are ripped at the knees, and cling close, snug against her slender legs and that ass. Damn. A firm ass like that will make you forget your own name.

When she returns from the bathroom, I smirk at her. "Now, don't you feel bad for not trusting me?"

"Thank you very much for watching my laptop," she says and hands back my driver's license. "I appreciate it."

I lift my hands and raise an eyebrow. "Understandable. I wouldn't want to give up my table either." I reach out my hand. "I'm Mac, by the way. Nice to meet you."

She gives me a firm shake. Her touch shoots heat through me, forcing my dick to jerk in my pants. I'm so glad I'm sitting behind a table. I glance down at her hand then back into her eyes. They're friendly now, not so intense.

"Just Mac? Surely that's short for something?" she says.

"You're right. Name is Mackensey, but people usually call me Mac."

"I'm Kelley. Nice to meet you, too. I don't think I've seen you in here—and I'm here a lot."

"Oh, I'm here about once a week. My sister lives nearby, and I have breakfast with her on Fridays. But no, you're right. I live in Midtown. We have our own Starbucks, but it's not quite as busy." I hesitate, trying to decide if I should tell her I saw her last week. "Actually, I was in here last week about the same time, and I think I saw you."

"Oh, funny. I'm usually here on Friday mornings, but I don't remember…" She stops and I can practically see the wheels turning behind her eyes. I watch the change as soon as she realizes and her cheeks grow a shade darker.

"Yeah." I wait a moment then say, "I saw you at the bus stop, right outside. You were upset."

"You saw me? Here?" Her eyes lift back to mine in question.

I'm tempted to let her save face and pretend it wasn't her, but I don't want to look like an idiot who doesn't recognize her. "Yes." I point to the bench at the bus stop outside. "You were talking on your cell phone, and you were crying."

She nods and purses her lips. "You saw that, huh?" She reaches up and tucks a strand of hair behind her ear. "It was a bad day… bad week, actually."

"I noticed." Should I tell her it brought out my inner caveman? Or should I let it rest?

It's probably not a good idea to tell her I was ready to track down and kill the person who'd hurt her. Whatever happened to her must have been pretty bad. People don't cry like that over just anything. "Is there someone I need to beat up for you?"

She looks back at her laptop, and I think maybe she's going to blow me off. But I'm not about to let her go that easily. "I'm sorry. Maybe I shouldn't have said that, but I was worried about you."

Kelley waves casually at me and breathes, "I'm fine. It's fine."

I'm an ass. I shouldn't have put her on the spot like that. Watching her face change from friendly to… God, I'm not even sure how to describe her new expression. Disappointment. Embarrassment. I have a sinking feeling in my stomach and I instantly want to make it up to her. Whatever *it* is.

"Thank you for being worried. I probably should've just stayed home last Friday instead of venturing out in public," she says.

I brush off her apology. "No harm."

Kelley watches me for a moment, then says, "So, are you a student?"

I almost spit out my coffee when I hear this. "Uh, no. I'm a little too old to be a student at Sac State. I work at the radio station, KQCC. Do you listen?"

"Sometimes," she says, and it sounds like she's trying to be polite. "I don't get a lot of time to listen to the radio. When I do listen to music, it's usually Spotify on my phone."

"Spotify? The good old radio DJ killer."

"Oh, no." She lifts her hand to her mouth in horror. "I'm sorry. Is that true?"

I shake my head and chuckle. "I'm only kidding. I feel pretty secure in my job. My listeners seem to like me."

"Good. I'm glad to know I'm not responsible for you possibly losing your job." She drops her hand. "I would hate that."

I peek over at her laptop screen. "So what do you do?"

She raises her eyebrows. "I actually am a student. And yes, I'm probably too old to be one." Her expression makes me think this bothers her. "I've been trying to finish for years but student loans are a killer and, well, life happens."

"I get it. I'm not quite finished paying off my loans yet."

"What do you do at the radio station? You said you're a DJ?"

"Technically, I'm a show host. We don't do a lot of slinging discs these days." I lay a hand on my chest. "I'm Mac from the morning show… *Mimi and Mac in the Morning*. You really don't listen, do you?"

She sucks air through her teeth and says, "No. Sorry."

"Ah, no biggie. That means you don't know enough about me to hold it against me. Probably a good thing."

Her eyes widen. "Are you that bad?"

I laugh. I can't help it. She's freaking adorable. "Only sometimes."

"Should I Google you?"

"No!" I shake my head fast. "Please don't."

"Oh, you really are that bad."

"Nah, I'm just kidding." I watch her for a moment, wondering if I should make a move. Her smile fades, and she starts packing up her laptop. "I'm sorry, am I too much of a distraction?"

"No. I wasn't really working, to be honest."

My heart starts racing. I can't just let her leave. "Do you have lunch plans?" I sound panicked, and that's not embarrassing *at all*. "Let me buy you lunch. That'll make up for your bad day last week."

"Um..." She stares, causing me to sweat around the collar. Those penetrating green eyes pin me down. "You must have better things to do," she says.

"I'm sure I can find something, but I'd much rather have a meal with you." I flash my famous, sideways grin that always works on the ladies, hoping it'll convince her.

She narrows her eyes. "Yeah, no, I don't think so, but thanks for the invitation."

I reach out for her hand. "Wait... why not?"

"Look, I appreciate it, but I really don't need drama in my life right now."

"It's just lunch. No drama at all."

"Yeah, right," she says. "I'm sure there are plenty of girls who would love to have lunch with you, you don't need me."

Again with the hard eyes. I'm intrigued. Who is this woman? "I'm inviting you because I like talking to you and I'd like to buy you lunch." I hold up my hand. "No strings."

She slips her laptop into her bag, along with the notepad and pen. With a heavy sigh, she glances back at me. "Just lunch, huh?"

"That's all. You can even pick the place."

"Well, aren't you sweet?" she says, her voice dripping with sarcasm.

I chuckle, not at all fazed. What can I say? I like the abuse. "How about one-thirty?"

She chews on the inside of her mouth as she stares at me. "Okay, but two o'clock is better. I have a class."

"Actually, that's better for me too since I just had brunch with my sister."

She nods and glances around. "Do you like Mexican? Ever been to El Placer on J Street?"

"I love El Placer. Great choice. See you at two o'clock."

She watches me closely for a moment and, with a nod, finally says, "Okay, Mac from the morning show. I'll see you then."

CHAPTER TWO

Kelley

I'm not sure what to think. On one hand, Mac seems super sweet; on the other hand, he seems incredibly arrogant. Hot as hell, but he knows it, too. What's his story? What made him talk to me? And why would he call me out so easily about my little emotional breakdown last week when I was on the phone with Mike? I'm still not sure if he was making fun of me or genuinely concerned, but I really don't need more trouble in my life right now—not with everything else going on. Even though it was nice to stop thinking about it for a while, especially since it's all I've thought about for a solid week. By distracting me, Mac's given me a much-appreciated gift.

My roommate and best friend Megan is with my ex-boyfriend Eric at my apartment—*together*. Which is why I've been spending every waking moment anywhere other than home.

How could they… how could *she*? I close my eyes, fighting to get the image out of my head. I'm gonna have to set fire to that sofa now. I can never sit there again after seeing their naked, sweaty asses draped over it. I ache with the disappointment I feel toward Megan. The heartache over losing a best friend far surpasses the heartache over a man… at least it does with Eric. I can't believe that after twenty years of friendship, Megan can so easily betray me the way she has.

I take a few cleansing breaths to fight back my tears. I'm not really surprised that Eric would do something like that. We're different, he and I. And that's become clearer with each passing day. Which is why I ended it with him. I just didn't expect to find him in bed with my best friend within hours of that breakup. It's not like we had a future; it's barely been a year since Megan and I met him. It's Megan's behavior that hurts. She didn't know I split up with him. At least, I hadn't told her. Eric could have. Lord knows what he said to convince her to sleep with him, but it doesn't matter. It wasn't right even if she did know about our breakup.

Last year, when Eric and I started dating, it was fun, but over the last couple months it had changed. He became possessive and jealous. Always questioning my whereabouts. He'd started checking up on me... snooping through my phone. He was even pushing me to let him move in with me and Megan. Years ago, Megan and I agreed never to let guys stay at our place for more than a couple of nights in a row. We didn't want anyone moving in with us and I told Eric that. Not only has Megan betrayed me by sleeping with him, she actually let the bastard move into our apartment. I had no idea she was capable of such betrayal.

Thinking back, I guess I'd be stupid to believe last Thursday was the first time they were together. I'm sure he stopped trusting me when his own guilty conscience started bothering him. My mom always warned me about that. She'd say, *if a man doesn't trust you, it's probably because he's guilty of something himself.* I can't prove they screwed around before last week, but it doesn't really matter now, does it?

I just need to move out. I can't carry on living with my ex-boyfriend and my ex-best friend. My search through the roommate ads on Craigslist today didn't turn up anything promising. I called two different ads and both sounded like creepers over the phone. I don't even want to find out what they were like in person. One old guy was renting out his kid's room and after he'd asked me what I looked like and my weight, I just hung up. I'm not sure what my weight has to do with my ability to pay rent.

I also did a little research and found out that since Megan is on the lease for the apartment, she's welcome to have Eric there as her *guest*, and I can't do anything to stop her. I'm afraid if I try talking to the apartment manager I could get us both in trouble, and I'll need the reference when I move.

I have no clue what to do. I can't afford the high rent in this area and tuition at the same time... but I have to leave. I can't stay there any longer than necessary. Nothing would make me happier than to never lay eyes on either one of them again.

The thought of going home is what made me accept Mac's invitation. I don't want to face them, not now, not ever. And while I really want to have lunch with Mac, I should spend the time looking for another apartment.

I glance at my phone as I head out of the lecture hall. I have time to drop off my backpack before meeting Mac for lunch, but I just can't go there. Instead of taking the light rail, I start walking toward El Placer. The fresh air will do me some good. It's a nice walk, too. Closer to Midtown, the sidewalk is lined with orange trees, and they're currently blossoming. It smells so good and has me smiling by the time I reach the restaurant.

I'm about a block away from El Placer when a bus passes me... with Mac's face on it. I've probably seen the ad a hundred times but I've never paid any attention to it. Now I'm feeling a little hesitant about my lunch date. What on earth can I possibly have in common with a guy who has his face plastered on the side of all the buses in Sacramento? When my phone buzzes in my pocket, I pull it out and read the text notification from my friend Mike.

Mike: *How are you doing? Find a place yet?*

He's always checking on me and I imagine this is what it would be like if he really were my big brother.

Me: *Not yet. Why don't you move to Sac and be my roomie?*

Mike: *No. You need to get away from that hellhole and move here and room with me. I even have a job waiting for you.*

I stop walking to punch out my next text.

Me: *First, Sac isn't a hellhole. Second, I can't drop out of school. And third, thank you. Really, Mike. One day some young hottie is going to swoop you up and keep you. I gotta lunch date. Talk later?*

Mike: *Lunch date! Damn, you move fast. I hope this guy is better than the last one. Call me tomorrow.*

Me: *Will do.* (smiley face)

I drop my phone in my pocket and enjoy the rest of my walk.

When I step inside the restaurant, Mac is already seated at a table. I'm a little early, so that means he's *really* early.

"Hey," I say. "You're really early." He stands as I approach and pulls a chair out for me. What a gentleman. I'm not used to such behavior. Eric never would've done that. The thought warms me. As arrogant as Mac seems, he's also considerate, a quality Eric always lacked.

"Sorry. Do I seem too eager?" he asks, without a hint of embarrassment. He's definitely confident.

"There's nothing wrong with eagerness. And there's nothing wrong with thoughtfulness. Thank you for inviting me to lunch." I try to be extra sweet to him, especially after my failed attempt to brush him off at Starbucks so abruptly this morning. I guess I'm not used to people being kind to me. After what happened with Megan and Eric, and everything else in my life leading up to it, it's no surprise I can't recognize kindness when it slaps me in the face.

"My pleasure. Seriously," Mac says. "Did you walk here?"

"Yes." I grin and say, "It's nice outside but hot as hell."

"I'm sorry. I didn't realize you didn't have a ride. I would have picked you up."

"No problem. I could have taken the light rail but I like walking."

"You chose well. I really do love it here. They have the best Southwestern salad with this great chipotle dressing. Have you tried it?"

I beam at him, a little surprised. "It's my favorite. Great minds, right?"

A giggle, followed by a small gasp, sounds behind me. I turn slowly and see a group of young women sitting at a table a row across from ours. They're watching us, smiling and pointing. I can't hear what they're talking about, so I glance back at Mac curiously. "Okay… wonder what that's about."

Mac peers around me and at the same time they grow silent. He shrugs and looks back at his menu. "No worries," he says. "We can ignore them."

Oh, okay. It's strange, but whatever. "So, do you like living in Midtown?"

Mac places his menu on the table and gives me his full attention. "I love Midtown. I used to live over on the East Side, closer to the university, but I much prefer living around here."

"I guess your sister still likes it in East Sac?"

"Yes, but she also works on that side of town, so it's easier for her to be over there."

The waitress approaches and asks for our drink orders. I order a margarita and suggest we get a full pitcher to share. Mac grins at me. "In need of a drink, are you?"

I widen my eyes. "You know it."

"Sounds good to me. I'll also have a glass of water," Mac says.

"Actually, I'll have some water too."

When she asks if we're ready to order food, we both nod at the same time. Mac waves a hand at me. "Go ahead."

"I'll have a Southwestern salad, with the dressing on the side. Extra dressing."

"I'll have the same thing. Exactly," Mac says with a smile.

The waitress rolls her eyes. She thinks we're trying to be cute, but really, we aren't. She has no idea we just met this morning. Whatever. I don't care what she thinks. I need some fun, and I think this lunch is it.

"So, you don't have a car?" he asks.

"I don't drive so I don't need one. I get around fine on public transportation."

He gives me a curious look but I'm not about to tell him why I don't drive, so I say, "You know, lots of people in Sacramento do the same… that's why there's so much public transportation here."

His face relaxes and he says, "Yeah, I get it. It also explains why you don't listen to the radio. Most of our listeners are car commuters."

The giggling behind me increases and I have to wonder how Mac can ignore it. He's acting as if he doesn't care, but I'm super self-conscious about it. It makes me wonder if I have toilet paper sticking out the back of my pants or attached to my shoe.

Catching on to my discomfort, he brushes it off and says, "It's not you. It's me." He leans forward and whispers, "They probably know me from the radio show."

"Right." I give him an exaggerated nod and say, "And from the buses. Hard to miss your huge face as it passes by."

"Oh… I thought you didn't know who I was?"

"I didn't until about ten minutes ago when your face flew by me at forty miles an hour." I throw my thumb in the direction of the giggles. "Does this happen a lot?"

Mac shrugs his shoulders. "Often enough."

"That must get really annoying."

"What can I do? The show pays my bills."

Before I can respond, the waitress brings the pitcher of margarita and two frosted, salt-rimmed glasses.

"So… as the morning show DJ, you have to be there super early, right?"

He nods. "Yep, the show starts at five o'clock in the morning and I have the bedtime of an old man."

"Ew," I chuckle. "It's a damn good thing it pays the bills because that's freaking early."

He laughs, and I love the way his smile brightens his entire face. My pulse picks up and I have to take a deep breath. He's so damn good-looking with his dark blond hair that hangs a little too long and his beautiful, even tan, which brightens his big, pale blue eyes. He's tall, much taller than I am, and he seems pretty built. But not buff, more like an athlete. Lean and sculpted. Maybe a swimmer or a cyclist. No wonder those women are acting so childishly. It makes me wonder what kind of radio persona he has. He's got to be a player, and that makes me wonder why he asked me to lunch since I'm about as ordinary as they come.

"What's up?" He lifts his hand in question. "You were laughing a second ago."

"You didn't ask me to lunch out of pity, did you?" The question is out before I can censor myself and now I feel foolish. "I'm sorry. I just have to wonder, with all of these girls ogling you, why would you want to have lunch with me?"

He laughs when I say this and that really makes me feel stupid but then he narrows his eyes. "Is ogling even a word?"

"Yes!"

"Are you sure?"

I lean down, unzip my backpack, and pull out my dictionary. I flip to the page, hold it open, and hand it to him across the table. "See, it's right here."

"Huh, look at that. You're right." He grins again, and something flutters in my chest.

"You know, Kelley, they have these neat gadgets called cell phones." He holds up his phone and waves it around. "I'd be willing to bet you could find a dictionary app that would save you having to lug that thing around."

I hold the book to my chest, offended at the suggestion. "I love this dictionary. I've been using it since middle school. I have words highlighted and"—I hold it to my nose—"I love the smell of real books."

He grins and his eyes sparkle in amusement. "I respect that. I also love the smell of books."

"Oh, so you do know how to read?" I quip.

"Funny. Yes, I do read."

"I guess the girls you usually have lunch with don't have much of a vocabulary."

That really makes him laugh, and that makes me laugh in return. When the waitress delivers our salads, we're both dabbing at our eyes. Of course, this just annoys her further.

"I guess she doesn't know who you are either," I say.

He laughs again, but this time so hard it makes him snort. "You're hilarious."

"Ha! Wait till I have my second margarita."

He's still chuckling when he says, "I can't wait for that."

"How old are you, Mac from the morning show?"

"Does it matter? And I should be asking you that, green-eyed girl who insists she's too old to be in college." He leans forward and fills my glass from the pitcher the waitress left on our table.

"Hey, I didn't say I was too old, I said I was *probably* too old." I sip the margarita and my mouth puckers from the tangy flavor of lime and the strength of the tequila. I eye Mac over the rim of the glass before I set it down and say, "I'm twenty-five."

"Thirty. Old enough to know better, but young enough to do it again." He lifts his water glass to toast me. His gaze is alluring, almost seductive, and I feel a blush creep into my cheeks—and it's not from the alcohol.

I'm just about to ask Mac if he's going to pour himself a drink when I notice a man walking up behind him. I glance up and freeze. The air catches in my throat and a sharp pain stabs me between my shoulder blades. Without fail, whenever I feel acute stress, that spot reminds me I'm lucky to be alive.

"Hey, Kelley," Eric says and nods toward Mac. "You moved on quickly."

I nearly drop my drink when he stops at our table. I gently set my margarita down, fighting to find my words. Mac must see the discomfort in my expression because he turns to face Eric. He holds out his hand and says, "I'm Mac, nice to meet you. And you are?"

Eric's expression changes from snarky to curious. He must recognize Mac. "I'm Eric, a friend of Kelley's."

When I hear this, my hands start shaking. I can feel the heat rising in my body, all the way up to my eyebrows. I hate Eric. I don't want him here. And I make sure he can see it in my eyes.

Mac smirks at him as if Eric is just too stupid to get it. "A friend? Really?"

Eric waves a dismissive hand at me. "Oh, yeah, Kelley and I go way back."

Mac looks over at me and winks. He turns back toward Eric and says, "Well, if you don't mind, Kelley and I could use some more chips and salsa and... hey, babe, should we get another pitcher of margarita?"

It takes all I have not to laugh out loud when I lift my glass and say, "I think we're still good on drinks, but thanks."

Eric points to the floor as if to refer to the restaurant and shoots daggers at me then Mac. "Dude, I don't work here."

"Oh, my bad. I just assumed, you know, with the uniform."

Eric looks down at his jeans and then back up and says, "Yeah, okay, I gotta go."

"Too bad," says Mac. "But it was nice meeting you, Aaron."

"Eric," he says, narrowing his eyes at Mac. He looks over at me and says, "See you later."

When the bell on the door sounds, announcing Eric's retreat, I look over at Mac and burst out laughing. "I didn't know he was here."

"What a douche."

I roll my eyes. "You have no idea."

Mac stares at me for a long time, and as he watches me, the laughter dies, and the smile slowly slips from my face.

"Is he the one?"

I know right away that Mac's referring to my little breakdown outside Starbucks last week. I nod and say, "Last week I found him in bed with my best friend." I wish the visual of the vindictive smile Eric gave me didn't come to mind when I said that, but it did, and it was just as vivid as the day it happened. That's what he did when I found him with Megan. He smiled at me. A knowing smile that said, *see, I told you.*

Mac shakes his head. "I wish I'd known that ten minutes ago. I wouldn't have been so kind to him."

I lift my brows at him. "That was kind?"

"Kinder than I wanted to be." He places a napkin over his lap and says, "It was painfully obvious how uncomfortable you were with him. I just wasn't sure why."

"Well… it's not a nice story," I reply, trying to sound stronger than I feel.

"So you lost your best friend and your boyfriend on the same day?" he says. "When I saw how upset you were last week, I thought you looked like you'd lost your whole world. I'm sorry."

I shrug, feeling sorry that the laughter died and wishing Eric could just disappear from my life. If only this was just about my best friend and boyfriend. If only this was just a broken heart. If only this was just embarrassment over not recognizing what a horrible person he is sooner. But, no, this is so much more, and I really don't want to talk about it. I don't even want to think about how I did indeed lose my whole world and five years later, I'm still paying for it. So, instead of thinking about it, I pour myself another drink and dig into my salad.

"So, Mac, what's your story?" I ask, hoping to take the spotlight off me.

"I have no real story," he says. "I'm from the East Bay. I moved to Sacramento for the radio gig. I have a sister, she's the oldest, and my mom, who still lives in the East Bay."

"Are you close with your sister? How much older is she?"

"We're extremely close. Emily's thirty-two and widowed. She lost her husband a few years ago. After losing Tuck, I try to always be around for her, and she's always there for me."

"Oh, wow, I'm sorry. That must have been hard," I say, and I'm also sorry to dampen Mac's mood. Nobody wants to be reminded of their losses. I understand that more than anyone.

"Thank you. It was tough, but Emily is doing better—time heals."

"Ha. Yeah, sure it does."

His expression turns curious, and I want to bang my head against the table for being so stupid. "What I mean is," I rush to say, "I can't imagine going through that. It can't be easy losing a spouse."

"You sound like you know something about that."

I fight for indifference but the reminder causes another aching pain between my shoulder blades and I get a flash of memory, an unwelcome image of waking up in a hospital bed. It's just a flash though and I fight to push it away because I don't want to remember. I place my hand on my chest and say, "Me? No. I've never been married. Have you?"

"Oh, hell no." He laughs when he says it, and I'm hoping I've dodged the rest of his questions. "I'm the guy who always tries to talk his friends out of getting married."

"Oh? Don't believe in commitments, huh?"

"Not so much." His eyes search the table as though looking for a new topic, and then he says, "What about you? Do you have any siblings?"

"No." I shake my head. "Just me and my mom. She lives in Oregon, so I don't get to see her often."

"Is that where you're from?"

"Yes."

He watches me, as if waiting for me to say more but I don't.

"Did you move here for school?" he asks.

"Yeah, my best friend was attending Sac State and convinced me to try Sacramento."

He purses his lips and nods in understanding. "And then she slept with your boyfriend?"

"… and then she slept with my boyfriend," I confirm and I'm about to change the subject again when my phone chimes—it sounds like a calendar reminder. I don't want to be rude by taking it out while we're eating, so I slightly lift it from the side pocket of backpack to glance at the display. Ouch… bad idea. It was a calendar notification of a Lake Tahoe trip I had planned with Eric for this weekend. It was supposed to be a relaxing getaway for my birthday. I actually hate celebrating my birthday, but Eric and Megan pushed me into making plans.

"Something wrong?" Mac asks.

I shake my head and drop my phone back in my backpack. "A reminder for a weekend away I had planned, but it's been canceled."

He gestures toward the door. "Was it with the douche?"

I shrug, trying to act like I don't care, but I'm sure he can see it on my face. "I don't need to go to Lake Tahoe, there's plenty of booze here." I grin and pour more margarita into my glass. "Don't you like it?"

He nods but doesn't drink any, and that makes me pause. I'm the only one drinking, and that's not fun… not to mention dangerous, since I hardly know him.

I put the drink down and pick up my fork.

"You going to be okay?" he asks.

"I'm totally fine and completely not interested in talking about exes while on a date with you."

He frowns and then smiles. "I get it. Your *exes* as in ex-boyfriend and ex-best friend, right?"

I wink at him and wonder if I'm already buzzed. "You got it." I start eating again, hoping the food will keep me from getting stupid drunk. The salad is so good, and I'm reminded of why I love this place. It's really fresh and the dressing is so spicy.

"So," Mac says. "What do you think of Reno?"

I scrunch my eyebrows together and say, "I think Reno is fine. Why do you ask?"

"Well, I'm spending my weekend in Reno, and I thought maybe you'd like to join me." He picks up his fork to take another bite. "You know, since your Tahoe trip isn't happening."

"I can't go to Reno with you. I don't even know you."

"What do you mean?" He waves his fork around and says, "Everybody in Sacramento knows me."

"Not everyone. I don't know you." I sip my margarita. "But I appreciate the invitation."

"If you don't have other plans, I don't see why you shouldn't go with me."

"I just told you, I don't know you."

"We don't have to share a room, I have a one-bedroom suite." He shrugs. "You can even have the bedroom with the locking door. I'll sleep on the sofa."

"That doesn't seem fair. I can't ask you to sleep on the sofa of your own suite. Besides, aren't you already going with other people? I'm sure they don't want a tag-along."

"Nope. I'll be on my own. It's a work trip. I'm MC'ing a gig tomorrow, it's a Comedy Fest. I'm working with a DJ from a Reno radio station who asked me to come and help. Also, one of the comedians is a friend of mine."

"Sounds like fun. I don't think I've ever been to a Comedy Festival."

"It'd be cool if you came with me." He casually reaches for my hand and begins to play with my fingers. It's distracting… almost intoxicating. I get a tingle up my spine from his touch, and it takes me a minute to digest what he says next. "You don't have to go to the Comedy Festival if you don't want, but I wouldn't mind hanging out with you for the weekend."

I stare at him for a long time, not sure what to think. Should I consider this a platonic invitation? I look down at my hand as he's caressing my palm with his thumb. No, positively not platonic. "Are you inviting me because you feel sorry for me?"

His thumb stops moving and he gives me a strange look. "Do I really look like the type of guy who offers trips to Reno for charity?"

I lift an eyebrow. "No, I guess you don't."

"I think it'd be a good time." His gaze travels down my body, and he says, "You shouldn't be so self-conscious. I can think of a hundred reasons to hang out with you, and none of them concern your exes."

Now I'm really feeling self-conscious. I watch him for a moment, wondering what's stopping me from saying yes. I pick up my drink, take a good sip, and pull my hand away from his. "How do I know you're not some axe murderer?"

He gestures toward the group of girls who've been giggling in the corner and says, "We could ask the mini fan club in the corner. I'm sure they can vouch for my character."

"Oh, I'm sure any one of those ladies would love to spend the weekend with you."

"Except I'm not inviting them. I'm inviting you."

I take another couple of bites of my salad and consider it. It's true. If he's a local celebrity, he's likely not dangerous. But that's not exactly a glowing recommendation. He's cute though, and I could really use a weekend away. Some fun wouldn't hurt either, and if Mac's anything, I'm sure he's fun. I'm still tingling from his touch, imagining what a weekend with him would be like. *Alone.* Then I think about how much I'd love to leave Megan and Eric wondering where I am all weekend. It'd serve them right. And it's that thought that pushes me into making the decision.

When I look up, I meet Mac's eyes. He watching me with an amused expression, his mouth teasing a lopsided grin. "It would be nice to have some company, but no pressure."

"You know, Mac, I think I would like to go to Reno with you."

"Nice." His face breaks out into a huge smile, and he glances down at his watch. "Can you be ready by six o'clock?"

"I'm ready right now."

"Yeah? You keep a change of clothes in that backpack of yours?"

"Who needs clothes?" I grin and say, "Just kidding. I can be ready by six."

"Sounds good."

Mac insists on dropping me off at my apartment. I would rather not have him see where I live since I didn't tell him the whole story about Megan and Eric, but it's hard to argue with him. I can already tell he's the type of man who always gets his way… and I think I like that.

He parks in front of my building, and when he gets out of the truck, I'm afraid he's going to walk me to the door. He circles the hood and rushes to open the passenger door before I can get out. When I step out of his pickup, I come face to face with him. Really close.

He leans forward, nearly nose to nose. "Have I told you how happy I am you're coming with me this weekend?" he says.

I can't hold back my smile. "Have I told you how happy I am to be coming with you this weekend?"

"So… we're in agreement."

I feel his hand snake around my waist and with a little tug he pulls me against him. It surprises me but what really knocks me off balance is the instant heat between us. It's almost unbearable. I'm not sure what it is, but there's something. Some weird connection I can't quite explain, and I think he feels it too. How could he not? When his lips touch mine, it's light at first. But then his tongue takes over, dominating the kiss. His hand around my waist tightens. He wants more, and I feel like he could eat me alive. I definitely *want* him to eat me alive.

I lift my hands and frame his face, then run my fingers through his hair. It's hard to breathe. Mac takes my breath away, and that has never happened before. It almost scares me, but I go with it because he feels incredible. I'm not sure I've ever been so thoroughly kissed before but it's powerful, and I feel powerful in his arms.

When he breaks the kiss, I'm a little off balance as my eyes focus on his huge grin. I think that's a good sign.

His hand loosens and lands on my hip. "Pick you up at six?"

I nod, unable to hide how flustered I am from his kiss. Mac leans into the truck, grabs my backpack. "I'll walk you to the door," he says.

"No!" I laugh. "I don't want you to see the mess. Next time?"

"Okay… I'll see you at six."

When he's gone, I'm left wondering if this day really happened or if I dreamed it.

CHAPTER THREE

Mackensey

I would've picked Kelley up at the door, but she surprised me by waiting in the parking lot.

"You're right on time," she says.

"I always try to be. It's hard to sneak in late when you work in radio." I grab her bag and toss it in the trunk. "You all set?"

She smiles widely, and I can't help but notice that she seems a million pounds lighter and less stressed than earlier. She's wearing a flowing, floral summer dress, ready for the ride. I try not to stare, but with a body like that, it's impossible not to.

"Yes! All set." She beams when she says, "Mac, thank you for inviting me. I'm so happy to get out of town for a few days."

"I'm sorry it's only Reno," I reply, wishing I had an exotic weekend of fun planned instead.

"No, Reno's great. I love hanging out there. I always run into the most unusual characters."

That makes me snort out a laugh. "No truer words were ever spoken."

I open the passenger door for her, and as she passes to get inside, I grab her hand and gently pull her in for another heart-stopping kiss. I can't help it, I'm still reeling from the last one, and I want to experience it again, and make sure it was real. It's the weirdest thing… these little flutterings I keep getting. I don't have feelings for women. At least, not the kind of feelings they usually want me to have. It's just not my way. But here I am, waiting to see her smile, and wanting to make her happy.

When I pull away from her lips, she's smiling. Her eyes drift open, and I'm glad to see she's relaxed as she slips into the passenger seat.

I walk around and slide into the driver's seat. Once my belt is on, she says, "This is my first time in a Tesla."

"You like?" I ask.

"Very much, but aren't you worried about driving so far? How many miles can you get on one battery charge?"

"Nah, I can get over three hundred miles. Reno is only about one hundred and thirty. The hotel has a charging station too, so we're good."

She runs her hand over the dash in admiration. "You gotta love a car that's good for the environment and drives fast. Right?"

I chuckle. "Absolutely." I clear my throat and say, "Except, I only drive the speed limit."

"Yeah, sure. I believe that like I believe the sky is green." She gives me a funny look and says, "Weren't you in a pickup truck earlier?"

"I was, but I thought this would be more comfortable for the ride."

"Whew!" she says. "I didn't think I drank quite that much at lunch."

"No, you're not drunk or crazy." I glance over at her and get a thrill at the thought of having her all to myself this weekend... if only it weren't for that damn Comedy Fest. "So... I have to be at this gig tomorrow at one o'clock. If you don't want to go, you can hang out in the casino, but I'd love it if you came with me."

"Of course I want to come with you. Why wouldn't I?"

"Well, as the MC I'll be getting a lot of attention. That means you'll be getting a lot of attention too." I shrug. "I don't know how comfortable that would be for you… but I'd love for you to be there. I think it'll be a lot of fun."

She brushes a hand at me. "I don't mind the attention. As long as it's the good kind. Will all the ladies be upset you brought a girl with you?"

I look over at her with a grin. "Ask me if I care."

"Of course you care. I'm sure a lot of your listeners will be there, and aren't you known as the hottest bachelor in town?"

"Where did you hear that? You didn't actually Google me, did you?"

"No. I didn't have to. I could've guessed that on my own."

The smile slips from my face. "Will you do me a favor?"

"Sure, anything."

"Please don't Google me. I'd much rather be judged at face value than for what you read online."

Her voice softens, and she says, "Of course. I would hate that too." She points a finger at me and says, "And from what I've seen, you're all good, Mr. Radio DJ. If other guys were half as considerate as you are, the world would be a better place."

"I don't know about that," I say. "But the radio thing… that's a character. It's not really me. I mean, it is, but it's been exploited by my producers so much that it's a skewed version of me."

"I understand. But I feel like I need to ask you the same favor." Her voice lowers for a moment, and I feel the atmosphere in the car change. I look over, not sure if I've misjudged the tension for something else. "Don't judge me based on what you saw last week."

That's a hard one. If I hadn't seen her cry, Kelley never would have caught my eye. But I get what she's saying, and it's a fair request. "Okay, so it's a deal. No Googling each other… and no prejudgments."

"That's a deal. Thank you."

"You know, Kelley, there's nothing wrong with… I mean, I get it, and I don't want you to feel self-conscious about the crying thing."

"It's impossible not to feel self-conscious about that."

"Please try. It's a normal reaction after what you've been through."

We've been on the road for a good forty-five minutes, and as we pass through Auburn, I feel a weight lift from my shoulders. Just like Kelley, I'm looking forward to getting out of town for a full weekend. Even though I have to work tomorrow, it's still nice to get out of the hustle and bustle of Sacramento. Kelley has gone quiet, and that makes me feel sorry for bringing it up. This is supposed to be a break for her too.

I look over to find her staring out the window. This gives me a few seconds to admire her beautifully toned legs. Her dress ends high on her thigh and when she shifts and crosses her knees, the crotch of my jeans grows tighter. Without thinking, I reach out for her hand. Once I've done it, I'm afraid she's going to pull away but to my surprise, she doesn't. When my eyes jump from her legs to her face, I'm hit with guilt. I'm such an ass. There's so much more to this woman than her looks. Here she is stressing over her life, and I can't stop looking at her body. "You want to talk about it?"

She looks down and tugs on her skirt. "You already know a lot of it. Besides catching my boyfriend in bed with my best friend, I'm also dealing with some stuff at school. It's not easy being a twenty-five-year-old student, and I can't work full-time when I need to take so many classes."

"How close are you to being finished?"

"Next week is finals week. Next fall I start my last year... at least, I hope so."

"So what's the problem? If you don't mind me asking."

"It's hard to find a decent paying job when I have to go to school. Rent in Sacramento is expensive, and you know, like I said before, life happens."

"At least it's only one more year. What are you studying?"

"Kinesiology with a minor in dance." She bobs her head back and forth a couple of times. "I'm also trying to get a teaching certificate. I figured it wouldn't hurt to have a back-up plan."

"Jesus! No wonder you're stressed."

"Yeah, it's a lot, but I want to be a full-time dance teacher... maybe even have my own studio someday."

"That's a reasonable dream. You seem like a hard worker, I'm sure you'll get there."

"Thank you." She sighs and snuggles into her seat, twisting to face me. "I don't hear that a lot. Usually, people tell me I'm doing too much, or I'm wasting my time. They might be right. I have no idea if I can support myself as a dance instructor."

I squeeze her hand. "You just have to take it one day at a time."

"Now you sound like a twelve-step program."

I laugh but it's more out of discomfort than humor. "Sorry about that. Maybe my response should have been suck it up and stop feeling sorry for yourself."

She looks over quickly, and I'm prepared for her to scream at me. I shouldn't have said that. What the hell was I thinking?

She stares at me for a moment then bursts out laughing. I chuckle along with her, glad it didn't go the other way.

"You're funny," she says. "But you're right. That's pretty much all I've been doing all week, feeling sorry for myself. Whew... it feels really good to laugh."

"You should do it every day."

"You probably do, don't you?" she asks. "Being on a radio show, I bet you laugh all day long."

"I do. It's definitely an enjoyable job. What about you? What do you do besides school?"

"I work part-time at a dance studio. I don't get a lot of hours, but I enjoy it." She shrugs and says, "The studio owner wants to retire soon, and she's talked about making me a partner and letting me take over when she's ready to stop working, but I have to finish school first."

"Oh, so you already have a plan, you just need to finish."

"Yep. That's all," Kelley says, but her tone isn't very convincing.

"So… you teach dance, but do you dance professionally? Like in competitions or anything?"

She's quiet for a long time and I feel a level of sadness cloud the conversation.

"I occasionally dance for fun, but not professionally. Not any longer."

"You did though?" I ask, wanting to understand.

"Years ago, I was signed with a touring dance company, but I was injured so I had to take a step back… sort of readjust my goals. That's why I started college so late."

"So after touring you settled here and started Sac State?"

"Yeah. Megan, my *former* best friend, and I grew up together. Right after high school, I started touring for the dance company, and she moved here for college." Kelley pauses for a moment and I get the impression she's not keen on talking about it, but she keeps going. "After touring, I wasn't sure what to do next. I'd always planned on a career in dance, but when that was over, I was a little lost. Megan was in her third year at Sac State. She convinced me to move down here. That was about four years ago."

"And I guess you like it here?"

She finally smiles. "I really like it in Sacramento. It's home now. I'll never move back to Oregon."

As much as I want to know more, I don't push. Her smile is back and I like it. This weekend was supposed to be fun. I don't want to bring her down by talking about the past.

As we enter Reno, I exit North Sierra Street to Virginia Street and follow it down a couple of miles to the Peppermill Resort. As we pass the strip, she asks, "Where are we staying?"

"The Comedy Fest is at the Silver Legacy, but my room is at the Peppermill." I glance at her, then say, "I like having some distance… keeps people out of my business."

"Out of your business? Who would get in your business?"

"Fans of the show… people working the festival. It's hard to have privacy sometimes. Especially when you're working a gig at a remote location and that remote location is also where you're sleeping."

"I guess that's smart. You don't want some drunk, horny ladies knocking on your door in the middle of the night," she says with a giggle.

She thinks it's funny, but she has no idea how close to the truth she actually is. "It's not the drunk, horny ladies that I have a problem with. It's their husbands."

When her mouth drops open, I laugh and say, "I'm just kidding. I happen to like the Peppermill. It's away from the strip, and the rooms are nice."

We pull into the parking lot and take our bags out of the trunk. I hand my keys over to the valet with a tip and ask him to make sure the car gets plugged into a charger. Once we're checked in, we take the elevator in the Tuscany Tower to our suite. I made sure to ask for a two-room suite so Kelley could have her own room.

When I open the door to the suite, I see Kelley's eyes light up, and I'm happy she likes it. I enter the room and walk around the granite, wraparound bar to place my bag in the seating area. The space is huge, with several cushy armchairs strategically placed around to create cozy nooks. There's also a long leather sofa and a cherrywood coffee table in the center. Kelley stops and glances around. On the opposite side of the room is a small breakfast table with two chairs facing a huge picture window. From where we're standing, we can see the sun is getting ready to set behind the distant hills.

"This is where I'll stay."

"Are you sure?" She gestures around and says, "I'm not going to be comfortable knowing you're sleeping on the sofa in your own hotel suite."

"You're my invited guest, remember?" I nod toward the bedroom so she'll follow me in. After two steps into the room, she stops abruptly.

"Nice." Her eyes are wide as she takes in the elaborately decorated room. The king-size bed is on an elevated platform near the window. There are burgundy and gold curtains draped between the bed and the seating area of the bedroom just in case she needs more privacy. The room is lit with small lamps, which creates a romantic setting. Watching Kelley's expression, I'm not sure she's ready for romance, which is why I made a point to leave my things in the other room.

"We'll need to share the shower, but I have my own half-bath in the other room."

She walks into the bathroom and hits the light switch with a gasp. "I've never seen such a huge bathtub before. That's crazy."

I point to the wall and say, "Your bathroom even has a big screen TV for your viewing pleasure."

"Oh, yeah, I'm definitely taking a swim in that tub this weekend."

I leave her alone in the bedroom to get comfortable and walk back into the seating area and to the window for a better look at the view. The sun is bright as it hovers over the horizon and I can see the light as it reflects off the windows of several other buildings in the area. Our room faces the southwest part of Reno and there's not much to see but a small part of town and the distant hills.

I don't have anything planned for the evening, but I'm hoping Kelley and I can hang out, maybe have a nice dinner tonight. I look over at her as she enters the room. "Where do you feel like having dinner?"

She walks toward me and faces the window. "I'm not sure... what sounds good?"

I fight the urge to suggest room service. I don't want to scare her away. Especially since we technically just met today. She doesn't seem like the type of girl who regularly hooks up with guys and takes off to Reno with them. Having her here is a little strange for me too. I don't normally invite women to join me on my trips out of town.

I don't always *sleep* alone while I'm traveling either, though. My line of work gives me the opportunity to meet lots of women, and there're usually one or two willing to join me in my room for the night.

I like having Kelley here. I look forward to spending the weekend with her, alone, even if it means we may be sleeping in different rooms....

CHAPTER FOUR

Kelley

After dinner, we wander through the casino, playing a few slot machines and joking about what utter failures we are at gambling. Fortunately, I had a little money saved for the trip to Tahoe I'd planned with Eric. I shouldn't really be spending it, but I can't help myself. I'm having a great time. Not that I'm given a chance to spend much of my own money. Every time I want to play a slot machine, Mac drops a twenty-dollar bill into it. I wish he wouldn't. I don't want him to think I came along to sponge off him. I really just needed a break and a good time. He's already given me both.

Mac sits at a quarter slot machine and starts winning. His twenty dollars slowly creeps up to a thousand, and I'm enjoying myself just watching him win. The drinks are free as long as you're gambling, so I take advantage and order a whiskey neat. I make sure to give the cocktail waitress a good tip so she returns regularly. Of course, the way she flirts with Mac tells me I'll be seeing plenty of her anyway. Next time, I'm not tipping her at all.

When I sip the drink, I realize it's not the smooth top-shelf stuff I was hoping for. I cringe a little and knock it back quickly to keep from tasting it. It goes straight to my head.

When Mac gets up to about fifteen hundred dollars, the winning streak slows and after a short while he drops back down to a thousand dollars. Not wanting to lose any more, he cashes out, and we head up to our room.

Leaving the casino, I nudge Mac to stop at one of the gift shops. I'm worried about waking up with a headache from the cheap whiskey so I want to grab some painkillers just in case. Mac grabs beef jerky and a deck of playing cards and then checks out.

On our way to the elevator, we pass a group of showgirls dressed in full costume. With magenta feathers flowing down their backs, spiked silver stilettos on their feet, and top hats decorated with silver rhinestones, they walk toward the ballroom as if they were dressed in business suits heading to the boardroom. Mac discreetly points to them and whispers, "If the teaching gig doesn't work out, you can always get a job here."

Feeling the alcohol, I giggle like a schoolgirl and pirouette into the open elevator. After my third spin, Mac catches me around the waist and pulls me against him. "That was pretty good." His voice is husky, deeper than usual, and the intense heat between us sobers me.

I rest my hands on his firm shoulders and nearly stutter my response. "Th-thank you."

He slowly releases me as his eyes slide to my lips. "Do you miss it?"

I tug on my dress nervously as I lean against the elevator wall. Mac props himself against the wall too with his long legs stretched out in front of him. He's lean and tall and staring at him brings heat to my face. "Yeah, I do." I avert my eyes at the admission and say, "I miss the shows and the audience… and my dance friends… but I still dance. I just do it in the privacy of the studio."

"Maybe you'll let me watch you sometime."

"Sure, yeah, that would be nice."

We both go quiet and a second later, the doors open to our floor. I'm fidgety as I walk next to him even though I'm trying to be calm. I'm not sure what's going to happen once we reach the room. I know what I want to happen, but I also don't want Mac to have the wrong impression of me.

I'm just so incredibly attracted to him, and I'm not sure I want to be the good girl this weekend. Besides, where has that ever gotten me? I've always tried to be good, always tried to do the right thing. And that's only left me with a broken heart. At this point, I feel like, if I'm getting my heart broken, I need to make it worth it. I want to make sure that when I leave, I won't have any regrets. I'll have had fun, I'll have met a really great guy who I'm sure isn't interested in anything more than a good time, and then I'll walk away. That's how I want this to play out.

My stomach is fluttering like crazy, and I wonder what Mac's thinking. I glance at him, and I see the heat in his eyes. I can't miss it because he's staring at me. When we enter the room, I walk in hesitantly. I'm nervous, and I look over at Mac, wondering how he's feeling. He's so well put together. I bet he never even sweats. He's smooth and confident, and I admire that. I wish I could be more like that. I lean against the bar and stare back at him. We hold each other's gaze for a long moment before he looks away. That's a tell, and now I'm sure he's going to keep his distance. I can see why Mac plays the slot machines in the casino instead of the tables. He can't hide his thoughts well enough to win at the table games. He's probably going to be a perfect gentleman because he thinks he'll scare me away, which I appreciate, but tonight, for once, I want to emerge from my good girl shell and have a little fun.

"The minibar is covered, if you want a drink. It's a package deal for working the gig. Help yourself to whatever you want."

"Are you serious? They really cover the minibar charges?"

"Yep. That's how these things work."

"Okay." I raise a single brow and say, "Would you like a drink?"

He looks at me intently and shakes his head. "No. But you go ahead."

I open the bar and inspect my choices. They actually have beer, and as soon as I see the bottles, that's all I want. I pull out a Sierra Nevada Pale Ale and grab the provided bottle opener to crack it open. I take a few sips and look over at Mac. He's watching me with a strange expression, and I'm not sure what to think. He almost looks envious, but that doesn't make any sense.

With my beer in hand, I walk to the window and look out. It's almost midnight and the main strip is lit up like Christmas with the other hotels' colorful neon lights. To the left, it's mostly darkness from the area terrain and the Nevada Hills.

When I turn and find Mac standing behind me, I watch him for a moment and then say, "I hope you're not afraid of me." Just saying those words sends my stomach into a dive. I'm not sure where my sudden bravado is coming from.

"Afraid of you?" he whispers.

"Yeah, like... afraid of offending me or afraid you'll push me too far, or maybe afraid it's too soon. And, you know, maybe it is... but maybe I don't care."

He watches me as if trying to decide what to do next. Then he says, "I like you, and maybe I am afraid I'll scare you away... but I don't have the option of not caring. I'm not allowed to cross that line." He shakes his head. "What I mean is, I don't want to cross the line and screw this up. So... you just need to be honest and stop me if I do push too hard... or too far."

"I can do that," I whisper.

Our eyes are locked and after a long moment, he says, "Know how to play poker?"

I watch as he turns his back on me and I'm totally confused. Does he want to return to the casino? "I know how to play poker. Why?"

He removes the deck of cards from the gift shop bag. "Care for a game?"

I smirk at him and say, "What are the stakes?"

He pulls out a chair at the breakfast table and opens the pack of cards. I'm feeling a bit nervous about it because I'm not an experienced poker player, but I also know he has trouble hiding his feelings and that could play in my favor.

"Hmm…" He cocks an eyebrow as he shuffles the cards. "Would clothes be taking it too far?"

"Oh… ah." My brain freezes as I realize I've misjudged him. He has no problem putting it all out there… or with *me* putting it all out there. "Clothes… as in, lose a hand, lose an article of clothing?"

"Yup." His gaze travels from my feet to my eyes and he's grinning wide.

"You do realize I only have three articles of clothing on, right?" I'm trying not to laugh at the expression on his face.

"Hmm…" he says again, assessing my summer dress. "Okay, let's make it fair." He stands and kicks off his shoes and socks, then removes his belt. "Now we both have only three articles of clothing on. Fair?"

A gentleman to a fault. I can't help but laugh, but I agree. "Let's do it."

"Five card draw, jokers wild, okay with you?"

"Yeah, um hum, that's fine with me." I'm trying not to stutter as I agree. I pull out a chair and take a seat across from him. "So…" I say. "Ante up?"

"No, babe, you can keep your clothes on until you lose a hand."

"Oh, okay. I've never actually played strip poker before."

He deals a hand and I'm fighting with everything I have not to laugh. I can't believe I'm in Reno, playing strip poker with a hot DJ. I glance at him and he's grinning ear to ear too. I'm hoping it's not because he has a great poker hand.

I glance at my cards and realize I have two pair, aces high. I hold my smile and glance at him. He's staring at his hand and it's as if I can see the thoughts processing in his head.

"Do you need a card?" he finally asks.

I lay down a card and say, "I'll take one."

He slides a card across the table and I can see he's trying to keep his eyes down. I wonder what that could mean. I pick up the card but it's no help to my hand. I watch as he replaces two of his cards and when he does, the smile returns to his face.

Once his cards are in place, he looks up at me and winks. What the hell does that mean? I gesture to him and say, "So, now what? Do we just lay down our hands?"

His smile widens and he says, "Are you calling me?"

"Ah, yes, I'm calling you."

Mac lays his hand down, face up. He has a full house.

"Holy shit, I'm going to lose," I mutter.

He chuckles and says, "Do I get to pick what you take off?"

I glance up to see a sultry expression. Testing the waters, I say, "What would you pick if it was your choice?"

His eyes travel downward and my heart is fluttering like crazy. I've *never* done this before. It's crazy, but damn, I'm enjoying myself.

Mac purses his lips and says, "I'd pick the dress, of course."

"Of course." I lay down my two pair. "Two pair. Did you actually shuffle those cards?"

He collects the cards and slides them across the table. "You can deal the next hand."

"Dammit." I stand and lean against the table for a moment, trying to figure out how to start.

Dress? No. Panties? I can slide them off and keep the dress on. "Screw it," I say as I tug the dress off and pull it over my head.

Mac's grin falters a little and he shifts in his seat. Good. I hope he has to bear a raging hard-on for the next several hands. I glance down at myself, thanking God I wore beautiful, matching nude lace under my dress. The only problem with nude underwear is that now I look completely naked.

"Bold move," he says. "I admire your spirit."

I start shuffling the deck, watching him the entire time, making sure his eyes stay up. No peeking. I deal five cards each and lay the deck in the center. Then I pick up my hand. "Jesus."

"Oh, she's losing her poker face already."

I have a throwaway hand. Nothing really but a ten and Jack of Spades. "Do you need any cards?"

"I'll take three," he says, and that makes me feel a little better about my hand.

I push three cards across the table. Mac's hand covers mine as he takes the cards I've offered. The touch is electrifying, like a jolt to my midsection. I lift my eyes to his and he's staring at me.

"You don't need to be self-conscious. You're beautiful, Kelley."

Oh, damn. This guy is good. "Thank you." It comes out as a whisper and I think that's because the atmosphere in the room has changed. We're no longer smiling and I feel like I'm playing a game of chess, instead of poker. As if I'm waiting for his ultimate move or he's waiting for mine.

I take my three new cards and when I see another ten and Jack, I'm relieved. Two pair is better than nothing. I actually feel pretty good about it. He couldn't possibly get lucky two hands in a row.

I glance up at him and say, "I call." Of course, there's nothing else to do, it's not like I can bet more clothing. Not that I would with a measly two pair.

Mac lays his cards down and he has two pair as well, but he's got two fours and two eights.

"Jesus! Thank you," I say as I lay down my two pair, Jacks high. I grin at him and say, "Do I get to pick what you take off?"

He stands, turning in a circle. "Your choice."

"Please, please take the shirt off."

He grabs the hem and swipes his t-shirt off in one smooth move. I'm trying to keep my mouth closed. Holy shit! I'm absolutely sure I'm blushing… I can't help it. He sits back down and

I can't help my stare. His muscles ripple as he moves and I can't take my eyes off him.

He folds his arms over his chest and leans forward, trying to catch my eye. When I look up, he says, "What?"

"Ah, oh… um, don't feel self-conscious, Mac. You're beautiful."

Now I think he's blushing. His eyes are locked on mine when he says, "Thank you."

I watch as he shuffles, wondering what happens if I lose another hand. What goes next? The thought makes me nervous and the tension in the room builds as we watch each other. I have to give the man credit, he is genuinely trying to keep his eyes on my face and he's doing far better than I am because I can't keep my eyes off his chest.

I grab my five cards and almost moan. Nothing good. At least not good enough to get his pants off. If these cards are good for anything, they're good for blocking Mac's view of my chest.

I tap the table. "Three cards, please."

Mac tosses me three cards and says, "I'll take two this time."

When I pick up the cards he hands me, I breathe a sigh of relief. It's not great but three of a kind is better than nothing.

"I call you," Mac says.

I lay down my hand and say, "Three of a kind. Kings."

Mac grins big and lays his cards on the table. "Flush. Take it off, sweetheart."

"Shit, dammit." I drop my cards and shake my head. "How is that possible?"

I'm so embarrassed my face is hot. I lift my beer and swig it, hoping for some liquid courage. Jesus. Now what? Panties or bra? "Whatever," I say as I stand and walk to the small kitchenette. I seriously need a drink of water.

I grab us each a bottle and turn to find him standing and staring out the large window. I'm holding a water in each hand, trying not to let the cold bottles touch my naked skin but also trying to cover myself, which isn't easy.

When I return to the table and set down the bottles, Mac reaches up and pulls the curtains closed. "Sorry, I guess I should have done that before you lost the dress."

I shrug. "I don't think people can see much all the way up here."

He turns toward me and his blue eyes are blazing. That sends a swarm of butterflies floating around my stomach. With our eyes locked, I unhook my bra and let it fall to the floor.

I can't help but let my eyes drop again to his bare chest. He may be a gentleman, but I'm not. I've been dying to see him without a shirt all day.

When my eyes dart back to his, he says, "You okay?"

"I promised I'd tell you if I felt uncomfortable, and I will."

He takes a step toward me. "Yes, you did."

"Then why are you so worried about me?"

He takes another step toward me and before I have the chance to take another breath, his lips are on mine and I'm up against the wall. The coolness of the surface behind me contrasts with the heat of him, and I'm so glad because if it weren't for that, I'd probably melt into a puddle of lust on the floor.

His hands rest on either side of me, his front pushes against me, and his lips, oh God, those lips are all over, searing my skin. But it's not enough. I want his hands on me too. I slide mine down his chest to caress his hard abs. The feel of his skin makes me shudder in nervous anticipation and I'm a little taken aback by my own boldness.

I can't believe I'm here, doing this, but I want it so badly. Mac's smooth and so hot... almost feverish, and it makes me hot. My pulse is pounding and my stomach is flipping. I'm not sure how he's keeping control or why he's not touching me, but it's driving me insane.

When his teeth graze the curve of my neck, I feel like I'm about to combust. I tug on the button of his jeans, wanting him as naked as I am, but when his hot mouth surrounds my nipple, I can't quite get them undone.

His mouth is wet, firm, and all over me. "Oh God, Mac." I can barely get the words out, but as soon as he hears my voice, his hands are finally on my body, and it feels so good. Now he's everywhere, both hands cupping my breasts, his mouth on my nipple and when I moan again, he wraps his arms around me and grips my ass firmly, lifting me off the ground and pulling me against him.

"Bedroom," he grunts.

I nod vigorously. "Yes, yes." I feel myself lifting higher before he carries me into the other room. I take his mouth with mine and lose myself in the kiss. So much so that I don't even comprehend where we are until he lays me on the bed. He leans over me with our lips still locked, having never broken contact, and when he finally pulls away, our eyes meet. It's darker in the bedroom. I can barely see his face, but his eyes are bright and clear. As I look at him, I wonder what the hell has gotten into me. Mac brings out a boldness I didn't know was hiding inside me.

This is dangerous.

He is dangerous.

I barely know him, but I know plenty of guys like him, and this should scare the shit out of me. It doesn't, though. He feels too damn good for this to be anything but right and maybe rebound sex is precisely what I need to move on.

"Don't move," he orders.

And then he's gone.

I reach up and pull at the comforter to get it out of my way. I want to stretch out on the huge bed and feel the crisp clean sheets beneath me. Once I've kicked off the elaborate bedcover, I spread out on luxurious cotton and enjoy the coolness against my burning skin.

With a deep breath, I try to relax and look around the dark room. It's beautiful, with the rich burgundy and gold accents. The cherrywood bedposts spiral up and become lost in the abundance of the sheer gold embroidered fabric canopied over the bed. The window curtains are open to the glittering city lights and I realize as I lie here waiting for him, listening to the hum of the air conditioner, that I've gone against every one of my personal rules just by being here. Maybe now is the perfect time to reconsider those rules I've lived by so strictly.

Where have they gotten me? Alone, broken-hearted, and most of all, in a hell of a lot of debt.

A moment later, Mac returns with his duffle bag. He sets it next to the bed, and as he pulls out a strip of condoms, my pulse kicks into overdrive. Damn, he's sexy. His jeans are unbuttoned and unzipped. I can see the bulge beneath them, and I'm simultaneously turned on and scared shitless. I squeeze my eyes closed, trying to push the feelings away. I want this so badly, why am I suddenly hesitant? *Bravado, don't abandon me now.*

I almost laugh as this thought crosses my mind and when I open my eyes, his face is there, and he's watching me. "Are you okay?" He looks concerned, and that makes me feel bad. Especially since I've already reassured him that I'm not afraid.

I watch him for a moment as I try to sift through my feelings. I'm not afraid of him… but I am afraid of where this relationship goes – or doesn't go. Can I really be a woman who has a one-night stand and then walks away? Mac has heartbreak written all over him, and I don't need to go down that road again.

"It's okay, Kelley. I understand this is… not a normal thing for you."

I sit up on my elbow so that we're nose to nose. "You're right. This isn't a normal thing for me at all. But that doesn't mean I'm not down to do this. I just have to push away that nagging voice that tells me I'm getting myself into trouble." *And by trouble, I mean emotionally.*

With a smile on his face he says, "Oh, you are getting yourself into trouble. Don't doubt that, sweetheart."

And, oh, that smile. *Damn*. I really wish I had Googled him just so I would know exactly what I'm getting into. Then I remember what he said about the skewed version I'd find online and compare that with what I've seen from him. He's been nothing but considerate and generous with me. Generous with his time, his compliments, his money... I feel like he really just wants me to enjoy myself. How can that be wrong?

"Do you want me to stop, Kelley?" He pulls back. "It's okay, honestly. I can go back to the other room."

"No." I wrap my hand around his arm because I'm seriously afraid he's going to leave and I want his hands on me again. "I'm just nervous, but I want you to stay."

Mac leans in and kisses me again, long and slow, his hand reaching around to cup the back of my head and bringing me closer. My pulse kicks into overdrive and every cell in my body is awake and trembling with anticipation of his next touch. I feel like I'm on fire and he's the only one capable of extinguishing it. I need this. I need him and I need him now.

He ends the kiss with a tug on my bottom lip and says, "There's nothing to be nervous about. This is supposed to be fun. Let's just... keep it light, okay?" His eyes dart from my lips to my eyes and he mutters, "Uncomplicated."

When I nod in agreement, he grins and the stress of our conversation melts away from his expression. The next moment, he's over me, his lips melding with mine, and just as quickly, those negative thoughts clouding my head fade away.

CHAPTER FIVE

Mackensey

She's so fucking incredible. I've been with a lot of women in my life, and they're as varied as you can possibly imagine, but I can't think of anyone who comes even close to Kelley.

It's the weirdest damn thing. I don't know what I'm feeling, and that scares the crap out of me. I'm not the kind of person who carries a lot of doubt. I'm always sure. Sure of who I am. Sure of who my friends are. Sure of my goals. I know what I want and what I don't want... at least I did until today.

Right now, everything's different. I'm willing to get off this bed, go into the next room, and close the door behind me. Because the most important thing to me right now is seeing this woman smile. And the last thing I want is to pressure her into something she's not ready for. I don't want to do something tonight that could possibly destroy my chances of having tomorrow with her. And that's a first for me. With women, I'm usually just living in the moment, not worrying about a future.

I've always prided myself on my ability to gauge other people's feelings. I've always been a little too empathetic, and due to that, I live within carefully constructed walls. In truth, I'd never pressure any lady into doing something she's not ready for, not on purpose anyway. That's not the kind of guy I am. But I can honestly say

I've never cared more about making someone comfortable as I do right now, with Kelley.

I'm hovering over her, and I can feel the squirm beneath me. You know the one, that give-away sign that the anticipation of the woman you're with has reached a peak level. That part of the sexual encounter where you realize you have complete control over her pleasure. It's my favorite part and I want nothing more than to give Kelley pleasure.

I ease her nipple into my mouth and circle it with my tongue as I slip my hand between her legs. She's still wearing her lace panties, but they're drenched with her desire. I push them aside as I lower my hand. I can feel her breathing increase, and it makes me rock hard. She's so wet and ready.

I enter her with one finger and push inside gently, then pull out and add another finger. She's tight, and I'm afraid of hurting her, but when she lifts her knees and tilts her pelvis toward me, I know she's enjoying herself. When I pull out, I link those same fingers around the strap of her panties and tug downward. She's wiggling and lifting her legs to help, and it's obvious her urgency has increased. But I'm keeping a slow pace… I'm in no hurry. We have all night.

I lick my way down to the neatly trimmed V between her legs. When my hands slide between her thighs and under the globes of her perfectly formed ass, she lifts slightly, and I bring her closer. One lick and her sultry flavor explodes on my tongue. I take another taste then another and she's fisting the sheets beneath her as her heels dig into the bed. She so sweet and feminine. I'm already addicted to the essence of Kelley and I want more but I know she's close to losing control. I surround her clit with my mouth and suck. A gasp breaks from between her lips as she pushes herself closer to me. I can feel the vibration as if her entire body is a live wire, full of electricity.

The sound of the sweet little noises and moans she makes fills the room and I'm very nearly bursting out of my jeans watching her, but watch her I do, and it's a beautiful thing.

The time it takes me to get my jeans off is just enough for her to catch her breath, and when I join her on the bed, she grabs me and pulls me closer. Her lips attack mine, tongue exploring my mouth, hands running down my chest and around my hips. Her nails are urgent, biting, but I don't care. I love watching her completely uninhibited and free, hair wild around her head, limbs flowing, her dancer's body taut and ready for more. It's almost got me coming before I can even get inside her.

I sit up on the bed and quickly grab a condom before ripping the wrapper off. The seconds it takes me are almost too long for Kelley to wait. Before I grasp what's happening, she's on her knees, straddling me.

I groan as she slides down, taking all of me in one swift move. She's tight, and dammit, I can barely contain myself when she starts moving. I've got my hands around her waist as she travels up and down, riding me. It's fucking hot as hell, and I can't keep myself from grabbing her nipple with my teeth and sucking it into my mouth.

Another gasp and she's picking up speed, and I have to hold her tightly to slow her down. I'm in no hurry. I want this to last as long as it can, but with the way she's moving, I'll be coming in seconds.

She grinds a couple more times, groaning as she moves, and then I feel her clamp down as her body jerks. Another moan and I lift my eyes to watch her lose control. The expression on her face is so beautiful. The sound that escapes her lips is unreal. The arch of her body is a work of art.

When she lowers her head to my shoulder, I take hold of her and slowly lift to my knees. Then I lay her down gently and finish what she started. As my momentum builds, she opens her eyes, and they focus intently on mine. I fight the urge to look away. Usually, the intimacy would scare me, but tonight it feels right. I want it. I want to watch her come undone again. I want her to watch me come undone. With that thought, I surge forward one more time.

The release is body-racking. Strong. And it steals the breath from my lungs.

I can barely breathe as I lower myself next to her. She curls up in my arms like a kitten, and I pull her close, rubbing my hands up and down her slick body. She's as quiet as I am—it's as if we don't want to break the spell. I feel like such a girl when I start to wonder what she's thinking. I've never been like this. Ever. But I can't help myself. I brush the hair off her face and kiss her forehead.

"Oh my God," she finally says with a relaxing sigh.

I have to agree with her. "I know, right?"

When she starts laughing, I get it, because I feel the same way. That feeling of overwhelming relaxation and calmness. That feeling of… I don't know… release.

"It's a good thing I'm a self-assured man. Laughing is not usually what I want to hear after something like that."

This makes her giggle again, and I can feel her body move with it. "I'm sorry, but you *know* that's not why I'm laughing."

I grin at her and feel a little jitter in my belly as I look down into her eyes. "Yeah, I know."

CHAPTER SIX

Kelley

I wake up slowly. Mac and I failed to close the curtains before we fell asleep last night, so the sun is shining right in my eyes. I gently roll over, away from the window, and there he is. Lying next to me, naked, and looking like a Greek god. I can't stop the grin that spreads across my face as I watch him sleep. My eyes travel down the length of his body. He's barely covered and I like what I see. With the smoothness of his well-defined chest and his glowing, sun-kissed skin, I have to fight the urge to reach out and touch him. My gaze travels the center line, down to his navel and the treasure trail of hair that gets lost behind the sheet draped over his hip. This sight makes my cheeks heat from the blush, and I feel a little giddy about my own behavior last night, but I don't regret it, at least not yet.

We took a bath last night after making love. *A bath.* I can honestly say, I've never taken a bath with a man. Fortunately, the bathtub in our room is huge, and it was fabulous. That's probably why I'm not sore this morning.

I was stunned when he got out of bed last night and started running the bathwater. I expected him to go into the other room and sleep on the couch. I expected him to be uncomfortable in bed with me. I expected him to be like every other player.

But he's full of surprises.

We talked a lot too. About everything, and about nothing. Mac is so down-to-earth, which isn't the impression I got from him the first time we met. I think that's what draws me in. I expect him to be a snob, but he never is. Every once in a while his arrogance will rear its ugly head, but I'm not so sure it's out of place. He's a great guy, and he's hot as hell... why shouldn't he know it, provided he uses his powers for good? I laugh a little, remembering how he used his powers for good last night.

He stirs a little so I creep out of bed reluctantly. I sneak from the bedroom and into the little kitchenette, thinking of coffee. The hotel is one step ahead of me. They have a coffee-maker, but it's a Keurig, so there's no need to brew an entire pot. I look over at the closed bedroom door and wonder if I'll wake him if I make myself a cup. After judging the distance from the kitchenette to the bedroom door, I think I can get away with it... because coffee is needed, stat.

Once I have a hot coffee in hand, I stroll over and open the curtains to stare out at the bright morning. I sit down at the breakfast table and take my first heavenly sip, then I lean back, raise my feet to rest them on the other chair, and enjoy the quiet. When I look out the window, I'm happy to see a perfect, cornflower blue, cloudless sky. Reno seems quiet but I guess that's typical for a Saturday morning. It's also already warm out. I can tell from the heat coming off the window that it's going to be a scorching day.

I can't help but wonder what Megan and Eric are doing right now. They have no idea where I am, and that makes me exceptionally happy. I've been trying to stay away from the apartment most of the week, popping in and out to change clothes or manage my laundry. It feels incredible not to be there now.

I sigh, wishing I could forget about it. I hate that this heart-sinking, sickening reality has crept into my weekend, but I can't continue to couch surf. Lexi, the barista at Starbucks, has been incredible, letting me crash at her house, but it's only a temporary solution to a permanent problem. Next week, I have exams, and I'll need to be home, sleeping in my own bed, so I can be at my best. I can't keep taking advantage of friends anyway, but what are my options? I can't stay in that apartment with them. After next week, I'll have to leave.

I shake my head and close my eyes. How could they both be so savage? And especially Megan—screwing Eric in our living room when I was bound to walk in on them... and then agreeing to let him move into our apartment the day after I catch them together, with zero consideration for how I might feel about it. Twenty years of friendship up in smoke over a guy. I can never trust her again. I need to move on and forget them both. Eric got what he wanted and there's nothing Megan can do to redeem herself. Eric knew that too. He knew sleeping with Megan would be an unforgivable act.

After a couple more sips of coffee, strong, bitter, and restorative, I look around and recognize the significance of where I'm sitting—this is where Mac and I started last night. With that thought, a rush of memories cloud my brain. His hands... mouth... tongue... Jesus. Everything was too good to be true. I can hardly believe I'm even here. Seriously. Who am I right now? I place my hand over my mouth as I remember the poker game, and it's like every detail is seared into my brain. This is so unlike me, but that's what he seems to do to me. He brings out a part of me I didn't know existed.

It's not that I'm in physical danger. Mac wouldn't hurt me, I'm sure... but I know I'm playing with fire. It would be different if I didn't like him and if I didn't enjoy his company so much, but I do. He made it clear last night that he's looking for "uncomplicated" and here I am, already conflicted about my feelings for him. But I can't. I just need to... what did he say? *Keep it light*, because I don't need any more grief in my life right now.

I lean forward, brush the playing cards aside, and grab the magazine on top of the table. It's an entertainment calendar for the

Reno Tahoe area. The cover announces the Comedy Festival that Mac is working today. I flip the page, and there's his picture. He looks perfect with his bright, shining, blue eyes and million-dollar grin with perfect, white teeth, and I'm sure it's not Photoshopped. He really does look *that* good. What the hell does this person see in me? Because I'm just a freaking mess. I'm broken. This guy, he totally has his shit together in a way that I can only dream about.

I read the article accompanying the pictures and the list of comedians. There's a couple of pretty big names. James Foster… that guy is hilarious. I just watched his HBO special a month ago. And Carmen Beatty, I love her. Most of the other names I don't know, but I don't follow comedy that closely—I'm always too wrapped up in my own life. Between school, work, and everything else on my plate, I don't have time for things like this.

I stare at Mac's picture. It's the same one from the bus advertisements. I can't honestly say I've never heard his radio show, but I can say I don't remember if I have. It's not like I'm a loyal radio listener, but I'm pretty sure I'm about to become one. The thought makes me grin, and as I flip the page on the magazine, I hear the bedroom door open.

Mac steps out of the bedroom, shirtless and wearing a pair of faded pajama pants. It's hard not to gasp at the sight of his lusciousness. His hair is all over the place, and he's a little blurry-eyed, but he grins at me, and I feel a shift inside. This man is here with me. *He's mine.* And I sure wish I could keep him forever. I set the magazine down and drop my feet to the floor. "Have a seat, I'll make you a cup of coffee."

He waves me off. "Stay put. I got it."

I watch the city come to life as I stare out the window, drinking my coffee, and I can't help but wish every morning was this relaxed. Slowly, the streets fill with more and more cars and the sun lifts higher in the sky. I glance at my phone to see the time and I wish it would slow down. From behind me, I can hear Mac prepare his coffee and the domesticity of it seems remarkable to me, especially since I only met him yesterday.

When he sits in the chair next to mine, I lift my eyes from the magazine photo of Mac to stare at the real, flesh-and-blood Mac. Damn, he's beautiful. "I didn't wake you, did I?"

He points to his chest. "Morning show guy, remember?" He sips his coffee and says, "I only slept this late because someone kept me up last night."

I chuckle and say, "I'm sorry. I'll be sure to let you sleep tonight."

He grabs me and pulls me into his lap. "Don't you dare even think about it."

I turn my body so that I'm straddling him. "Okay, I promise to keep you up again tonight..."

When our lips meet, I feel him grow hard beneath me. That makes me smile against his lips. I grind a little and pull a moan from him.

"I wish I didn't have to work today," he says. "If it weren't for that, I'd never let you leave the bed."

"Promises, promises," I say and I lift my phone so he can see the time. "We only have a few hours to clean up and get breakfast before you need to be there."

He tilts his hips, rubbing his erection against me. "That's all the time I need."

I wasn't sure what to pack for the trip and had no idea what to wear. I've never been to anything like a Comedy Festival. Is it like a concert? I decide on a form-fitting miniskirt and a flowing tank, and wear my hair down. I have some high-heeled strappy sandals to wear, too. When we arrive, I'm glad to see I don't stick out. Mac looks so sexy in his tailored button-down shirt and jeans.

He's happy too, and I revel in how easy-going he seems. He's so relaxed among all these people, where I'm a little wide-eyed at the entire experience. Having him next to me calms me.

It's a little nerve-wracking, the hustle backstage, and it makes me miss dancing. Our shows were always hectic, but the energy was different. I remember it being more stressful, probably because I was performing in those shows, nervous energy zipping through me as I waited to go on stage.

I close my eyes at the memory and swell with the unexpected grief that washes over me. I wish I could go back there, to those times, even if it were just for a moment. Just a moment on stage, with the music... and Bradley.

But I can't, and I need to remember that.

I shake the memory away and focus on today.

I've met so many people, and I can't remember all of their names. The comedians are hilarious and the drinks are plentiful; for that I'm grateful. I'm having a good time, but I've seen very little of Mac since he started working and I'm kind of missing him. How is that even possible? I've only known the guy for twenty-four hours. After an hour or so of being backstage, I head into the crowd to check out what the festival has to offer. I don't want to be in Mac's way, and I don't want to be a distraction.

I'm surprised at the variety of booths. There're charity organizations, craft stands, food stalls, and a lot of local companies advertising their businesses. People are everywhere, hundreds of them, and they're all having a good time. I'm not sure what's more prevalent, the smell of fried food or pot smoke. The scent of both surrounds me as I walk through all the exhibits. When I see the Sierra Nevada beer stall, I stop and order a drink before heading over to the side stage, where Mac's expected to make the next introduction.

As I approach the area, I'm just in time to watch him charm the crowd. He's so good at winning people over. Who needs a comedian with him at the mic? He's fascinating to watch and I'm not the only one who thinks so from the looks of the ladies in the crowd. I'm not even sure what he's saying, but every woman within sight is staring at him and they're smiling. I weave through, dodging elbows, trying to get a better look, and to hear what he's saying, but just as I get close enough, the crowd whoops and claps for the next comedian. I get close enough in time to catch Mac say, "Give it up for Corey Proctor!" And then he's gone.

I laugh at myself and skirt the rest of the crowd to head backstage. After getting through security, I'm searching for him but he surprises me when he sneaks up behind me and grabs my arm. "There you are." He draws me to him and kisses me until my knees grow weak. When he pulls away, his cheeks are flushed with excitement and a grin creases his face. I'm a little flustered, and it takes me a minute to realize he's asking me a question.

"What's that?"

"I said, are you having fun?"

"Yeah. I'm having a blast. How about you?"

"It's great. Come this way, I have someone I want you to meet."

I follow him to the other side of the stage and walk behind the curtains. It's not quite as busy over here as it was on the venue's main stage, but there are still a lot of people. When I see we're approaching James Foster, my eyes go wide. "Hey, is that James Foster?"

"Yes. He's a friend of mine. Come on." He pulls me by the hand and approaches James. "Hey, Jim, this is Kelley."

"Kelley, nice to meet you." James smiles and nods at me. "Mac's been talking about you all day. You having a good time?"

I shake the hand he offers me, not sure how to respond to that. Mac's been talking about *me* to James Foster? *Holy shit!* When I get my bearings I say, "I'm having a great time. I've never been to a Comedy Festival before so I wasn't sure what to expect. But this is awesome."

"*… But this is awesome.*" I hear a mocking voice behind me. We all turn, and I see Sammie Collins, a pretty famous comedian. I'm taken aback by her appearance because she's much prettier in person than on TV. "Is this your flavor of the month, Mac?"

Mac's body goes ridged and he curses under his breath. With pursed lips, he shakes his head. "Can you attempt to be nice, Sammie?"

"Why should I?"

"Time does not heal all wounds," James says. "And that's my cue to leave. Kelley, it was lovely to meet you. I hope you enjoy my set." He glances at Mac. "We'll try to catch up later."

"Yeah. See you in a bit," Mac says.

Sammie glares at Mac. "So, back again this year?"

"Maybe I should ask you that, since it's been a couple of years. How are you, Sammie?" Mac's expression turns sad, and I wonder what it is about this woman that can so quickly alter his mood.

"Don't ask me how I am," she says. "I see some things haven't changed." She looks directly at me. "Good luck with this one, honey, you're gonna need it."

At first I'm stunned by what she said, but still quick with my comeback: "No worries, I'm sure I can handle him."

She laughs, which surprises me, but I guess if you're going to dish it out then you should be able to take it back in turn.

"Sammie," Mac says.

She lifts an eyebrow at him and walks away, her raven hair swinging down her back as she leaves.

"I am so sorry about that," Mac says.

"What's her problem?"

"We hooked up a few years ago… it didn't end well."

"Well, she certainly hasn't forgotten."

"I'm sorry she was so rude to you, but you handled her well."

"Rough history?" I ask.

He grabs my elbow and pulls me closer. "Very rough." He snakes his hands through my hair and pulls my face closer to his, making me shiver at his touch. "But it's not going to interfere with our evening." He kisses me deeply and that certainly helps me forget Sammie Collins.

Mac pulls away and lays his seductive eyes on me. "I'm almost done, and then we can get the hell out of here."

I inhale the atmosphere and take a moment to enjoy being here with him. Then I smile. "I'm ready whenever you are."

I watch James Foster deliver an incredibly funny set, but when Sammie Collins takes the stage, I retreat and look for Mac. He's finishing up, and making plans to meet James later at Death and Taxes, a local bar down the street. I'm watching his animated expression as he's chatting with James and I'm still in awe of him, in awe of the fact that this sexy beast is here with me. My eyes drift down his body and memories of the night before roll through my head. I can't wait to have him and his broad chest to myself again. I look at my phone, and I'm thrilled to see it's only four-thirty. That means we still have the entire evening together.

The promotions company that booked Mac for the show provided him with a limo for the evening. Which makes me very grateful. I'm not the type who goes out partying and I definitely don't like to drive. I'd much more of a homebody, where it's safe and I don't have to travel.

When we climb inside, I'm surprised at how huge the interior is. There are easily ten empty seats and a fully stocked bar. I guess they were expecting a party, but it's just me and Mac.

I'm reminded of my dance days and how Bradley and I were carted around in limos to parties and charity events. We were just kids and it never occurred to me at the time that what we did was special or extraordinary. The memory almost makes me laugh since now my usual mode of transportation is the light rail.

This car has running lights that go along the ceiling from front to back and as soon as the driver closes my door, Mac reaches over and turns them off. There's still a dim glow of light around the mirrored minibar, but it's dark enough that I don't realize how close Mac is when his hands touch my face and his lips take my mouth. I'm immediately overcome with butterflies from his touch but I don't get to enjoy it for very long. The ride is over almost before it began and I'm disappointed when the car stops in front of the bar.

Death and Taxes is a great place with the perfect ambiance, buzzing but not super loud like most of the clubs in the area. We sit in one of the leather loveseats, and I order a whiskey sour. Mac orders a ginger ale, which surprises me, but when I think back to lunch yesterday, I remember he didn't actually touch the margarita pitcher then either.

"You don't drink, do you?" I ask.

"Oh, I can drink with the best of them."

I lean forward, closer to him. "But you don't."

"I want to keep my wits when I'm out with you. I can't afford to not be at my best."

His thoughtfulness isn't missed by me. I'm not so young and inexperienced not to appreciate the meaning behind the statement, but I feel like there's more to it. We have a car service and we're not that far from our hotel. Not drinking because he wants to be at his best seems like overkill to me. I stare at him for a while, trying to understand what's really going on. "I want you to be yourself with me… I thought that's what you were doing."

"I've been more myself with you than I have been with anyone else," Mac says, and as he plants a gentle kiss on my lips, a group of women walk up to us. They compliment him on the show and ask about his partner Mimi, and to my surprise, they're actually trying to join us for drinks. That's not cool. I want him to myself… at least until his friend arrives later. After chatting with them for a few more minutes, he politely brushes them off when the waitress shows up with our drinks.

Somehow, three of the women managed to leave Mac their phone numbers. I didn't notice until he rips them up and drops them into an empty glass. I'm struck speechless at how they did it right under my nose. He apologizes, but it's not necessary. I clearly remember him telling me why he stays at a hotel off the strip, and now I understand.

"So, tell me about Sammie," I say, when we're alone again.

"There's not much to tell. We went out for a while… she got more attached than I did and things ended badly."

"Oh… so, you broke her heart."

"I guess I did. I honestly don't remember doing anything to make her believe we were more serious than we were, but apparently, she got that idea anyway." He pauses and sips his ginger ale. "I didn't mean any malicious intent… I just didn't have feelings for her beyond friendship. I feel bad about it, but I can't pretend I have feelings when I don't."

I dip my head in acknowledgment because I believe him, but I also sympathize with her. I know what it's like to be heartbroken. I take a deep breath and remind myself that Mac and I are *keeping it light* and *uncomplicated*. I glance up at him and say, "Now I feel bad for her."

His eyes meet mine. "Yeah, me too."

Before he can say any more, James arrives, and he's all hopped up on the adrenaline high from his set. I've never seen such a hyperactive adult before. He doesn't sit still, and he barely stops talking, but he's hilarious, so it's okay. He insists on paying for all the drinks, and when he orders a double round of whiskey sours for the three of us, the drinks barely fit on our small round table.

Sitting with James is like having our own private comedy show. He pushes us into playing liar's dice and then consistently beats us at the game. I'm a horrible liar, which is proven pretty quickly, and

I find them both laughing at my expense. I don't mind, because we're all just having a good time.

Mac's always watching me, which I find endearing. It's as if he wants to make sure I'm comfortable. His attentiveness is constant and that encourages James to make fun of him for it. This is when I realize you need some pretty thick skin to keep a comedian as a good friend. Of course, it doesn't bother Mac. He's not rattled in the least... until he is.

I'm not exactly sure what changes, or why things change, but they do.

I'm a few drinks in when I see Mac pick up a cocktail.

I only notice because of the expression on his face. He's staring at the drink as if weighing up whether he should finish it.

He looks at me and beams. I return his smile, and he says, "I think you're absolute perfection." Then tips the drink back to the whoops of James.

He kills the drink, grabs me, and pulls me in for a kiss. I'm stunned and happy and excited... but in the back of my mind I'm wondering if this is how Sammie Collins got her heart broken. With his kiss, I can taste the alcohol on his warm lips, and I'm so thrown by his words, all I can do is sink into the kiss and enjoy the roller coaster of emotions I'm riding with Mac.

CHAPTER SEVEN

Mackensey

My head is pounding. Literally, like a bass drum on my skull. Am I dying? I might be dying. I lift one lid and look out at the bright blue sky through the open curtains. It takes me several seconds to figure out where I am. I raise my head and try to focus, but that only causes more pain. I close my eyes and think… think about anything that makes sense. It's been a damn long time since I've woke up feeling… Fuck! I bolt upright and look around again. I'm naked… in a hotel room in Reno. Did I drink last night?

I rub my hands over my face, and I'm surprised by the gold band on my left ring finger. What the…? I stare at it for several seconds, turning my hand as the light glitters off the shiny surface.

Kelley? *Shit.*

I look around, but she's not in bed with me. I throw my jeans on and creep out of bed, trying not to jostle my thumping head.

What the hell have I done?

I walk into the other room of our suite, and she's there, sitting with her cup of coffee, watching the world outside. She looks miserable. I walk over to the seating area and look down at the official-looking certificate of marriage on the table next to her mug. Sitting there is another gold band that matches the one on my hand.

Nausea rolls around in my stomach, and I rush to the bathroom to puke. It hurts, and I'm painfully reminded why I stopped drinking three years ago. I rest my head on the toilet seat, praying that getting married was the only stupid thing I did last night. What the hell was I thinking?

I hear Kelley enter the bathroom and then the water turn on. A moment later I feel a wet towel as she rests it against the back of my neck. Then I hear her soft voice. "Are you okay?" She sounds like she's been crying and that only makes me feel worse.

I close my eyes and nod. "Are *you* okay?" I croak, fighting the next wave of nausea when it ebbs over me.

"Can I get you something? Water?" The fact that she hasn't answered my question doesn't escape me, even in this condition.

"Please." I glance up at her and say, "Will you bring me my phone?" I'm defeated... and I know it. There's only one thing I can do. *Must do.*

When Kelley hands me the water and my phone, I give her an apologetic look. I know I need to talk to her, but it has to wait. I've got to do something first.

I dial Jeff's number and wait for him to answer. I scoot back and lean against the bathroom wall, craving oblivion. When I hear his voice, I breathe a sigh of relief. "Jeff, am I glad you answered."

"That's my job, man. What's going on?"

It takes me several seconds to find my voice, and I'm sure that's all the time Jeff needs to figure out what my problem is. "Mac, where are you?"

"Reno."

"I can be there in two hours."

"Jeff, I screwed up." I'm almost crying when I say it, and I should be embarrassed about that, but I'm much, much more embarrassed about what I did last night. Instinctively, I glance up to see that Kelley is standing in the doorway, watching me.

"Where are you?" he asks again.

"You don't have to come," I say.

"Yeah, I think I do."

"No, I'm… I'll be fine." When I say it, I realize it's true. I'm not teetering over an edge. I screwed up, but I don't feel like I've completely lost control.

"Talk to me, Mac. What's happening?"

"I just… lost it last night."

"I gathered that. How are you feeling right now?"

"Hungover like a son of a bitch. But… I'm okay."

"Listen, man, this happens… but that doesn't mean you give up on all your progress. This isn't a free ticket to ride, know what I mean?"

"I do, and I get it. I'm not drinking again. I drank enough last night to last me a lifetime."

"I think I should come to get you."

"No, it's a bad idea." I look up at Kelley and hold her gaze. "I'm not alone."

Jeff's quiet for a long time, then he finally says, "Is she going to be a problem?"

"No, it's not like that. This was all me… I promise." When I say this, Kelley's eyes lower to the floor, her hair falling like curtains on both sides of her face, and a fat tear slides down her cheek. That tear feels like a punch to my chest.

"If she didn't drive you to drink last night, if it really was all you, why? What caused it, Mac?"

I think about that for a long moment but I don't have an answer. "I don't know."

"Be straight with me, Mac. I need to know exactly what's happening if I'm going to help you through this."

I take a few moments to evaluate how I'm feeling. Hungover for sure, but I don't feel the slightest desire to binge. I don't feel any different than I did before last night, other than an enormous headache and the shame radiating through my body. "I'm fine. I'd tell you if I wasn't… I just needed to… I don't know, tell someone. Come clean before I started looking for false excuses."

"Get something to eat. Drink lots of water, flush out your system. And call me when you get home. I'll stop by and pick you up for a meeting tonight."

As I stare at the intricate tiled floor of the bathroom, it occurs to me that I can no longer say I'm eleven-hundred and eighty-two days sober. I have to start at zero. The thought crushes me. "Thanks for being there, Jeff. I'll talk to you later."

I pull the phone away and hit the disconnect button. Then I look up at Kelley. She looks so sad, and I feel terrible about that. I drink the glass of water she gave me, get up and approach her. Her eyes are glued to the floor as if she can't stand to look at me.

"Kelley, I'm so sorry."

"*I'm* sorry," she whispers. "This is my fault."

"No, please don't do that. It's me." I lay my hand on my chest. "I do stupid shit when I drink."

She nods, and I see another tear fall from her face. "Apparently, so do I." She turns and walks away.

When I enter the bedroom, I see that she's packing. "You don't have to worry, we can fix this." And even as I say it, I feel the weight of it on my chest. I approach her and try to get her to look at me, but she won't. "I think we should talk about this."

"It's a little too late for that." She shakes her head and drops her duffle bag, sitting on the edge of the bed. "Probably should've talked about it before we signed the marriage license."

"Honestly, I'm not so sure we didn't. I just don't remember." The statement makes me want to laugh, but I know this is not the time.

"I feel sick," she says, eyes brimming with tears. "I shouldn't have encouraged you to drink." She rests her elbows on her knees and drops her head into her hands. "Let me guess… Jeff is your sponsor?"

I nod my head. "Yes."

She drops her hands and looks up at me. "Why didn't you tell me?"

"I don't know. I guess I just didn't want you to see me as that guy." I sigh heavily, wishing I could turn the clock back. "I didn't want to be the broken guy."

"Mac, everybody has demons. Everybody is broken in some way. Do you think knowing this would've made a difference to me?"

I think about her statement and lower myself to the floor in front of her. "What can I say? I liked being with someone who didn't know my history. I liked having a clean slate."

"Well, you're pretty much stuck with me now. At least for a while."

"Fuck..." I draw the word out and then say, "We actually got married last night."

She nods her head, but I can see she doesn't think it's funny like I do.

"Who the hell does that?" I ask with a shrug.

I see a faint lift to one side of her mouth. "This isn't funny."

"We'll figure it out, Kelley, okay?"

Her face falls, and as I watch her eyes grow misty, I get that I have no idea what she's been going through. Not really. When I reach for her, she pulls away, and that hurts. It hurts more than I want to admit.

I slowly get to my feet, and as I do, I recognize I may still be a little drunk. I feel pretty off-kilter, and all I can think about is getting this poison out of my system. I know Kelley needs me, but I don't think she wants me. It's a punch to the gut.

I stare at her for a moment and say, "I'll leave you alone for a while." When she doesn't respond, I say, "I need an hour to go work some shit out with myself. I'll be back."

She nods, and there's nothing else to do but leave her alone. I grab some sweats and a t-shirt out of my bag and change in the bathroom. Then I head down to the hotel gym with my phone and earbuds. When I step inside, I'm relieved to see it's empty. I hop on the nearest treadmill and bring up my iTunes app. I shuffle Slayer, knowing it's the only thing I can tolerate right now. It's masochistic, but I need something that will keep the self-destructive thoughts away while I sweat out the alcohol.

I start out slow, to warm up the right way, but I stumble, and it's a stark reminder of how I destroyed three years of sobriety in one blurry evening. That one stagger is all it takes for my carefully structured façade to collapse. I'm second-guessing my insistence that Jeff not come to get me. I'm not so sure I can pull myself out of this. I think about Kelley, and my heart sinks. I wanted her. I wanted her so bad last night that I was willing to throw away my career, my sobriety, and every relationship I've managed to salvage in the three years I've been sober. I wish I could explain why. I wish I knew what about Kelley—or our time together—drove me to pick up a drink. All I know is, it's different with her. I'm different with her, and I don't know what that means.

I turn up the music and speed up the treadmill. Forget the warm-up, I need to purge this shit from my system. Within five minutes I've set my pace on the treadmill, and then I spend the next hour running for my life, fighting the entire time for a clear head, to escape last night.

Exhausted and dripping with sweat, I finally find my way back to the elevator. When the doors open on my floor, I run directly into Kelley, bag in hand. She freezes, her eyes wide.

I step out of the elevator and let the doors close behind me. "What are you doing?"

She stares at me for a few seconds before she finally says, "I've, um, caused enough trouble for you... so I'm going."

I place my hands on her hips and say, "No. No, you're not, Kelley."

"Mac, I can't..." She's fidgety and nervous, and her eyes are red and swollen. I'm starting to think I've done something to scare her. "I need to leave," she finally blurts out.

"No. Forget it. I brought you here, I'm taking you home."

"That's not necessary. I'm perfectly capable of getting myself back to Sacramento."

"Capable, yes, but you're going with me." My adrenaline is flaring again, and I feel gross from all the sweat, but that doesn't mean I'm going to let her sneak out and leave without me. I place my hand under her elbow and lead her back to the room. She doesn't fight me or even complain. She just walks with me quietly, as if I'm taking her to the Principal's office.

When we're back in the room, I turn to face her. "Look, Kelley, I'm freaking out about this too, but we need to figure it out together, okay? You can't just take off like that."

"I don't know what's to work out," she says. "It was a mistake. You were drunk, I was drunk, and we stumbled into an all-night wedding chapel." She folds herself into a chair and says, "Now we're sober and faced with the reality of our mistake. The only thing to work out is an annulment." Her voice raises as she says the word annulment and it drives a spike through me too.

"Kelley…"

She looks up at me with sad eyes, and I'm not sure what to say. I mean, fucking Christ, am I seriously thinking about staying married? I don't want to be married. I've never wanted to be married. That's insanity talking. I'm not the marrying type. I'm the one-night stand type, not a husband, and I would know since… well, since my relationships never last longer than one night. At least, not since the disastrous couple of weeks I spent with Sammie. My chest tightens at the reminder, but I try not to let Kelley see my feelings.

Her stare is intense, visceral. She's pinning me down again with those eyes, and I feel like I can't hide anything from her, and that makes me ashamed. Of who I am. Of what I've done. "I don't think this is something we're going to sort out today. Can we just give it a day or two? Give our bodies time to recover from the alcohol, and our minds time to clear. I don't feel equal to it yet, and I can't just jump, I need to think first."

She slaps her hand on the arm of the chair. "Well, a lot of good that does us today. Why didn't you think first last night?"

"I'm pretty sure this isn't entirely my fault, but I understand why you're pissed." I let out a heavy sigh. "Sneaking out when I'm not looking isn't cool, you know. I would've come back here and been worried sick... or was that your plan?"

She gives me a dirty look and points to the bar around the kitchenette. "I left you a note, asshole."

"Kelley, that doesn't make it okay." My voice raises when I consider how bad I would have felt if I'd missed her. "At the very least, we need to be fair to each other. Sneaking out isn't okay."

She nods and closes her eyes. "I know. You're right, I'm sorry."

All I want is to take her into my arms, kiss the pain right off her, but I know she'd pull away from me. My head is hammering, and I know I won't feel any better until I shower and eat something. I look at my phone; we have two hours before we need to check out. "I need to shower... will you be okay for a while longer?"

She nods but doesn't look up at me.

I can't walk away. I try, but my feet won't move. The need to touch her, the need to make this right, roots me in place. I stare at her for a long time. Eventually she looks up at me. I don't know what to say, emotion choking me, so I spit out the first thing that comes to mind. "Please don't take off while I'm in the shower."

She shakes her head. "I won't. I promise."

I squat down next to her and take her hand. "Kelley..." I press my lips together, not sure what to say, but certain I need to say something. "I'm so sorry."

She squeezes my hand. "I know... I am too."

CHAPTER EIGHT

Kelley

When he finally leaves me alone, I drop my head between my knees and take several deep breaths. How could I have let this happen? Why didn't I follow my instincts last night when I realized he wasn't drinking? I knew it. I've seen it before; I know what this looks like. Yet I ignored the warning signals. I feel terrible. This is going to be a massive problem for me, but I know that's nothing compared to how it's going to affect him.

When my phone rings, I glance down to see Mike's face pop up on my caller ID. Just seeing him makes me emotional. I hit the ignore button. There's no way I can talk to him today. I won't be capable of holding it together and I can't tell him about this. He'll flip out. I tap out a text so he doesn't worry.

I set my phone down and get up to pace the room. I stop at the small table holding our souvenir marriage certificate, given to us by the wedding chapel, and rings. Mac removed his ring like I did, and now they lay side by side. I pick them up and hold them in the palm of my hand, feeling their weight, trying with everything I have to remember the night before. A few things are clear, but only a few. The words he mouthed seconds before his first drink.

I think you're absolute perfection.

I scoff at that and roll my eyes. He has no idea just how far from perfect I really am.

That moment is the sharpest memory from the entire day. I remember picking out these rings at the jewelry store inside one of the casinos. We seriously shopped for the perfect matching pair, grinning the entire time. I remember that... smiling until my face hurt. I remember that moment and how sure I felt. How giddy it felt to do something so spontaneous. How different from my usual life, sticking to the rules. What on earth was I doing? How could I have jumped into this without a second thought?

Was I really that drunk?

Was he?

I sit down and rest my head again. It hurts, and that's making it hard for me to think, and impossible to remember. The rest is a blur. Those two moments are all I have from the entire evening, at least until we returned to our room. Watching Mac down that first drink and looking over at James and his whooping and encouragement... that's the last thing I want to remember. I don't want to remember the moment I screwed up this man's life. But James? Did he know? Did he encourage Mac on purpose? My mind drifts over the evening again, to piece together bits of this broken puzzle, trying to remember the moment we made the decision to get married, or who made the suggestion. Did Mac propose? Did I propose?

I sit in silence, staring out the window. For some reason, I want to believe it was James who made the suggestion, to shift the blame from us. But why would he? The thought lingers in my mind for a moment, and I ask myself again... why would he?

What a great bit that would be... this is the line that flows through me, and then... *what a great story to tell your grandkids.*

Wonderful. We've turned our lives upside down to give Mac's comedian friend fodder for his comedy act. I groan and throw my head back. We're so stupid.

I try to remember the rest of the night, but the only thing that comes to mind is the incredible time we had after we returned to our room. I vaguely remember him calling me his wife. I remember the smile on his face as we stripped down to our wedding bands. I remember him tossing me on the bed, his lips all over me. I remember an overwhelming feeling of belonging... which is quite the opposite of how I'm feeling this morning.

Why didn't he tell me? I remember what he said about wanting a clean slate, and I can't fault him for it. That's how I was feeling as well. I wanted to wipe Megan and Eric—and everything else—from my head, and I wanted to focus on him. *Just him.* It's odd how similar our motives were, yet our situations are so different. We both wanted a clean slate and we both have stuff we wanted to hide. It makes it hard to be mad at him, makes it easy to be mad at myself. I should have recognized it and done something last night. I should've stopped drinking. Number one rule, don't drink too much with strangers. Don't drink too much when you don't have a backup. Don't drink too much when you don't have a friend to make sure you get home safe. Of all people, I should know this.

But I did. I did have a friend to make sure I got home safe.

This thought pushes on my chest because above all, I still feel like I can trust Mac, even though he lied. He should've told me he was an alcoholic, but that doesn't make him a bad guy. I chuckle but without humor... I guess it just makes him my husband.

"What's so funny?" I hear him ask from the doorway.

I jerk my head up, surprised he's there. I didn't hear the water shut off. He's wearing only a towel, and that almost takes my breath away. Tiny water droplets shimmer on his broad chest and I can't stop staring at him. He's staring back at me, and all I want is for him to hold me, take me in his arms as a husband would. I know that's stupid. *I'm* stupid.

I laugh hollowly again and hold up the rings, echoing his words from before. "We're married. Who the hell does that?" I'm laughing like a maniac, and that makes me think I'm cracking up, but then he joins in too.

When our laughter dies we look at each other, and he says, "It is going to be okay."

"Is it though?" I shake my head, the heaviness returning to my chest. "Is it really?"

He grabs my hand and pulls me against him. "I'll make sure of it, I promise. You just have to trust me."

I nod into his chest and breathe him in. He smells clean, he feels warm, he feels safe. I'm going to miss all of this about him.

When he turns off J Street and into an alley, I'm not sure why. "Where are we going?"

Mac glances over at me. "I have to meet Jeff at my house. He's already there waiting for me."

"Okay. You don't want to drop me off first?"

"No. I want Jeff to understand, and know for sure this isn't your fault. The only way to make sure of that is for him to meet you in person."

"Look, Mac, I understand why this is important to you. I get the whole steps to recovery thing. I know you need to take responsibility, and that's easier for you if you can prove to your sponsor that someone didn't talk you into taking a drink. But I'm not going to pretend I don't have any responsibility in this. I recognized last night that you were trying not to drink. And I'm sorry I didn't stop you."

"See, there's where you're wrong. You asked me outright, and I didn't tell you the truth. Do you remember that?"

I think about it for a moment. "Yeah, I remember. And I'm stupid for not following my instincts. That's my fault."

"You trusted me, and I abused that trust." His hands are white-knuckled on the steering wheel. I know he wants to take full responsibility for this, but he shouldn't. I had a hand in it too. I can't deny that. "I apologize for breaking your trust, Kelley."

Mac's sincerity is clear in his voice, so is his hesitation about seeing his sponsor. I certainly don't want to face this Jeff guy, but I'm torn because I don't want to abandon Mac either. Not to mention, I really don't want to go home and face Megan and Eric. Thank God they don't know about this.

Mac takes another left turn, and I see he's pulling into an open garage. My heart starts racing, and my palms are getting sweaty. I feel like I'm about to face my executioner and I can only imagine how Mac's feeling. When he pops his door handle, I reach out and rest my hand on top of his. "Are you okay?"

He nods. "I will be. This is going to be hard, but I'll be better when it's over." He leans forward and wraps his fingers around my head as he pulls me in for a kiss. I feel the flutter in my belly, and I wish it would stop. I have to stop thinking about us as a couple. It's not going to happen. He's a playboy. Even if he is my husband. When Mac breaks the kiss, our eyes meet in the darkness. "I'm sorry for everything… but no matter what, I'm still happy you came with me to Reno."

The building emotion robs me of words, but I know for sure that I also don't regret going with him. I slowly get out of the car, giving myself time to get it together.

The Sacramento heat hits me as I exit the car and I'm fanning myself, hoping I don't have to meet his sponsor covered in a layer of sweat. As I follow Mac into the backyard, I'm almost plowed over by a large chocolate Lab.

"No!" Mac shouts and grabs the dog's collar, but I'm instantly in love.

"Oh, my God! Hi, sweetie. Oh, my." I rub his head and let him lick my hand until he's familiar with me. "He's beautiful."

"He's a she… and she's still learning her manners." Mac lowers himself to his knees and lets the dog lick his face. "Luna," he croons, and the dog is whacking my leg with her tail, she's so excited to see him. "Hi, Luna… can you be a good girl?"

I squat next to them and rub my hand over her back. I'm a little taken aback. I had no idea he had a dog and this is a stark reminder that I don't really know much about Mac at all. "What a good girl. Hi, Luna." She licks my face, and I know instantly that we're going to be best friends. I hug her neck and glance at Mac. "I love her."

He chuckles and says, "I think she loves you too." He helps me to my feet, and with a couple more rub downs, Luna settles.

I watch Mac as he takes a deep breath before leading me up the back stairs, onto the back deck, and into his house. His home is an early twentieth-century Craftsman, and it's so beautiful. There must be at least three bedrooms, with a basement and an attic, and I wonder if he shares the house with roommates.

The back door enters into a mudroom that leads to the kitchen, and the house is cool from the air conditioning… almost cold. The first thing that catches my attention is how spotless everything is. Seriously. It's the cleanest kitchen I've ever seen. I look around with my mouth hanging open, not sure what to think. Most bachelors aren't quite so neat, are they? I've never seen a bachelor pad look like this.

All of his appliances are stainless steel. His stove is huge, with six burners and a double oven. "You cook?" I ask.

He nods and smiles faintly. A moment later Luna rushes into the kitchen with a dirty tennis ball in her mouth. Mac points to the back door. "Take that back outside, Luna. Go." Her ears drop, and she slumps away, back through the small doggie door.

I look around again and admire the space. There's a low counter with stools between the living room and dining room, which doesn't look like an original feature. I wonder if he knocked the wall down and added the bar himself or if he bought the house like this. The dining room has a six-person table, and that seems odd for a bachelor. It looks like solid oak, and it's stained a dark brown. The walls are a soft blue with white trim, and look beautiful with the wood furniture. There's a built-in bar in the dining room, but I can easily see there are zero liquor bottles behind the glass doors.

Mac has excellent taste. As clean and well decorated as his place is, I can still see signs that he's single. There are no silly knick-knacks, or fluff. Definitely no lace curtains and I don't expect to find knitted throws on his sofa, but there is beautiful art on the walls, one of which is covered with what looks like family photos.

We step through the kitchen into the dining room, and then into the living room. Two people are there waiting for us. The man, who I assume is Jeff, stands up and shakes Mac's hand, pulling him into a tight, one-armed hug. He's almost as tall as Mac and about the same size, but maybe a little older. He's good-looking for an older guy. Well-built, with an even tan and a friendly face.

When they break from the hug, Mac turns toward the woman and sighs. "What are you doing here?" He looks over at Jeff. "What were you thinking when you called her?"

Jeff holds up both hands in surrender. "I didn't call her. She called me."

She stands and gives me a look that tells me she'd love nothing more than to see me dead. She's dressed casually but she's fully tucked in and pristinely pressed, and as I look at her, I feel as if I'm dressed like a teenager in my ripped jeans and t-shirt. Her hair is perfectly coiffed, and I can tell by the lack of roots on her highlights that she's been to the salon recently. "Jeff didn't need to call me. I heard all about your escapades last night on Facebook."

Mac looks at me and says, "Oh, shit." Which echoes my thoughts exactly. I hold my breath, afraid of exactly what everyone knows.

"Yeah," she says. "I'm sure the entire world knows now."

Mac looks from her to Jeff. "Knows what exactly?"

The woman places her hands on her hips. "What do you think, Mackensey? That you got drunk last night in Reno."

"Is that all they know?" he asks, and I let the breath out in a long whoosh in relief.

She narrows her eyes at him. "What else is there?"

"Um... Emily, this is Kelley. My wife."

Holy shit! Does the man have *any* impulse control? I'm so embarrassed. How could he just blurt it out like that?

"What?" Emily and Jeff say at the same time and then Emily starts laughing maniacally. I get this horrible sinking feeling in my stomach.

"Emily," Mac says, obviously trying to shut her up, but all it does is make her laugh harder and point to me, then to him.

"Married," she manages to spit out. "You got married? *You?*"

"Emily, stop." Mac's face is turning bright red, and I'm sure mine has lost all its color. "Kelley and I went to an all-night chapel last night and got married." As he says this, I feel the two gold bands grow warm in my front pocket.

Mac rests his hands on his hips in response to Emily's laughing. "I guess it's safe to assume that wasn't reported on Facebook last night."

"Ah, no," Jeff says. "I don't think anybody knows about that yet."

"Probably a good thing since everyone knows you think marriage is for idiots," Emily says, and she looks over at me. "What were you thinking last night?"

"Don't, Emily," says Mac and his expression grows hard. I can see his jaw tick as he stares at her. "Don't get your hackles up at her. This isn't her fault."

"No?" she says and waves a hand in his direction. "You don't think she has a bet with her BFFs on who can tame the beast first? She obviously didn't try to stop you from drinking."

"She didn't know," Mac says. "I lied to her. I didn't tell her I was an alcoholic."

"The hell she didn't." Emily's eyebrows draw together. "Everyone in Sacramento knows you're an alcoholic, Mac. She's not fooling anyone but you." As she says this last line, she glares at me.

"As much as I'd love to say that every single person in Sacramento listens to my show, I can't. She doesn't, and she didn't know who I was."

"What a way to sing her praises. Do you always give it up so easily to strangers?" Emily says, her voice full of sarcasm.

I can't listen any more. Partly because she's right, and partly because I just don't have it in me today to take the abuse. Especially from someone I don't even know. I turn from the room and retreat through the house and out the back door. I'm fighting tears but I'll be damned if that bitch gets to see me cry. I rush back out into hot day and through the yard, petting the dog as I go to keep her from jumping on me and slowing me down. I exit through the gate and into the alley toward K Street. I have no problem taking the light rail home; he's got more important things to take care of anyway.

A block and a half away, I hear footsteps running toward me. Mac catches my elbow from behind and stops me. "I'm sorry, Kelley. My sister can be a bitch, I know."

I shrug in an effort to pretend I don't care, but I do and I'm afraid to say anything because I'm not sure how much longer I can hold back the tears. "No need to be sorry. She's right about everything."

"No. She's not." He grabs my other arm and pulls me closer. He's quite a bit taller than me, so I have to look straight up at him to see his face. Looking at him is what breaks me. I don't want to cry in front of Mac, but I'm too tired and too emotionally drained to control it. When tears leak out, he reaches up and swipes one away.

"She's wrong," he says. "And I'm sorry. She shouldn't have treated you like that."

"It doesn't matter anyway, Mac."

"Yes, it does. I'm not going to let her talk to you like that. I'm not going to let *anyone* talk to you like that."

"Thank you, really, but you need to stop worrying about me and worry about repairing all of the relationships we've damaged by what we did last night."

"I can't stop worrying about you." He drops his hands, and his expression grows soft. "What about this…"

"Mess?" I ask. "Because that's what this is. A mess."

He takes a step back. "Kelley, don't be like this."

I force back my emotions and face him, and this situation, for what it really is. I have no choice. "Seriously, Mac? Your sister's right, you're not a relationship guy. I don't need to listen to your radio show to know that. And don't worry, I'm not like Sammie Collins. I'm not going to blame you for this and hold a grudge forever. I'm a big girl, I can take the rejection." A pained expression crosses his face, and I feel sorry for being so blunt with him, but we both need to face reality.

He doesn't say anything, he just stands there and stares at me. So, I turn and walk away from him, even though it feels like I'm walking away from something that could've been great… and every step hurts. With a heavy heart, I head down to R Street to catch the Gold Line toward campus.

Before I reach the light rail stop, a car pulls up next to me. It's Jeff, and he's waving me over. "Kelley, hon, get in and let me drive you home." I stop and stare at the car for a minute, not sure what to do and in no hurry to get home.

I finally open the passenger door and get into his car. Sitting down, I realize I don't have my duffle bag. It's still in Mac's trunk, but I'm not about to go back to get it. Jeff greets me politely with an apologetic expression on his face. I give him the address, and he heads toward my building.

"I'm sorry Emily was so rough on you. I know it's hard to believe, but she actually is a nice person. She's just anxious about Mac."

"I know that," I say. "I'd be worried too… I *am* worried. I never meant for any of this to happen. I had no idea Mac was an alcoholic."

"I'm sure you didn't. Mac can be quite charming when he wants to be. He's good at… well, let's just say, he's good at being who people want him to be."

That statement makes me a little sick to my stomach. Because when Mac and I were together, I didn't have any expectations. I didn't want him to be somebody else. I was just trying to go with the flow, have a good time—for once. Look where I've ended up. "I'm sorry for the mess. I'm sorry about his drinking. I'm sure you're disappointed in him." I look over and say, "If it helps, you should know, he's more pissed at himself than we could ever be at him."

"I know." He frowns and says, "I'm sure he'll be fine. One night of drinking isn't going to destroy all the work he's put into his sobriety. I just hope nothing else does."

I'm not sure what that means. And I'm not sure how to respond. "What are you trying to say?"

"Well… he's fine today, and he'll probably be fine tomorrow, but I'm little worried about the outcome of your relationship. You know what I mean?"

"No. I don't think I do."

"May I be frank with you?" he asks.

"I wish you would."

"Mac doesn't usually grow close to women. He's a serial dater. He doesn't commit… as a rule." He pauses for a moment and then says, "I think women use the term 'commitment-phobe' to describe him."

"Oh." I think about that for a minute and about what that means. "Honestly, Jeff, I could have guessed that about Mac, but it doesn't mean he's incapable of being in a relationship or committing to one person. He's personable and affectionate… at least he was with me."

"You really don't listen to his show, do you?" He chuckles and glances over at me. "Look, I just don't want to see you get hurt. I don't know what you're expecting from him, but he's not likely to pursue a relationship, even after what happened in Reno. He's a player, and he's well known for it, which is why Emily said some of the things she did."

I can feel the heat in my cheeks, and now I feel like an idiot. What can I say to that?

"I guess I'll just consider myself well played."

CHAPTER NINE

Mackensey

I stare her down, fighting to contain my anger. "How could you?" I pace in front of her, unable to sit still. "Emily, that woman has done nothing to you."

"Yeah, she has. She's hurt you, and you can't be mad at me for hating her for that."

"She's done nothing wrong. She genuinely didn't know my history, and we've hurt *her*, not the other way around." That statement hits me hard. I've hurt Kelley and that's the last thing I wanted to do. Jesus. I'm fucking toxic. What the hell happened last night that caused us to *get married*? For someone like me, getting married is about as much fun as getting the death penalty.

I'm still feeling a little sick from all the alcohol last night. I walk into the kitchen, pull open the refrigerator, and grab a bottle of water. I need a little space from my sister. We don't usually fight. We're close, we talk to each other, we barely argue. But I'm having a hard time forgiving her for treating Kelley the way she did.

"What are you going to do about this marriage, Mackensey?" She says from the dining room. "It won't go away if you ignore it. You've pretty much written that girl a blank check, and I bet you don't even know her last name."

"Her full name is Kelley Michelle Kontos, and you're a bitch for treating her like that." I point my water at her and say, "Go home. I can't stand to look at you right now."

"What the hell did I do?" she shouts.

"Go home!" I turn away from her and walk outside. Luna is there, and she's so happy to see me. Dogs are great like that. They don't hold grudges, they're not judgmental, and they give all of their love unconditionally. Unlike most people.

"Hi, baby girl, did you have a great weekend hanging out with Jeff?" I give her a good rubdown, using my nails the way she likes. She rolls over onto her back, showing me her belly. She's such a good girl, and I feel a little guilty for being gone all weekend. That thought makes me think of Kelley again, and then I feel worse.

I spend the next twenty minutes playing catch with Luna, trying to clear my head until Jeff gets back. But clearing my head is easier in theory than in practice. I can't stop thinking about Kelley and what we did last night. I don't remember much, but I remember how radiant she looked when we got back to our room. I remember the happy glow as we undressed. I remember feeling completely smitten and not being afraid of signing my name next to hers. Alcohol does that. Erases my fear. Erases my fear of *everything*, which is why drinking is so dangerous for me.

When Jeff returns, I can't judge what he thinks from the look on his face, so I ask him. "How was Kelley when you dropped her off?"

"Quiet," he says.

"I feel terrible. I can't believe how horrible Emily was to her."

Jeff pats my back as he sits next to me on the step. "Don't be so hard on Emily. She's worried about you, you can't fault her for that."

"I can when she treats someone I care about like that."

Jeff starts to chuckle, but I'm not sure why. I look over at him, and he says, "You care about her? Okay…"

"What are you saying?"

"Like you care about all the women you date?"

"What do you mean?"

Jeff shakes his head and says, "How long have you known Kelley?"

I puff up my chest, even though I'm trying to be open-minded and not get offended by his questions. "What difference does it make?"

"It all makes a difference. You say you care about her, but I have to ask if you even know her." He grunts another laugh and says, "Careful, man, you don't want to turn into a cliché."

That pisses me off. Now I am offended. I expect this shit at work, but I don't expect it from my sponsor. "Fuck off."

Jeff leans back, obviously surprised. "You're serious?"

"Yeah, I'm serious. Why wouldn't I be?"

He shrugs. "You never are, Mac. Usually, when you say that, you don't really mean it." He waves a hand and says, "Yes, you mean it. You care about everyone, but you never *care* in the way that means anything. Your care and affection never amount to love." He points to me and says, "You can get angry with us, and act like Emily and I are misjudging your relationship, but our behavior hasn't changed, yours has."

"I'm telling you I care about this woman. Why is that so hard to believe?"

"Yeah, and you cared about Angela, and Jess, and Christine, and Sammie—"

"All right! I get your damn point." Hearing him say Sammie's name forces me to instantly recoil. It's bad enough that I drank with Kelley, but then getting so drunk I don't remember everything… If that doesn't give me déjà vu of my time with Sammie, nothing will.

I stand up and toss the ball for Luna. When she brings it back, I juggle it from hand to hand.

"Mac, look, I'm sorry I brought up Sammie. It's unfair... I know you're a different person now."

"I just don't see any point in leading anyone on. I can't pretend I want more when I don't, but maybe it's different this time. You don't know." The normal pang of guilt I feel when I think about Sammie hits me hard. As much as I don't want history to repeat itself, I feel like things with Kelley are different. Typically, after spending the weekend with a woman, I wouldn't be interested in seeing her again, but I can't seem to get Kelley off my mind... and I don't think it has anything to do with getting married. Dammit, or getting drunk with her.

"Okay, maybe it is, but you can't get pissed off at us when you bring home a woman, and we see your relationship with her exactly the same way we see all the others. We have no way of knowing that it's different with Kelley... if it is." He stares at me for a moment and says, "It must be... if you married her."

"I was drunk, remember?"

"Yeah, I know, Mac, but does it matter?" He stands, takes the ball from my hand, and tosses it for Luna, who's become frustrated that I've held onto it. "The question is, did you marry her because you were drunk, or did you marry her because you love her?"

I look at him sharply, not sure what to say. He must understand because he gives me a knowing look and says, "Tonight's meeting was canceled so we'll go tomorrow. Call me if you need me before then."

Four o'clock in the morning comes awfully quick, especially when you can't sleep. The last time I looked at the clock, it was midnight. That's less than four hours of sleep. Sometimes I really hate my job. I drag myself into the station, dreading what I'm going to face from my co-host today.

As soon as I enter the studio, Mimi's frowning at me. I hold my hands up. "I'm fine. It was one night, and it won't happen again."

"Mac, you do understand that if you get fired, I'll get fired too. We're partners, I can't do the show without you."

"I'm sorry. I'm here, right? I screwed up one time, it won't happen again."

"I hope you're right." I see her eyes shift to something behind me. I turn around and see Kurt staring me down from his producer's booth. "Morning, Kurt."

"Not that I need to ask, but how was Reno?" he says.

"It was fine. Sammie was a complete bitch. Thanks for the warning, by the way."

"Oh, she showed? Good to hear." He grins. "Would you have gone if you knew she'd be there?"

"Kurt, you asshole. That's probably what drove him to drink," Mimi says.

Kurt pales a little, and I like watching him squirm. It only takes him a moment to recover before he says, "Maybe you should've come to that meeting on Friday."

I grin at him. "Sorry... got tied up with a woman."

"You little jerk. Are you telling me you didn't come to the meeting because you were with a girl?"

I laugh at the annoyed expression on his face. "A woman, Kurt, a woman. Not a girl." I pull out my chair, plop down, and grab the headphones, feeling good about rattling his cage. "And, yeah, of course, it was a woman. What'd ya think?"

I put my headphones on and pull the mic closer. A moment later, I hear Mimi in my ear. "You're such a slut, Mac."

I glance up at her and wink. "Yeah, but that's what you guys love about me."

Then I stare down at my notes, trying to focus on the Monday morning schedule and what I have to do today while I wait for Mimi's introduction. I have to shake off what happened over the weekend and remember I'm Mac, from *Mimi and Mac in the Morning*. Not Mac, the alcoholic who destroyed his sobriety over the weekend.

Mimi leans into the microphone and says, "This is Mimi Swan with Mac Thomas, and we're Mimi and Mac in the Morning. Happy Monday. How are you this morning, Mac? Besides hungover?"

I laugh and say, "Right for the jugular first thing in the morning, huh?" So much for shaking off the weekend.

"That's what happens when you leave me to learn about your life on Facebook."

"You'll be happy to know I'm just fine this morning. I survived the weekend and the Comedy Festival."

"Caller on line two." I hear Kurt say through my headphones.

"Line two, what say you this fine Monday morning?" Mimi says.

"Hey, Mimi and Mac. So, this is Bree, long-time listener, and I ran into Mac in Reno this weekend. He was hanging out at Death and Taxes with James Foster and some girl."

"Oh, so you were drinking with a woman… what a surprise," Mimi says.

"Hey." I shrug and say, "You know what they say… when in Rome…"

The caller pipes up before Mimi has a chance to say anything else. "And they were pretty close all night. Faces glued, if you know what I mean."

"Is that so?" Mimi says. "Do tell, Mac."

"A gentleman never kisses and tells."

Kurt is in my headphones again. "Caller line three." Mimi disconnects line two and clicks to line three.

"Caller, line three, what say you?" Mimi says.

"Yeah, I saw Mac in Reno too, at the Comedy Festival. He was curled up with some pretty brunette, but I'm sure he was completely sober. I think we should give them a break."

Mimi chuckles. "Oh, you think we should give them a break?"

Kurt chimes in. "I don't think we should give them a break."

"I do," I say. "It's a new day, guys. Let's start this Monday off with that movie review. Kurt, you got that ready?"

"The movie review isn't scheduled until seven-thirty. We have plenty of time to talk about the weekend, Mac," Mimi says, and I see her grin from across the room. I shoot her the bird, and that just makes her laugh.

"Caller line one, what say you?" Mimi says again and I'm really hoping this one is about something else. Anything else.

"Hey, Mimi, this is Josie and I just called to tell Mac, I'm available to join him in Reno anytime he needs a date."

"Thanks for the call, Josie. Mac's always looking for a date, especially the kind that doesn't mind him sneaking out before sunrise."

"You know me too well, Mimi." I give her a challenging stare and pipe in with my usual comment. "Josie, feel free to leave your number with Kurt and maybe we can hook up later."

So this is how my morning's going to go. It's no different than any other day, except that I feel the need to protect Kelley from it. As each caller comes on the line and each text is read, I'm worried someone is going to out her... or tell everyone about our little trip to the wedding chapel.

"We have a text from the nine-one-six area code," Mimi says and then she reads the message. "I think Mac spent the weekend with my BF."

My eyes go wide, and I stare at Mimi, giving her the cut sign with my hand slicing across my neck.

"Hey, Mac, do you think she means best friend or boyfriend?"

"Haha, very funny," I say before giving Mimi the cut sign again.

She breaks for a commercial and a song, then pulls off her headphones.

"What's your problem, Mac?" she asks.

"I do not want this woman's name shared on our show. She's local, and I don't want this brought to her door."

Mimi looks me up and down and finally says, "Fine. I won't let the callers or the texters out her if you promise to give me the scoop later."

I tilt my head and glare at her. "You already know I will."

CHAPTER TEN

Kelley

I couldn't sleep, which seems like the norm for this week. I drag my ass into Starbucks, walk straight to the counter, and order a Venti mocha. I don't want to look over at the table where I met Mac. I don't want to think about it or about how much I miss him. He's a distraction I don't need today. If it weren't for finals, I'd skip class and go back to bed. It'd be a perfect time too since Meg and Eric are both at work.

When Lexi, the barista, hands over my coffee, I almost want to weep with joy.

"Thank you so much." I whisper as I smile at her.

"Anytime, sweets," she says. "Oh, yeah, you know you left some stuff at my apartment."

I roll my eyes. "I have crap spread all over Sacramento. That's what I get for not wanting to go home."

"My couch is available anytime you want to crash."

"Thank you so much, Lexi. I have finals this week. I'm trying to stay home so I can be on my normal schedule but we'll see how it goes with Megan."

"Good luck with that." She gives me a nod goodbye and gets to work on the next drink.

I grab my mocha, head toward the back exit, and run smack into Emily, Mac's sister. Now I *really* wish I'd stayed in bed. This is the last person I need to see right now. So much for avoiding distractions.

I'm frozen in place, and she seems a little surprised too. She points and spins her finger in a circle. "Do you live around here?"

I nod, unable to use my voice yet.

"Oh, I didn't know that." She glances at her watch and says, "Do you have a few minutes?"

She seems like she's over her anger, but it's hard to forget the nasty things she said to me on Sunday. I clear my throat and say, "I have an exam in half an hour."

"You're a student?"

I nod. "Yes."

"I won't need that long, but can I order coffee first? I haven't had any yet and I can't function without caffeine."

"Sure." I look around and luck out with an empty table. It's the same table I was sitting at when I met Mac and that sinks my spirits even further. I slide down into the chair and try not to remember his broad smile and friendly laugh or how good it felt to be with him.

I sip my mocha and savor the bitter chocolate while I wait for the caffeine to kick in. I need it so badly today. I watch as Emily approaches the counter. The staff seem to know her, and only take a moment to get her drink ready. I look her up and down. She's wearing a blue business suit with spiked heels. She's gorgeous and tall... well put together, just like Mac. I look down at my yoga pants and flip-flops, cringing as she sits down across from me.

"Thank you for staying," she says. "So... a student? How old are you?"

"I'm twenty-five," I say, and I'm about to ask why when she interrupts me.

"Graduate school?"

"No, undergrad. I got a late start."

When she gives me a confused look, I say, "I'm a dancer. I went on tour with a dance company right out of high school. Due to that, I started college a few years late."

"Oh, that makes sense." She seems a little uncomfortable.

"Is that what you wanted to talk to me about?" I asked.

"No... sorry. Actually, I'm glad I ran into you. It saves me from having to track you down."

This statement makes me nervous. I've already spent my morning stressing over crazed Mimi and Mac fans wanting to hunt me down and string me up for thoughtlessly getting the man drunk and ruining his life. Now I have to worry about his aggressive sister too. "Why would you need to track me down?"

"I want to apologize. I shouldn't have spoken to you the way I did. Mackensey is my baby brother, and he's had a hard time with alcohol. And women never usually have his best interests in mind. So... I was worried. I freaked out, and that's why I acted the way I did."

I stare at her, not sure what to say. It takes me a minute, but when I finally find my voice, I try for politeness. "Thank you. I understand. I'm a little worried about him myself. But I hope you know I didn't set out to find Mac or to cause him trouble. I really didn't know who he was when I met him."

"I didn't believe it at first, but Mac explained it, and I know now that I was wrong. I'm sorry about that."

I'm a little taken aback. I'm not used to people admitting when they're wrong and actually apologizing for it. I guess between Megan, Eric, and dealing with my past, I'm conditioned for the opposite. Megan has never admitted that she was wrong to sleep with Eric. She never admits she's wrong about anything.

"I appreciate that," I say. "I just started listening to his show this week."

She grimaces and says, "Oh, no! You picked a horrible time to start, you poor thing."

I'm not sure how I feel about her pity, but I chuckle anyway. "They definitely seem to hate me."

She sucks air through her teeth and says, "Wait until they find out you're married."

I feel the blood drain from my face. "Great. Can't wait for that."

She holds a hand up and says, "Don't worry, they don't need to find out if you guys take care of it right away."

I wasn't expecting to have this conversation with Emily. This is about me and Mac, not his sister. I nod without saying anything, but that doesn't slow her down.

"What are you guys planning to do about it?" she asks.

I shrug. "I don't know… we haven't had a chance to talk about it."

"Really?" Her eyebrows scrunch together. "You haven't talked about it at all?"

I stare at her for a moment. "No." I lean back in my chair, fighting to remain calm. "We were too busy discussing his drinking problem. That seemed like the bigger issue at the time."

"Of course, sorry." She nibbles on the inside of her mouth for a moment then says, "But what's your plan?"

"I don't have a plan, except for getting to class and doing the best I can on my exam."

"You know, Mac isn't the marrying sort of man, right? He's a complete commitment-phobe."

"Funny," I say. "People keep telling me that, yet he's proven to be the exact opposite since the moment I met him." I'm pretty sure she can hear the annoyance in my voice.

"So you haven't even thought about what you're going to do yet? About the marriage?"

I stare at her for a moment, and I'm wondering if she's heard anything I've said. "I've thought of little else since I woke up Sunday morning. So much so that I haven't had any sleep. Listen, Emily, my class starts in ten minutes, and it takes eight minutes to walk there. I need to go."

"Right. Of course, I'm sorry for keeping you. Good luck on your exam."

I stand up, trying hard to smile at her as I leave. I'm halfway to class when my phone chimes in my pocket. It's a text from Mac.

Mac: *Good morning, beautiful.*

I want to ignore him, but my stomach knots up, and I know I won't be able to concentrate if I don't respond before my exam. He's texted me several times this week and even tried to meet up with me, but after my conversation with Jeff, and now Emily, I'm not sure I should, even though I really want to see him. I'm still trying to decide if I'm being played... or should I say, how badly I'm being played. The funny thing is, as often as Mac messages or calls, it's hard to believe he's not genuine. I know his reputation but I see a completely different side to him. Not that it matters since I haven't had the time to devote to him anyway. But it's interesting he's texting me minutes after I talked to his sister. Did she call him?

Me: *Hi*

Mac: *Plans today?*

Me: *Class. It's finals week. Got a lot going on.*

Mac: *Right, sorry. I hope you kill it! Call me when you get a break*

Me: *Okay*

No way am I calling him later. I stuff my phone back in my pocket and pick up the pace because now I'm a minute behind.

Between Megan, Eric, and Mac, it'll be a miracle if I survive this week.

I stumble in the door, so damn relieved about having the apartment to myself. I have a few hours before my next exam, and that's all the time I need for lunch and a good long nap. When I reach my bedroom, there's a note stuck to my door from Meg.

Coffee later?

I crinkle it up and toss it on the floor. As if...

We used to leave notes for each other all the time. We'd meet for coffee, make dates to hang out, or even just plan a movie night through little Post-its. But that ended when I caught her with Eric.

Does she think I forgot what she did to me?

I'm too tired to care much. I lock the bedroom door behind me and crawl into bed. Just a couple more days. A couple more days of school, then I can figure out what to do next. Mary, my boss, mentioned that she may know of an attic apartment available near the dance studio. At this point, I think it's my best option... if I can even qualify. I'll have to find another part-time job over summer though. Otherwise I won't be able to afford it.

I close my eyes, halfway between asleep and awake, when someone knocks on my bedroom door. Who the hell...? Eric and Meg should both be at work, so I'm not sure what to think. I lay still, hoping they go away.

"Kelley?"

It's Megan, and I want to scream at her for waking me up. I ignore her, but she knocks again. "Kelley, I know you're in there since my note is gone."

"I'm tired. Taking a nap. Go away."

"You don't sound like you're sleeping."

Has she always been this selfish and I just didn't recognize it? "Kelley?"

"What do you want?"

I hear the door handle jiggle. "Can I come in?"

I sit up and pound the mattress with my fist. I just want to sleep. I walk over and swing the door open wide, keeping my hand on it so she doesn't try to enter. "Megan, I have another class in a couple of hours. I'm trying to take a nap. What do you want?"

Her navy blue suit tells me she's just come from work. The flash of pink silk peeking out from her buttoned jacket softens the sharp edges of the blazer. I would have complimented her normally… in another life, but in this life, she doesn't deserve kind words from me. Her soft, blonde curls look a bit wild and windblown as she brushes them off her face. "I've barely seen you in two weeks, and I've been worried. I just want to make sure you're okay."

"Were you though? Were you really worried about me?" It's impossible to miss the sarcasm in my voice.

"Yeah, I was. Why don't you believe that?"

"Should I list those reasons in random order or do you want them alphabetically?"

"Wow! You're so angry. I thought you'd be over this by now."

"Are you kidding me?" I throw my hand in the air. "I'll never be *over this*, Megan."

She watches me closely, as if she's afraid to say what she needs to say. Finally, she spits it out. "You've been complaining about him for weeks, Kelley, and you were planning to break up with him anyway."

I feel the heat rise to my cheeks. So, she didn't know we broke up. I though Eric might have told her when he was trying to convince her to sleep with him. Of course. It's all very clear to me now. If only I could've seen her for who she truly was years ago maybe I'd have a different best friend. And perhaps that best friend would be a decent person. "You're right." I nod and purse my lips. "I actually did break up with him. Hours before finding you two screwing on our couch. However, that isn't the green light for you to sleep with him. What kind of friend does that?"

"If you ended it with him, why is this such a big deal? Come on, Kelley, give me a break."

I give her a hard look and say, "Megan, you have no idea what you've done."

"I've scored us another roommate. We can both use a break on the rent. You should be happy about it."

"Oh, no. I have one foot out the door already. I'm not staying here. But you have a nice life because you and Eric are made for each other." I glance at her and then at the door in my hand. "Is there something else you needed?" I get the feeling she has more to say and that's why she's being hesitant. It's not like her to sit around and take abuse. Normally she would've already retreated from the conversation.

"I know you can't afford to move out."

"You're right, I can't afford it. But I definitely can't afford to stay either. I don't want to have anything to do with you or Eric. And don't worry about my finances, I'll work it out. I always do."

"Eric said he saw you out with Mac Thomas, from KQCC."

My hearts starts pounding hard in my chest. One of the reasons I'm so tired is because I've gotten up at five every morning this week to listen to the radio. I've barely managed to escape being named outright on Mac's show. I've sat in pure anxiety for four hours every day, waiting to hear my name. Thankfully, he and Mimi divert the conversation whenever 'the girl' Mac was with comes up. What the hell am I going to tell Megan?

"Why do you care, Megan?"

"You know he's an alcoholic, right?"

I stare at her for a moment, fighting to understand the point she's trying to make. "I'm not sure what that has to do with me?"

"Because of what happened, you know, with Bradley," she says innocently, and then it hits me like a punch to the stomach.

"So, what? What does Brad have to do with my lunch date?"

"I'm just saying, you should watch out. I would hate to see you get into trouble again."

"Well, gee, thanks for the warning, but stop, okay? What happens to me is no longer any of your concern. We are no longer friends. First chance I get, I'm out of here, and you and Eric can carry on." I close the door and lock it. I rest against the cool wood, and it takes every ounce of strength I have not to hammer my head against it over and over.

I go back to bed, curl under the covers, and pray for sleep, but I can't. Megan planted the seed, and now it's spreading its branches, blossoming into a fully grown tree. I immediately start making comparisons between Brad and Mac. I'm sure that's what she was expecting me to do. But there aren't a lot of similarities, especially since Mac no longer drinks. Something tells me it's completely unfair to hold that one night against him, but... I don't really know him, do I? I only think I do.

I poke my head out from under the blankets and stare up at the photo of Brad and me. The memories of when the photo was taken flood my brain. The dance, the music, the applause... it was so powerful, the energy was incredible. I wish I could see his face. The photo only shows his profile as he's holding me high above his head, my toes pointed into the splits. It was The Cheshire Cat lift from *Alice in Wonderland*.

I grab my phone and pull up a picture of his face. It's been five years. They flew by in a heartbreaking blur, but they also crept by like a snail. I so clearly remember some things, like they happened yesterday, but then have no memories of others. As if on cue, I can feel my pulse in the back of my neck, tendrils of pain snaking from my old scar. It hurts my heart to think about Bradley, and that makes me feel like an awful person because I actively try to forget him. *I'm sorry, Brad. I'm so sorry.* I close my eyes and try to picture his face from that night, but I can't. I can barely remember anything from my twentieth birthday or that entire year. As the emotion builds in my chest, it makes me so angry at Megan. She did this on purpose. She wanted me to feel horrible… to remind me of what I've lost. No matter how hard I fight them, tears slip out. It's too hard to fight it when I'm this tired so I let them fall.

A moment later, my phone dings in my hand. It's a message from Mac. I click the notification and read it.

Mac: *Lunch?*

With a deep sigh, I stare at the message for a long time. I need a distraction, which is the complete opposite to how I felt this morning, but I'm absolutely sure I'm not going to sleep, thanks to Megan. And, as much as I don't want to tangle with Mac, I really do miss him. Bradley is gone and there's nothing I can do to change that… but Mac is here and he wants me. Why not give him a chance?

I type out a text.

Me: *Sure. I have a couple of hours before my next exam.*

Mac: *You like Joe's Deli?*

Me: *Yes! Meet me in front of my building in five*

Mac: *Give me ten, and I'll bring it with me. Do you mind eating at my house? I need to check on Luna.*

Me: *Of course! BTW I like roast beef*

Mac: *You got it, babe*

My heart jumps at his endearment, and I can't hold back the smile. I hop out of bed and quickly scan my closet for something decent to wear. I don't want him to see me in my yoga pants and flip-flops… it's just too pathetic.

Once I'm dressed, I stare at myself in the mirror, jittery with nerves. I'm playing with fire and have a feeling I'm going to get burned… but I can't help myself.

CHAPTER ELEVEN

Mackensey

I pull up, and she's standing there waiting, with a smile. She's wearing a sexy little yellow summer dress and I can't help but stare at her long, toned legs. I'm incapable of controlling the grin that takes over my face. I'm not sure why but I'm nervous. Seeing her kicks my heart into overdrive and I feel like a damn teenager with a hard-on.

After she fastens her seatbelt, I lean over and pull her closer for a kiss. She smells like coconut and summer. I run my nose over her warm skin, and I want to take a bite out of her rosy cheek, but I settle for a kiss. The anxiety I've felt over the last couple of days fades away as I taste her. She gives me an instant and natural high and I have to wonder how dangerous she is for my addiction, but right now, I don't care. I just want to enjoy her.

When I pull back to look at her face, I'm stunned by the dark circles under her eyes. "Kelley… Are you okay?"

She nods as her hand rests against my face, and I like it. I grab it and kiss her palm. "You look tired. Did you sleep last night?"

"Not at all." She looks away sheepishly and says, "I haven't slept much all week. Finals week is always hard."

"I'm sorry. Is there anything I can do to make things easier?"

She nods toward the deli bag. "You already have… and thank you for thinking of me."

"Thank you for agreeing to see me, finally. I've been worried about you… and how we left things on Sunday."

"I appreciate your persistence. I guess I should thank you for not giving up on me."

I give her a good long look before I say, "I won't be giving up, Kelley. You can count on that." I put the truck into drive and head to my house. I'm feeling a little selfish. I don't want to share her with an audience. Not to mention that, after today's show, I really don't want any of my listeners to see us together. Not because I'm embarrassed, not at all. But I don't want the drama to seep into Kelley's life.

"You know, Mac, we're going to have to talk about it. Make some decisions."

My chest tightens a little because I don't know what to do. The anxiety I feel about being married is a little more than I can handle at the moment. I still can't believe I did something so damn stupid. I've spent a good portion of my life drunk and I've never done anything as careless—reckless—as getting married. I can't be a husband, I have no idea how, and more than that, I don't want to force her into keeping a commitment she isn't ready to make. "I know," is all I can say, since I'm not prepared to talk about it at all. I think she can tell because she lets me off the hook.

"If it's okay with you, I'd rather deal with it when I don't have to think about school."

I nod, afraid to speak for fear I might sound indifferent about it—and I do not feel indifferent about her. After a moment I say, "We have time."

She rests her head back and closes her eyes. "I think I'm gonna spend the entire weekend sleeping," she says. "I can't wait for this week to end. I'll be done with school for the summer."

"What are your plans for summer?" I ask.

She lets out a heavy sigh, and I can almost feel the stress that accompanies it. "I have no idea yet."

"Do you go visit your family in Oregon?"

"I usually try to make it up there for a week or two, spend some time with my mom, but not much longer than that."

"Why not? You're not close with her?"

"No, not really, but we get along fine. I'm the black sheep of the family, especially with my extended family. They're a bit... toxic." She lifts one shoulder in a shrug. "It's also a financial hit to leave the dance studio for that long."

"*You're* the black sheep? I never would have guessed that. You seem so normal... put together."

She frowns and says, "It's the professional dance thing. They all think I've destroyed my life because I'm not touring."

"But you were injured?" I glance over and say, "That doesn't seem right and it doesn't matter if you're doing what you want to do." I brush my hand at her. "Screw them."

She points at me and says, "That's what I said too."

"If the dance studio doesn't pay you enough, why do you work there? Maybe you should try a different studio."

"Mary, the owner, has offered to make me a partner when I graduate."

"Oh, right, I remember you telling me that before. Isn't that exactly what you want?"

She smiles faintly. "Yeah, if I can survive that long."

I grab her knee, give it a shake. "One more year, right?"

She takes my hand in hers and entwines our fingers. "Yes, one more year." Her voice is heavy, and I wish I could do something to make things easier.

I park the truck in front of the house and get out so I can open her door for her. I really want to kiss her again, but I'm trying to give her a little space. I don't know why but I'm fighting the urge to tell her that I've missed her. It's only been a few days—hell, I've only known her for a few days—but it's still true.

I carry the bag of sandwiches up the front steps and unlock the door to let her inside. When she enters, Luna is there bouncing up and down, jumping on us both. I shout her down and tell her to sit. She does, and Kelley says, "Oh, good girl."

"She's getting better." I point to Luna and then toward the back door. "Okay, Luna, let's go outside."

I walk through the house as she rushes to the back door. I set the sandwiches on the table as I pass and head into the kitchen. I flip open the lock on the doggie door, and Luna rushes out.

When I return to the dining room, Kelley is looking around, wide-eyed. For some reason that makes me nervous. "What is it?"

She shakes her head. "Your place is so clean. I guess it just surprises me."

"It's weird, right?" When she glances at me, I say, "It's weird that we feel like old friends, but we really know very little about each other."

It's as if I can feel her relax at this acknowledgment. "So it's not just me?" she says. "One minute, I feel like I've known you my whole life, but then the next, I get a stark reminder that I haven't."

"Yep, me too. And the freakishly clean house is part of my sobriety. If my space is clean, my mind is clear, and I can make better decisions." I reach inside the bag for the sandwiches. "I follow a pretty strict schedule. The structure makes things easier."

She sits in one of the chairs and says, "Do you find it hard? I mean, besides Saturday night, have you had other setbacks?"

"No. Not one. Saturday was the first time I've had a drink in over three years."

"I'm sorry," she says, guilt written all over her face.

"Please don't." I place my palms on the table and lean toward her. "Please don't blame yourself. You and I know the truth, and the truth is, I didn't tell you."

"Why did you do it, Mac?" I see her eyes dance around nervously. "I want to understand. Why did you drink? What about me, or about our time together, drove you to pick up that drink?"

"I'm not sure." I shrug and say, "I've been asking myself the same question. I guess I just got caught up in the evening. James was egging me on, and I didn't want to admit to you that I had a problem. Something inside me snapped, and I had this sudden urge to be reckless." I sit down in the chair across from her, trying to remember what I was feeling at the time, but it's just too blurry. Blocking out the emotions, I try to focus on the moments without feeling. I remember watching Kelley laugh, and I remember being in awe of her... of her beauty, her grace. I remember how much fun she was having, and how just once I wanted to enjoy myself without working for it. Without always being conscious of my actions and conscious of what's coming out of my mouth. I wanted to be free.

This thought levels me. I can have fun without drinking—I do it all the time. So why did I feel like I needed to drink that night? I glance over at Kelley, and she's watching me. I can't help but think about how cautious I am around women all the time. I have to be careful about what I say to them to make sure they don't get the wrong idea. I specifically remember not wanting to be so cautious around Kelley that night. It's almost as if I wanted to be reckless with her. I wanted to be unboxed by her. Because that's what I am, boxed. I have to be. I have to be carefully contained.

I lock myself in a box to avoid emotional attachments. It saves me from leading women on and making them believe that one or two dates will turn into a long-term relationship. I've never been interested in that. Never.

"I don't want to be the person who drives you to drink," she says, and I can hear the emotion in her voice. I stand and walk around the table, grab her elbow and pull her to her feet so that we're nose to nose.

"It wasn't you, Kelley. I was cowardly by not telling you. It was me attempting to be macho when I should have been strong enough to have a good time with you and James without taking a drink."

I reach out and touch her face, and when our skin connects, it sets off a fire inside me that I can't control. "Is it crazy that I missed you?" After saying this, I want to roll my eyes because I don't say shit like that to women. What the hell is wrong with me?

She shakes her head and says, "No. I haven't been able to stop thinking about you all week either." Hearing this stokes the flames within me, and suddenly I don't care about being reserved with her. I don't care about anything but touching her a little more.

I lean in and take her mouth in mine. I want to taste her. I want to drag her to the floor and listen to her cries of pleasure as I drive inside her. I deepen the kiss and pull her closer. I'm hard and can't help grinding my erection against her. When she presses back, I run my hands behind her head and grab fistfuls of hair, fighting against the desire to bend her over the table.

I drag my mouth from hers. "What time do you have class?"

"I have to be there at three-fifteen," she breathes and nips at my bottom lip with her teeth. "Screw it," she says. "I'll skip it."

"No." I pull away. "No, I can't let you do that. This wasn't my intention when I brought you here." I rest my forehead against hers, and it takes me a minute to slow my pulse. "I just wanted to see you and make sure you're alright after last weekend."

"And now you're going to send me off to class besotted and horny. Kind of a dick move, if you ask me."

I crack out a laugh. I can't help it. Kelley's smiling, but at the same time, she's reaching for my belt buckle. I grab her hand and pull her to the bedroom. As much as I want to bend her over my dining-room table, I won't. I want her to feel cherished, not trashy, even though I plan to screw her until she walks funny.

The bedroom curtains are open but with the shadows from the trees outside, it's still pretty shaded, so I can't see the details of her face clearly. She's already got my belt off and my pants unzipped, and that's a good sign that she doesn't mind about the curtains. She circles my waist with her hands and locks her thumbs into my waistband before pushing downward. A second later, she's on her knees with her hot, wet mouth around my length. Not what I was expecting. Not at all, but I'm not about to complain.

"Oh, Christ, Kelley." It feels so good as she takes all of me, then pulls away, circling me with her tongue. I'm not sure how much more I can take. This wasn't—isn't—I wanted to make her cry out, not the other way around. "Kelley… I can't… you're going to make me come, babe."

I wrap my hand around her cheek and gently pull her away. "Come here," I say.

She lifts to her feet and reaches for my t-shirt, before pulling it over my head. I do the same with her dress, tossing it on the chair in the corner. She's not wearing a bra, and the sight of her beautiful breasts causes my dick to twitch. I reach out and take them in both hands, gently caressing her nipples before leaning forward and taking them between my lips, one at a time. They pucker and stick out in points and that makes them easier to suck between my teeth, rolling my tongue over them. She sways a little with a moan. I'm so on edge, so ready for her; I don't want to play, I want to be inside her. Now.

I back her against the bed and lay her down. Then I retrieve a condom from the bedside drawer. She's shifted to her side, and she's watching me. I can't help but wonder what she's thinking. She looks amazing. Her curves are so natural. She's slim but firm, with long limbs and a swan-like neck. A dancer's body. *My body.*

I slide the condom on, then reach out and gently slide her panties off. When I lean over her, our eyes lock, and it's as if our heartbeats are in sync when I push inside her. She feels so comfortable yet so deliciously new at the same time. Her eyes squeeze closed, and she cries out, but not in pain. She likes it. I thrust forward again, harder this time, and watch the smile spread across her face.

"Oh, damn, Mackensey," she whispers, and I like the sound of my name on her lips. I pump inside her, one, two, three more times, and then slow down, taking my time.

She opens her eyes, and her sultry expression is killing me.

"Say it again, Kelley."

She grins teasingly. "Your name?"

"Please…" I slide in again, slowly, and I can tell by the way she lifts against me that it's not enough. She wants more.

"Mac," she cries. "Mackensey, do it again. Please, don't stop." Her words sound breathless, and goddammit, I want her. Her voice, every little sound she makes, is like a drug and I want more. I pound again and again and again until I'm sweating and out of breath, chest heaving. Finally, she digs her heels into the bed and lifts against me; her body is rigid and quivering from her orgasm, her voice crying out in ecstasy. I even my pace but when I feel my balls tighten, I pound against her again. My release is explosive too and I let out a long moan until I'm empty and exhausted.

I drop down next to her, fighting to catch my breath. She curls against me, and we're both sweaty, but I don't care. I wrap my arms around her and pull her close. Within seconds, her breathing evens out, and she's asleep.

I glance at the clock to see it's one-thirty. That's plenty of time for a nap, and so I let her sleep. I've never been the type of guy to cuddle after sex, but I like this. I don't think it has anything to do with me. It's Kelley. I want to be near her. The desire is strong. Since the day I met her, I've had this overwhelming feeling… a need to protect her. I'd like to say it's because of the day I watched her cry on the bus stop bench, but I don't think that's it. I genuinely care about her, and not in the way Jeff was talking shit about on Sunday. This is different. And seeing how exhausted she is digs at me, makes me wonder what else is happening in her life.

I know there's something she's not telling me. I get that she's upset over Megan and Eric, but I sense there's more to the story. Whatever it is, I'm going to be there for her. After losing her best friend, she's going to need someone. This makes me wonder about her other friends. Where are they? What about roommates? I roll my eyes because it's pathetic that I don't even know who she lives with or which apartment is hers.

I lean down, plant a kiss on the top of her head, and close my eyes for a moment. Her hair smells freshly washed and I bury my nose in the chestnut waves. I won't sleep because I don't want her to be late for class, but I'm going to enjoy the peace I have with her while she's here.

Lying with her is a practice in patience, especially since she's naked. I keep my eyes closed and focus on my breathing, trying to think about anything but sex.

Who am I kidding?

Men think about sex… that's what we do. All the time. It's always first and foremost on our minds. And as I contemplate how I'm not going to think about sex, it ends up being the only thing I can think about.

I crack an eye open and shift my head so I can see the clock. It's a quarter after two, and I think that's a good time to wake her up. She'll have time to eat and relax a little before her exam. Not to mention, if I try hard enough, I can probably make her come again. I lift my head to stare down at our entwined, naked bodies. Lying like this, it's hard to tell where I end and she begins. Her pale skin is a shade lighter than mine and her limbs are much narrower, and that ass of hers is a work of art. I run my hand down her side and over the contours of her body; she's warm to the touch and smooth as silk. Touching her has made me grow stiff between us and I know naptime is over.

I grind against her and place a hand on her cheek to shift her face up toward mine. Then I gently kiss her, her neck, her lips, her cheeks, the space between her eyes, and then back to her lips again, slowly and softly. After a moment she's kissing me back, and I hear a sweet sigh escape as I grind against her again.

"Kelley, baby, you need to wake up. I want you to have time to eat lunch before your class."

"Not going," she moans.

"No, you can't skip class because of me. I'm not going to be that person for you." I rub up against her again, and I feel her push back. "Kelley, are you awake?"

"You're not giving me much choice."

"I want you again… May I have you?" I shift so that my hand is hovering between her legs, inches from being inside, waiting for permission, desperate for it.

A coy smile spreads across her face, and she whispers, "I thought you'd never ask."

With one finger, I slide inside her and God, she's snug and swollen from before. I massage her gently and lower my mouth to her erect nipple, tugging it inside my mouth. I pull away and as my breath grazes her now wet nipple, goosebumps rise to attention. I brush the tip of my nose along the underside of her breast and inhale the scent of coconut that lingers there. She's so beautiful, so irresistible.

My finger slides out and then two slide back in as my thumb rubs gently over her clit. Kelley's goosebumps fade with the warmth that rises from her core. Her body is moving with my touch now and I feel a slight quiver as her breathing increases. With every stroke of my thumb she's lifting to me.

"Does that feel good?"

"You're such a tease," she says in a voice higher than normal.

"Am I?"

"Oh my God, Mac. What are you trying to do to me?"

I flick her nipple with my tongue. "Is that what you want?"

"I want you, inside me. Now."

Just hearing her say the words makes me rock hard. Who am I to refuse such a demand? I lift and hover over her, sucking her other nipple into my mouth and clenching it with my teeth as I slowly push inside her. Kelley cries out as I do, spreading her legs for me, and lifting her hands to my hips. She's gripping me tightly, helping me keep the pace, and it drives me faster and harder. She's so damn sexy, so unassumingly sexy. Sexy in a way that's natural and feminine, and I cannot get enough of her.

"Oh God," she moans. "That feels so good, just like that. Mackensey, keep going just like that."

"Dammit, I love when you give me directions. I just want to make you feel good. Does it feel good?"

"Hell yeah. Jesus, yeah, just like that." Her eyes are squeezed tight, and I can see the tension in her jaw and then watch as it relaxes. It does feel good, even better than earlier, and I'm on the verge too, but I want to hold off. I shift slightly, and within another minute, her nails clamp down on my hips, and she's lifting off the bed to meet me, thrust for thrust. Then she arches and cries out the sweetest sound I've ever heard.

I sit back on my knees and lift her legs so that they're resting on my shoulders. With my hands on her hips, I pull her closer, wanting to get deeper. She's limber and relaxed from her orgasm, and I'm hoping I can drive her to it again. I pump in and out a couple of times, slowly at first, then faster until I see her hands grip the sheets beneath her and I know she's close again. I am too, and watching her breasts bounce up and down as I pump inside her pushes me along. She's so amazing. Watching her fills me with pleasure... and hope.

When she opens her eyes and meets mine, I can see that she's waiting for me.

"Can you come with me, baby?" I ask, fighting to maintain control for another second longer.

"Oh, God, Mac. I can't wait." She arches and tightens. I can feel it… I can feel it a little too well, and that's when it occurs to me that I forgot to wear a condom. I quickly pull out and pump up and down until I've emptied myself across her belly and breasts. I'm panting, watching her as she watches me come all over her beautiful, naked body.

I fall forward, and now we're both covered in my cum. I don't care. I'm just fighting to catch my breath and keep from freaking out. I never forget to wear a condom, I just don't. What the hell is wrong with me?

When my breathing settles, I shift her legs so that they're wrapped around my waist. "Hold onto me."

She wraps her arms around me and locks her ankles. I sit up, tuck my hand under her ass, and stand. She rests her head on my shoulder as I carry her into the bathroom. I flip on the shower, and while waiting for the water to warm, I turn so that I can see her face. She smiles, and I'm struck by how badly I already want her again. She lifts her head, and I reach out with my free hand to cup her neck and bring her closer so I can devour her perfect lips. It's intimate, almost too intimate for my taste, but I want her so much more than I care to admit. It scares the hell out of me.

CHAPTER TWELVE

Kelley

I don't want to go. My belly is full of Joe's Deli special roast beef sandwich. I'm freshly satisfied and showered, thanks to Mac, and I'm not in the mood to go to class. But he insists, and I understand. Just like I don't want to be the person who drives him to drink, he doesn't want to be the person who causes me to fail at school. Not that I would ever let that happen, but it's a tempting scenario when I remember his sinewy, naked body in bed next to me. And so, we're stopped in front of the math building, and I'm kissing him goodbye.

I'm practically straddling his lap because I don't want to leave him. I want to stay in his warm bed and sleep the night away. I'm still exhausted. Not to mention, I don't want to go back to my apartment.

"Will you call me when you're finished?"

"I will. But I have to study tonight for my exam tomorrow, so I can't talk for long."

"I'm sorry. I wish there were something I could do to make this week easier."

I grin against his lips and chuckle. "You already have, sir."

"Oh, yeah. I love it when you call me sir." He chuckles and pats my ass. "Get going, or you'll be late."

I grin wickedly and say, "See you later, master." Then I pull away, slide back over to the passenger seat, and pop the door handle as he groans.

"Bye, you little minx. Don't forget to call me when you get home otherwise I'll worry."

I nod and bounce into Newsom Hall for my exam.

An hour later, I'm finished with the exam, and I'm thrilled to be done with that class. If I never see another math problem for as long as I live, I'll be happy. I walk home, and all I can think about is how much I want to sleep. The nap helped considerably, but it wasn't long enough. Not that I'm complaining. There's no better way to wake up than to have some sexy beast asking to please you.

I didn't realize he didn't have a condom on and from the look on his face, he didn't either until it was too late. I'm not likely to get pregnant since I'm on the pill. I'd like to assume I don't have to worry about Mac being clean—I mean hell, after looking at his house, I can't imagine he's any less diligent with his own health. I laugh at myself; he's probably at the doctor right now, getting himself checked out.

When I enter the apartment, Eric and Meg are in the kitchen making dinner together. My stomach bottoms out and I try like hell to ignore them. I put on a neutral expression—I don't want them to know I'm affected by them. They both peer around the corner when I pass, and Eric looks like he's waiting for me to sit down. As if I'd actually eat a meal with them. Hell no. If I weren't so tired, I'd study at Starbucks and hang out with Lexi, but I've got the other half of my Joe's sandwich, and after I eat that, I'm going to bed.

Since they're staring at me expectantly, I decide to act completely unbothered by the two of them. "'Night," I say as I walk past the kitchen.

"You're going to bed already?" Megan asks. "But it's not even six o'clock."

"I told you earlier, I didn't sleep last night."

"So, how long have you been seeing Mac Thomas?" Eric asks.

I stop in my tracks and shift toward him with my hand raised, palms up. "Excuse me? How long have you been screwing my best friend?"

"You asked for it, Kelley," Eric says with a wink and an evil sneer.

I hate him. I hate him with the power of a thousand fiery deaths for taking my best friend away from me, and he knows it. He's conniving and manipulative. I never should have trusted him.

"Go to hell." I wave with a sarcastic smile as I walk into my bedroom and slam the door.

I really need to get out of this place. I plop down on my bed, unzip my backpack, and take out the rest of the sandwich. Then I grab my phone and text Mac.

Me: *Thank you so much for spending the afternoon with me and for lunch!*

Mac: *You're welcome. Are you home now?*

Me: *Yes, I'm taking an hour to study then I'm sleeping. Wish me luck.*

Mac: *Good luck and good night, beautiful. I have an afternoon appearance tomorrow but call me if you need anything. Lunch… or anything else. I'm here for you.*

I sigh and thank my lucky stars for him. It's been a long time since anyone has had my back.

Me: *Thank you, sincerely. You've already done so much. Thank you for caring. Tomorrow will be fine so don't worry about me. Enjoy your gig and have fun.*

Mac: *Before you go, I want to tell you that I'm sorry about earlier. The condom…*

Me: *Accidents happen. No worries. I'm on the pill and clean. I got thoroughly checked the day after I found out about Eric and Meg. I can show you the paperwork from Planned Parenthood if you like.*

Mac: *LOL! I'll take your word for it. I also have paperwork from my last checkup from a few weeks ago. Also clean. I'll show you if you like.*

Me: *Call me crazy, but I still trust you.*

Mac: *That makes me feel good. Thank you.*

Me: *Mwah. Night, night.*

I drop my phone on the nightstand and finish my sandwich. I settle in with my anatomy textbook to prepare for tomorrow's exam, realizing that the anxiety from my run-in with Eric and Meg is completely forgotten. I have Mac to thank for that.

I set my alarm for five so I can wake up in time to listen to Mac's show. I love that I can hear his voice even though he's not in the room. And he has an amazing voice. I can see why the ladies flock to him, and who can blame them? He's smart, sexy, and a free agent.

This thought sinks in, and it makes me pause… technically, he's not a free agent.

We're married, and that marriage is still legal. We haven't had any real time to talk about what we're going to do yet, and I wonder if Mac's made plans I don't know about. Is he going to spring annulment papers on me any day now? If we're even eligible for an annulment… Divorce papers, then?

I know this is something we're going to have to address, but the pending conversation makes me sad. It's not that I'd planned to get married or that I even wanted it, but with each day, I remember the evening more and more. I remember the feeling I had as I walked down the aisle. I remember the hope I felt as I stepped toward him. Every time I see him, I grow closer to him and more attached. Yes. The conversation is inevitable but I can't take another hit to my heart, not this week. I'll deal with it when I don't have to focus on school.

I lean back against my pillow, remembering Mac's hands on me yesterday. Every caress a whisper across my skin. Every jolting graze of his teeth burning me from the inside out. He fills me in a way no one ever has, physically and emotionally. I've never felt so desirable, or desired. He's intoxicating… or we're intoxicating together. The chemistry between us is undeniable. Mac is considerate in bed, so sure and smooth. My stomach flutters as I remember him washing my hair in the shower, the amazing shoulder rub, and the feel of his heat pressed against me under the flow of the raining shower head.

As I listen, I remember him saying the show portrays a skewed version of him and I have to agree. His co-host and producers exploit his lack of an attachment. They openly encourage him to flirt with the ladies and even try to set him up on dates. They have one segment they call Matchmaking Mac, where Mimi basically plays his pimp. The entire idea makes me nauseated. Why is he okay with it?

Mimi is interviewing the final girl and so far, she and Mac have laughed off all of his potential dates. "So…" Mimi says, "Camille, tell us about yourself and why Mac would want to go out on a date with you?"

"Well, let's see… I'm tall, almost six feet, and I have long blonde hair. I work out… like a lot. You know, running and swimming. I like to do kickboxing."

"That sounds promising," Mimi says. "What else?"

"I have brown eyes and wear a double D bra size—"

"Wait, Camille," Mac interrupts. "Did you say running? Where do you like to run? Outside? Treadmill?"

"Um… well, like… my neighborhood and I jog around where I live. I also like River Walk Park."

"Camille, didn't you say you're a double D bra size?" Mimi asks. "How do you run with such huge knockers?"

"Oh… hahaha! You're so funny, Mimi. I just, like… run, you know. It's not a problem. Why would that be a problem?"

I roll my eyes and mock her in a high voice. "*I just, like, run, you know.*"

Mimi laughs too and then she says, "Yeah, I don't think it's going to work out with you, Camille. Goodbye, hon, thanks for playing."

After Mimi disconnects the line, she says, "I just, like, run," making fun of the girl the same way I did. And I start laughing because I'm so relieved.

When the segment ends, and Mac hasn't been matched, I know it's all for the show and relief floods me. With each and every girl, they portray him as too picky, too snobby, or too shallow. Even with Camille, they portrayed him as a jerk. He didn't say anything mean about her, but by Mimi mocking the girl, it also makes Mac look like an ass. In reality, he's none of those things, and I know the entire bit is an act. I don't care what people have to say about this man. With me, he's constant. I haven't had to question his interest or his sincerity once since the moment we met. He's made it very clear he cares about me and he wants me around. At this point in our relationship, what more can I ask for? I decide to text him while I'm listening.

Me: *So glad Mimi didn't find you a match this morning!*

It takes a moment, but then he replies.

Mac: *She never does. Are you listening?*

Me: *Of course!*

I hit send, and when I do, I can hear a slight ping through my radio.

"Was that," I hear Mimi say through the radio, "a phone?"

"Nope." Mac replies. "Not a phone."

"Mimi, he was on his phone," Kurt says.

"Nope," Mac says. "No phone."

"Give it up," Mimi says. "You know the rules. If you're on the phone during the show, you have to share with the class."

There's a rustle over the mic, and then Mac says, "Whatever."

There's laughter and Mimi says, "Oh, now it's *whatever*?"

"It's nothing so, you know, go ahead and read it."

Mimi reads my text over the radio, and my face is so hot, I can barely stand it.

"So, Mac, this chick's contact name in your phone is Babe. Is that her real name?"

Mac chuckles and says, "Yep. Babe McHottee."

This has the entire crew giggling, and I have to snicker at that too.

"Is Babe McHottee the woman you took to Reno?"

"Nope, that was Baby McSexy."

Mimi chortles and says, "Shut up. You're such a dog! No wonder we can't find you a match." Then she says, "Good luck, Babe McHottee, you're gonna need it."

CHAPTER THIRTEEN

Mackensey

I'm so happy when the Friday show ends, I'm out of the studio and on the light rail home within minutes of signing off. My usual Friday would consist of brunch with Emily, but I'm still pissed at her, so I'm not meeting her today. I also have to return to the studio at two for our Friday meeting. After flaking last week and breaking my sobriety over the weekend, I'm not going to push my luck. I'll be at the meeting today, faithfully, and on time.

I walk from the light rail to my house and hop in my truck to run some errands. I want to make dinner for Kelley since it's her last day of the semester. I can't wait to have her alone and relaxed. I know she needs the break and I'm praying she agrees to take the weekend off from work and spend it with me.

I've selected a couple of beautiful New York strip steaks, potatoes for baking, and all the fixings for a salad. I walk through the produce section and grab some strawberries to go with the pound cake for dessert. I've also gotten everything I need to make breakfast… it doesn't hurt to hope for the best. When I'm done getting ingredients for the salad, I walk over to the fresh flowers. I look over what the store offers and pick up several bouquets and smell them. Once I find one I think Kelley will like, I read the label. Lilies, it is. I'm sure Kelley likes flowers. Most women do, don't they?

After checking out at the grocery store, I decide to drive by Starbucks to see if she's there. I can't help it, I just have to see her. I peer inside but she's not there. Her mid-morning class was rescheduled for 8 a.m., so I'm sure she's finished by now. I drive the three blocks to her house and get a glimpse of her as she turns into the corridor of her building.

I call out to her, but she doesn't hear me, so I park and follow her, rushing to catch up since I'm not sure which door is hers. I turn the corner just as a door on the second floor snaps closed. I run up the stairs and knock. It takes a moment but then it opens.

I stare at him for a long moment, and at first, I'm not sure where I know him from, but then it occurs to me, this is Eric... Kelley's ex.

I point, unable to find my voice.

"Are you looking for Kelley?" he asks.

I nod, still not sure any words will come out. Eric turns and calls out to her, and at the same time, another woman steps into the picture. Her face is blank, but then her expression changes the longer she looks at me.

"You're Mac from the radio," she says, pointing like I'm a zoo animal.

I nod again but don't speak. My pulse pounds in my ears as I stare at Eric, trying to figure out what the hell is going on. I'm not sure what to think. I want to punch Eric's smug face, but at the same time, the woman is staring so hard, I want to turn and leave. Before I can do any of those things, Kelley steps out from around the corner.

She has an angry look on her face as she focuses on Eric. "What do you want?" she says. Then she sees me, and her face relaxes... before tensing again.

Kelley lifts her eyebrows, points to the woman, and says, "This is Megan." Then she points to him. "And Eric..."

"Oh, my God," Megan says, rushing forward to shake my hand.

I pull my hand from her grasp as Kelley approaches. It takes me seconds to figure it out, and I'm pissed. Kelley steps between Megan and me and says, "You remember who Megan is, right?"

I can tell she thinks I'm jumping to the wrong conclusions, but I'm not. I see exactly what's happening. I understand precisely why Kelley's been so miserable and stressed. I'm staring at why she was crying on the bench, and the longer I think about it, the angrier I get.

I turn to meet her eyes. "Pack your things."

She looks hard at me for a long moment, but then nods. I can tell she's not sure what to think, but I'm too angry to say anything else. She silently takes my hand and leads me to her bedroom, closing the door. When she turns, I want to pull her against me, but I'm too mad… I don't want to touch her when I'm this upset.

"Mac, I'm sorry I didn't tell you—"

"Pack your things. You're not staying in this apartment for another day."

She nods, and as she moves toward her closet, I see that her hands are trembling. Have I frightened her? I take a deep breath and look around her room. It's tidy but too small a space for all her stuff. I remember living like this in college, always dealing with asshole roommates and shared space. On the wall across from her bed is a framed print. It's a couple in a ballet pose. A lift… and a complicated one from the looks of it. I take a closer look and recognize Kelley.

She's so beautiful. I focus on her face, and she looks relaxed. Determined, but relaxed… and healthy. No dark circles, no frown, and no stress line between her eyes. Her body is rigid and elegant, her lines are arrow-straight, and her toes are perfectly pointed. This is the woman I want to know. The strong one who knows who she is and knows her place in this world.

I take a deep breath and count to ten, hoping to push away some of my anger. Then I look back up at the photo. "Is this you?"

"Yes," she says, and she sounds like she's crying. I spin around to look at her and I'm so sad for her sake that I can't help but pull her to me. "Come here," I say as I fold her into my arms. I need to feel her now. I need to breathe her in to know that she's okay. "Why?" It's the only thing I can say at this point.

I feel her breathing hitch, and I cup the back of her head as I hold her against my chest. "You should've told me. I can help."

"I was too mortified." She lifts her hand to wipe her face and says, "She moved him in the same day I found out, but I didn't have anywhere else to go."

"You do now." I kiss the top of her head and say, "Grab some things. We'll come back for the rest later." I release her and nod toward the picture. "We're taking this now."

She nods in agreement without looking at the photo.

I help her pack three duffle bags worth of clothes, cosmetics, and all of her toiletries. There's still a lot more, but I'll come back with my truck and get the rest later. Right now, I just want to get her out of there.

As we're carrying the bags out, Megan says, "You can't just move out, Kelley. You're on the lease."

"You're right, I am on the lease." She points to Eric. "But he's not. If you report me to management, I'll report you. There are time limits on how long you're allowed to have a 'guest' stay over."

"I don't believe you would do that," Megan says.

I stop, pull out my wallet, and grab a business card before handing it to Megan. "Here, my lawyer's phone number. Make sure to include her in the meeting when you involve the apartment manager." Then I turn and walk out the door with Kelley in tow.

We load her stuff into the back of the truck, and then I open the passenger door for her. When I get into the driver's seat, she says, "I'm sorry I didn't tell you."

"Why didn't you?"

She shrugs and lowers her eyes. "I don't know. I guess I didn't see the point… and I was embarrassed."

This instantly makes me feel guilty. What have I done to make her think she can't talk to me? I know this is a new thing and we don't know each other that well, but after our drunken episode last week, I thought we were on the same page. But then again… I suspected she was going through more than she'd shared with me.

"I'm sorry," I say.

She finally looks up at me. "What are you sorry for?"

"I'm sorry you felt you couldn't trust me." I consider that for a moment and think maybe I don't know myself like I thought I did.

"This isn't about trust," she says.

"Isn't it though?"

"No!" she says, and her voice hits a higher octave. "It's not. Trusting you doesn't have anything to do with this situation."

I shake my head. "So… what, then? If you felt you could share this with me, you would have told me sooner."

"What if I told you, Mac?" she says, throwing her hands up. "What if I told you that Megan moved Eric into our apartment within twenty-four hours of me finding them together? What could you possibly do about it?"

"I just did it, Kelley."

She grows quiet, and so do I. I'm not sure what to say, and to be honest, I'm not exactly sure about what I just did. I reacted to the situation. A knee-jerk reaction to finding out she was living with her ex.

"I'll find a place quickly. Mary told me about an attic apartment near the dance studio. I'm supposed to go look at it tomorrow."

"Where's the dance studio?"

"It's off H Street, near Starbucks."

"I'll go with you," I say, because I'm not about to let her move into a dump or some other awful situation.

"It's okay," she says. "You've already done more than your share of helping me."

That pisses me off. I park in front of my house and turn toward her. "I didn't realize there was a limit to how much I'm supposed to care about you." Then I pop the door handle and jump out the truck. We unload in silence, and once we have all of her stuff in my living room and all of the groceries in the kitchen, I assess the situation. I have no idea where to put everything.

I walk into the bedroom and look around. Then I head back into the living room, and Kelley's just standing there among her bags, looking orphaned.

When our eyes meet, I try to reassure her. "It's fine, Kelley. I have plenty of space here."

She nods but doesn't say anything.

I point toward the hall. "The closet in the office is empty. You can have it for all of your stuff until we come up with a better solution."

Another curt nod and I'm starting to feel like I've really scared her with my anger. I approach her slowly and say, "Are you okay?"

Another nod.

"I hate to leave you alone right now, but I absolutely have to make it to my meeting today, or I'll probably be fired."

Yet another nod from her.

I take another step toward her, and we're only about eight inches from each other. I want to reach out to her, but I'm afraid of doing more damage. Thankfully, she takes the decision out of my hands and leans into my chest. I wrap my arms around her and hold her tightly. It's a relief to have her in my arms and to know I can help her, since I've only made her situation worse with that wedding debacle. I tilt my head and bury my nose in her hair; she smells like warmth and comfort and I hope when she smells me, she gets a sense of warmth and comfort too.

We stand like this for ages, and as I maintain a firm grip, I feel like this is what she needs right now. She doesn't need words. She needs action. She doesn't need another talking head in her life, she needs to be shown what it feels like to be cared for.

When she finally pulls away, I place a finger under her chin and lift it, so she has to look at me. Her eyes are sad, and all I want is to see the fiery expression of the dancer in the photo. Where is *that* girl? "It will be okay, trust me," I say, and her gaze drops again. I grip her chin and force her to look at me. "I've got you, Kelley."

CHAPTER FOURTEEN

Kelley

I watch Mac drive away, and I'm struck with a sudden wave of exhaustion. It's so acute, I have to sit immediately. I sink down on his couch and fall sideways. The door is open, and the breeze is flowing through the house. It's magical in its ability to make me feel better. I've always been the type of person who loves the wind. For some reason, it tends to remind me of the people I've lost. Like the brush of the breeze is their way of telling me they're here, looking out for me. It actually makes me think of my dad. The day he died, I remember standing outside and feeling the wind… but not like I'd ever felt it before. This was different… more familiar.

Luna lumbers over, tail wagging, and it makes me smile. She licks my face and then lifts her front end and drops her front paws on my chest. It nearly knocks the breath out of me. I rub behind her ears as I say, "You are too big to be a lapdog." She rests her head on my chest and stares into my eyes, and I'm happy she's there.

I look around Mac's home, and I'm struck by how odd it is that my things are sitting in his living room. On the floor of his immaculate house, that he shares with no one. And I'm absolutely sure he never planned to share it with anybody. This is probably why I'm so uncomfortable here. I feel like I've trapped him into doing something he never would've normally chosen.

He seems so genuine, so sincere, when he tells me he cares. And that's such a huge contrast to everything I've heard about him. It's the complete opposite of what he portrays to people—the playboy that everyone in Sacramento fawns over. It's confusing and heart-wrenching at the same time. I want to believe everything he says to me, and until today, I did. I'm not sure what has changed. It must have something to do with his insistence that I pack my bags and bring them here. I know this can't be what he wants. So why would he do it?

Maybe he's just too nice to leave me floundering. Then again, we are married, and perhaps he has some masochistic idea that he's responsible for me. Maybe he's afraid I'll try to stake some claim to what he has now that I'm legally his wife.

I would never do that.

The thought alone disgusts me.

The truth is, I never allow myself to rely on men. For the last twenty years I've relied on Megan. She and I have always taken care of each other. I could call her for anything, and she could come to me for anything… and now that's gone. Megan has always been more of a taker. Looking back, I see that more clearly now. That's just the way she is. I guess it took this act of betrayal for me to recognize it.

We're both far from perfect, but even with these imperfections, she was my constant for so long. I guess that's why I feel lost. What really hurts is knowing she's not going to be here for me but also that she no longer needs me. She chose Eric over me and I just don't understand why. What changed that would drive her to let a man come between us? I understand what drives Eric, but I can't figure out why Megan no longer cares about our relationship, why she would throw away so many years and so many memories.

I need to find my way. Be it with Mac, or without him. I like him. I think about that for a minute, and realize that I more than like him. He makes me feel special, and it's been a long time since

I've felt anywhere close. I think about him and the gold bands in my pocket and feel comforted. I've been carrying them with me every day as if they're a talisman or a good luck charm.

I sit up as Luna drops back down on the hardwood floor. Then I pull the rings out of my pocket. As I stare at them, resting in the palm of my hand, I admit I might even love him. These feelings I have, they're strong. Stronger than anything I've felt in a long time. This fact hits me hard because I've only known him for a couple of weeks. How does that happen? I'm not even sure how to feel about... about how I feel. Is it possible to love someone so quickly?

I glance over at the photo of Brad and me, the one Mac insisted on bringing. It's a beautiful picture. I was on top of the world then... before it all came crashing down around me. "Yes," I mutter to myself. "I've hit rock bottom before and survived." And I know I'll survive this too, so with a heavy sigh, I get to my feet. Groceries first. Then I can figure out where to put all my crap without messing up Mac's beautiful home.

As I unpack the bags, I'm surprised by Mac's attention to detail. He has a wonderful meal planned... dessert, salad and even breakfast. I grin at the thought. The idea of waking up next to him is so comforting.

Flowers. He bought flowers.

I search the kitchen for a vase and arrange them before placing them in the center of his dining-room table. They're gorgeous and their sweet, vibrant scent with bright white and pink petals really brighten the room. He has excellent taste—I love lilies.

Once the groceries are all put away, I head into the living room to deal with my crap.

I grab the first, largest duffle bag and carry it into his office. This space is just as clean as the rest of the house, and it's a little unnerving. I always expect people's offices to be a bit messy, but there is nothing untidy about Mac. I place the bag on the loveseat and look around. The walls are covered in old, framed concert posters. They're all signed too. Billy Joel, Elton John, Fleetwood Mac... Wow! He even has a vintage Beatles concert poster from their last show at Candlestick Park, and it's signed by Paul McCartney. I stare in awe for a few minutes but then return to the task at hand. I'd like to have everything cleaned up before he returns from his meeting.

I do a turn, taking in the space again. The closet is next to Mac's desk. I walk over and open it. He's right, it's pretty empty. Two winter coats are hanging up and there's a blanket in a plastic bag on the top shelf. It's a pretty big closet, and I'm glad because I don't want my stuff cluttering his space.

I sort through the duffle bag. As I lay a stack of socks on Mac's desk, I glance around and take in the sound recording equipment and then the notepads, pens, computer... normal office stuff. Everything is very tidy, except for two old and beat-up file folders sitting out. I freeze when I see my name handwritten on the top folder.

I stand there, rooted to the spot, staring like an idiot for a long time. I don't snoop, it goes against everything I believe in. But when you come across something that has your name on it, it's damn hard to look away.

Unable to resist any longer, I push the socks out of my way and lift the lid of the file. On top, is a photo of me lying in a hospital bed. My heart pounds so hard, I can feel it in my temples, and my breath catches. I've never seen this photo before. At least, I don't remember it. I barely remember anything from the months I spent in the hospital except for the pain... and the grief. I pull out the desk chair and sit down, laying the file in my lap.

As I flip through it, my heart sinks with every image. There are articles about me from newspapers all over the country. Some I've seen before, others I've never seen. Then I come across the financial information... information nobody should have access to. The total amount owed on my student loans, old hospital bills

I couldn't pay, and letters from creditors I still owe money to. He even has copies of old report cards, reviews from my shows, and private medical information from the accident.

With pain so intense I can barely breathe, I realize that Mac knows more about me than I know about myself. So much for our deal not to Google each other. Why did I trust him? How could I have been so stupid?

Hands trembling, I lay the file down and pick up the second one. I open it to find crisp, clean white pages of legal jargon from a local family law firm naming Mac as the petitioner and me as the respondent. Under our names, the 'Nullity of Marriage' box is checked. There are other documents, including a summons form and an injunction that bars me from selling any property. This actually makes me laugh. What property? How the hell did he get this done so quickly?

When I reach the waiver of service, I'm shaking so hard I can barely read what it says. I finally lay it on the desk, fisting and then shaking my hands as I pace in a circle around his office in an effort to calm myself. Once the trembling slows, I read the rest.

So… Mac was hoping I'd take this well and sign away my feelings like they're nothing. The comfort I felt earlier, the comfort he gave me, slips away and I'm back to wondering what to do next. I think about the groceries and the flowers… was he just trying to soften the blow? I don't understand. But that no longer matters because he's right; I'm willing to walk away. I never wanted any drama, I made that very clear from the beginning.

With a sinking heart, I grab a pen, complete the form, and sign my name. It's very nearly the most painful thing I've ever done. I can barely see the ink on the page through my tears, but I see no reason to drag this out. It's not like this was even a real marriage… it's not like it was ever going to be a real marriage. Mac wants out quick and easy, so I'll let him have it. I look over at the other file and know in my heart I can't blame him for that.

I'm not sure what hurts the most, the fact that he lied, or the fact that he wants to erase our relationship from the books completely... and without even discussing it with me first.

CHAPTER FIFTEEN

Mackensey

When I arrive at Café DeMilo, which is located in the courtyard of the KQCC office building, Mimi is there waiting for me. "You're late."

"I know, I'm sorry. Something came up," I say.

"You've had a lot come up lately, Mac." She slides half of her scone toward me, but I shake my head. I can't eat, I'm too on edge. Too thrown by what's happened today.

She gestures toward me and says, "You ready to tell me what's been happening?"

I watch her, waiting, not knowing how to begin. I decide to start with the obvious. "Babe McHottee."

"What about her?" She raises an eyebrow. "I assume she *is* the one you took with you to Reno last weekend. The same one you got drunk with on Saturday."

"She didn't know."

She rolls her eyes. "Really?"

"It's true." I raise my hands, palms up. "She doesn't listen to the show. At least, not until this week."

"How did you meet her if she doesn't know you from the show?" she asks.

I tell her the entire story, from Kelley crying on the bench outside Starbucks, to our drive to Reno and the incredible time we had at the Comedy Fest—then I stop dead in my tracks.

"So, what aren't you telling me?"

I stare at her for a moment, then I spit it out. "On Saturday, after all the drinks, we went to an all-night chapel and got married."

I'm waiting for her to start laughing like Emily did... but she doesn't. She just watches me.

"Say something, Mimi."

She tilts her head, examining me. "Mac, I've known you for what, eight, nine years, now?"

"Almost ten," I say. "I was your intern my senior year of college."

"What can I say? You're a bit neurotic, especially since you stopped drinking. You've definitely never done anything so unpredictable and impulsive. There must be something behind it." She shrugs. "Do you love her?"

I'm speechless. I wasn't expecting that. I was expecting... derision. "That's an interesting question."

"That's a no."

"It's complicated."

She draws her eyebrows together and says, "You either love her, Mac, or you don't. Which is it?"

Now I'm staring at her, and I'm speechless again. I'm not sure about anything. I widen my eyes and say, "Is that what this is? Is this what it feels like?"

Now she's laughing at me. "Oh, honey..."

"This isn't funny." I place my hands on my chest and say, "This is for real, Mimi, and I don't know what to do."

She covers her mouth with her hand and I know she's trying to hide her amusement. "I'm sorry, but you're so cute. You really don't recognize these emotions, do you?"

When I give her an incredulous look, she bobs her head and says, "Okay. Listen, don't do anything until you're sure. Don't push her away and don't pull her closer." She points at me. "Figure out what you want before you screw with her. If you're not sure, you're only going to do more damage."

"I think I kind of just moved her into my house."

She leans forward. "You what?"

"She was living in a bad, unhealthy situation, so I removed her from it. She's at my house right now."

"Okay, well…" She pops another bite of scone in her mouth. "That's another way to go."

"I had to come here, so I didn't really get a chance to talk to her about it, but it doesn't have to be permanent. She's looking at other apartments and I haven't made any promises."

"So don't… until you know what you want." She lifts her eyes toward the ceiling. "Are you telling the crew today?"

"I have to tell them something, I don't want her exploited on the show. The only way to avoid that is to be straight with them."

"What's her name?"

"Her name is Kelley, but don't tell the crew. I don't want them to 'slip' while we're on air."

"Yeah, they don't need to know. We'll stick with Babe, it's better that way." She looks at her watch. "Let's get up there and get it over with."

When Mimi and I enter the conference room, the entire team is already sitting around the table. Kurt's brewed some coffee, and there's a tray of brownies on the table. Of course, I can't touch them. My stomach is still doing somersaults at the thought of what I'm about to do… at what I just did.

I want to tell myself I'm stupid, but I can't bring myself to. Having Kelley as mine feels too right.

When I sit down, Kurt takes a moment to give me shit. "Well, look who decided to join us today."

I fight to hide my annoyance. I'm trying to be a good sport. "I told you I would be here. I missed one week, let's not dwell."

They all laugh, but I don't. I'm over it. I'm over the *let's screw with Mac* show. I sit quietly and listen as we review next week's bits. Mimi's responsible for all the entertainment news and gossip, and I cover all the local news and sports.

"I think we need to ditch Matchmaking Mac," Mimi says. I'm shocked as hell, but maybe she's starting to feel the same way I do. It's been taken too far. Everyone at this table knows I don't want to be matched on some stupid game from our show. It's as if Kurt and the others want to dehumanize me, feeling better about themselves if I come across as some shallow, uncaring jerk who's bound to be a lifelong bachelor. Like I'm emotionally stunted or something.

It's true, I don't get emotional with women, but that doesn't mean I'm not capable. Just the opposite. I keep myself at a distance on purpose. It's a defense mechanism and helps me avoid the hurtful crap that comes with it... I'm failing miserably with Kelley.

When Kelley's name enters my head, I glance at my phone to see the time. I hope she's getting comfortable. I hope Luna is behaving. I hope Emily doesn't show up at my house, unannounced.

"Mac?" Kurt says, trying to get my attention. "What do you think?"

"Think about ditching Matchmaking Mac? I think it's a great idea. I hate that bit, and I don't think my wife likes it much either." Chins all around the table drop. Except for Mimi's. She's smiling, but I know she's got my back.

"What the hell are you talking about?" Kurt asks.

I shrug like it's no big deal. "I got married in Reno last Saturday."

The sound guy, Dan, starts chuckling. "You're such an asshole."

"Me?" I say, pointing to my chest. "Why am I an asshole?"

"We've been talking about your Reno trip all damn week. Why didn't you tell us sooner?"

Mimi and I both give him a dirty look. "Excuse me?" I say. "I am entitled to a personal life. I don't have to tell you everything."

"Mac," Kurt says, "we could have used that all week. What a ratings boost that would have been."

Yeah, I'm the asshole, I think as I look over at Mimi. She rolls her eyes and leans forward. "By the way, Mac, congratulations on your marriage."

That shuts everyone up.

"Wait, Mac, did you really marry that chick you were with at the Comedy Festival? Hey, Dan, didn't someone email us a picture of the two of them together? Did we get that up on the blog? Or Instagram?" Kurt asks.

"Stop!" I shout. Now they're just pissing me off. "You are not posting her picture anywhere. I absolutely do not give permission for that."

"You don't have a choice," Kurt says. "It's in your contract."

"Wanna bet I don't have a choice? Have you read my contract lately? I have ten bucks and ten minutes that says if I call my lawyer and my agent they'll confirm it."

Kurt looks over at Mimi, and she smirks at him. "Mac's right. We had those items removed the last time we renegotiated." She clicks her tongue and says, "You gotta love a guy who has a lawyer for a sister."

Kurt shakes his head. "Damn that Emily."

"Haven't you noticed that I haven't said my kids' names on air for almost a year?" Mimi says.

Kurt stares at her, and his look of utter confusion almost makes me feel sorry for him. "Listen, guys, I don't want her exploited for ratings. We were both wasted when we signed the papers, we're not sure yet what we're going to do about it." I wave a hand around the table and say, "Until she and I figure it out, we'd rather not advertise it."

"That's unfair," Kurt says. "We're a team here, guys. We need to keep our ratings up, and this is exactly the type of thing that will boost us."

"Kurt, we're already the top-rated show. We don't need to push Mac's private life for a boost," Mimi says.

Kurt crosses his arms over his chest and stares at us for a long time.

"When she and I figure things out, I'll be a little more open, but right now, I don't want to overwhelm her. She's had a hard time lately, and I'd like to be the person who helps and doesn't make things harder on her. She's not used to the attention, unlike the rest of us."

Dan smiles like the Cheshire Cat. "Are you saying you're staying married to her?"

"No. I'm saying, I don't know yet."

He laughs now, his body bouncing in his chair. "But you're considering it."

"I don't know yet," I say, and it's nearly a growl. I don't want to talk about this with them, and I genuinely don't know what I want to do yet.

Dan looks over at Kurt and they both chuckle. "Wow, man, this must be some girl."

I can't deny it: Kelley is some girl. I nod without speaking, because she's special, and I know that. I knew it the first time I laid eyes on her. I don't know how, but I knew.

They continue to discuss plans for the following week, but I can barely sit still. I want to get home. I glance at my phone and see that I haven't received any messages from Kelley. That's good, she must be settling in well.

I'm going to like having her all to myself this weekend and I'm damn thrilled she's not in that living situation any longer. I wish she'd told me about Megan and Eric sooner. I can help her look for a decent apartment… or we can wait it out a little longer. I have plenty of room, and hopefully, she doesn't mind the dog.

In a million years, I never thought I'd be moving a woman into my house, especially after only knowing her for a few days, but somehow this feels like the right thing to do. I don't mind having her stay while she saves some money for a place.

"Mac, you listening?"

"Sorry, what's that?" I ask, when I look up to see them all focused on me.

"We're going to swap out Matchmaking Mac with Craigslist missed connections and personals. Maybe include callers too," says Kurt.

"Yeah, that sounds like fun."

Kurt lifts his hand and says, "Great. We all agree. We'll try it out the next couple of weeks and see how it goes."

"Perfect. We done? I'd like to get my weekend started," I say.

"No," Mimi says. "James Foster keeps calling. He wants on the show, but we've been avoiding him for your sake, Mac."

"Yeah," Kurt says. "What's up with that?"

I groan. "James was the best man at my wedding last weekend."

"Oh," Dan says. "So that's why you wouldn't let us put him on the show. Makes sense now."

"Can we put him off a little bit longer?" I ask.

"I guess we have to," Kurt says. "But you'd better make it worth my while."

"I will. I'll do my best to make it up to you guys."

"Great, in that case, we're done," Kurt replies. "And, Mac, let's stay sober this weekend, okay?"

"We're all good, boss. I have zero interest in having a drink."

I can't get out of there fast enough. Visions of spending the weekend with a naked Kelley in my bed drive me forward, and on my way out the door, I text to let her know I'm on my way home.

CHAPTER SIXTEEN

Kelley

Lexi greets me with a sad frown. "I hate that I'm seeing you under these circumstances."

"Are you sure you don't mind hanging onto my stuff for a few days?" I face her and say, "I'm sorry I keep putting you through this."

"Kelley, stop. You know I'm here to help." She glances at me as she turns onto L Street. "But maybe you should stay at my place this weekend?"

"Thank you, really, but I need to get out of town. I have to be back at the dance studio next week... maybe then I can stay? Is that okay, until I figure out something else?"

"Of course. Just call me when you get back into town, and I'll pick you up at the train station."

"Thank you so much." I lean forward and rest my face in my hands. "I can't tell you how thankful I am. Seriously."

"I understand... I can't believe what a shit he is for doing that to you."

"It's okay. It's not... I can't blame him completely." This is true, and I'm not going to bad-mouth him and give people a reason to spread rumors that could possibly hurt him. "It's not like we planned to get married and then he backed out. This was inevitable."

"Not like that, Kelley. He could have told you instead of leaving the paperwork out for you to find."

"I'm sure he didn't plan on me finding it, since I shouldn't have been there in the first place. He probably planned to tell me at dinner." I throw my sunglasses on to block out the bright, hot glare and lean back in the seat. "He was trying to do a nice thing by getting me out of that apartment. I'm sure he meant well, even though he obviously had no intention of continuing our relationship—which is just ridiculous anyway. I've known the man for a week. This was never going to be a thing. I know that, he knew that. I'm stupid for even having my heart broken."

"It's just so weird that he reacted the way he did when he found out you were living with Megan and Eric, yet he planned to hand you annulment papers."

"I don't get it either, but until today, I thought he cared about me. I don't doubt he likes me—and likes getting laid," I scoff. "He just never planned to get married. It needed to be resolved, one way or another."

"Maybe you shouldn't take off," she says. "Running away isn't going to fix anything. Why don't you stay and talk to him?"

"At this point, it's done. The paperwork was in order. Mac knew what he was doing, that was obvious. Besides, I can't be here. I just can't…" When my voice wavers, I stop talking. I'm not crying over him. It's ridiculous, just stupid, the entire situation.

He's not my husband!

He's some guy I got drunk with and out of a need to get back at Eric and Megan—out of a need to separate myself from them—I made a stupid decision. That's it, that's all. It was in the heat of the moment.

"Kelley, are you sure about this?"

I nod, and when I'm sure I can maintain a firm grip on myself, I say, "Absolutely."

"Oakland, though?" she says with a sour expression.

"I'll be fine, don't worry."

"At least leave me the address of where you're staying?"

"Yeah, sure, I'll text it to you as long as you don't share it with Megan. Don't even tell her I'm in Oakland."

"All right, I'll keep it to myself." Lexi pulls into the train station and parks. "Can I walk you inside?"

"No, don't worry, I've already taken enough of your time. Thanks, though. Get home before the Memorial Day weekend traffic gets bad." I lean over and give her a tight hug. "Lexi, thank you so much for being there for me."

"Anytime, toots. Let me know when your return train is and I'll be here to pick you up."

I climb out of her car and go to catch my train. It's a relief to be alone. I'm tired of pretending to be okay. I'm not, and I don't want to be. I want to wallow for a while. I thought Mac and I were moving forward. No, I didn't expect us to become this perfect, happily married couple, with a house, a dog, and two-point-five kids. But I thought we were being honest with each other. Granted, I didn't tell him about Megan and Eric, but why did he have such a fit about it, if he was also hiding something?

I work at shaking it off as I board my train and find a seat. When the train pulls away and out of Sacramento, I fight tears. It's the exact opposite of how I felt with Mac last Friday as we left Sacramento in his car. My, how things can change so quickly. I was so wrong to trust him... so stupid for not doing my research and not believing all the crap I heard about him. I should have known he was a player, and that I was about to get played.

I absolutely have the worst taste in men. I brush the tears off my face and hold my breath to keep the sob from escaping. As much as I wanted this thing with Mac to be different—as much as I wanted *him* to be different, I should have known better.

I pull my phone out and send a text to Lexi with the address of where I'll be staying. Then I stick the phone into my pocket, lean my head back, and close my eyes. Thirty seconds later, my phone chimes.

Mac: *You're not at the house? You okay?*

My heart hurts as I read his words. I'm not answering his text, I just can't. He'll figure it out soon enough. Maybe he should have been an actor with his ability to convince me he cares, even now. I roll toward the window, hoping nobody sits next to me, because I don't want to pretend I'm okay. I guess he hasn't found the paperwork I signed. Funny, I would've thought that'd be the first thing he'd check.

I put my phone on silent, stuff it in my purse, and rest my head back again. I have a while so I might as well take a nap. It doesn't happen, though. I can't sleep, and my phone is still buzzing in my purse. I'm not looking, I don't have it in me. I'm exhausted with it and with this life. If I have to, I'll block Mac's number. He got what he wanted, there's nothing left to say.

Two long hours later, the train is pulling into Oakland Station. Once I'm off, I quickly hit the Uber app, ignoring the line of messages in the queue. It takes me a half hour to get a car and trek to the building. Once I'm standing outside his door, I have to close my eyes and send up a little prayer to help me get through the weekend. My stomach's in knots and I'm seriously questioning my decision to come here. I know he'll be happy to see me, but that doesn't mean I'm ready to see *him*.

The nervous energy coursing through me makes my hand shake as I lift it. I make a fist, holding my breath as I knock. Before I have time to prepare, the door swings wide and he's there, in front of me. He snatches me up and lifts me off the ground in a bear hug, and I laugh because now that I'm in his arms, I'm relieved. He's always been there for me… or at least he's tried. He's one of the few things I have left from my old life. He's something to be happy about.

When he puts me down and pulls away, he frowns. "What the hell are you doing here?"

It takes me a minute to get my bearings. Talking to him on the phone and seeing him in person are two very different things. *I can do this. I can do this.*

It's been two years since I've seen him, and that was when he came to visit me in Sacramento. He, Megan, and I had a really good time that week and then he was gone again. He kept in touch though, calling me at least once a week. I've missed him hard. But I had to be honest with myself, it's difficult to be with him. He brings up memories I'd rather leave buried.

The distance makes it easy to ignore the fact that he looks so much like Brad. But in the flesh that fact is impossible to ignore: Michael is the spitting image of his brother.

But maybe being with him will help get my mind off Mac— and that's what I need right now. To forget Mac. It's ironic that I have to suffer through a weekend of constant reminders of Bradley in order to fight through losing Mac. My heart aches for Bradley and for what could have been… for our life together, now lost. For his life, cut short. For his family, who like me, will always have an emptiness because he's gone.

I miss him every day. I'll always miss him, but I don't miss the craziness that always surrounded him. I don't miss the drunken weekends, with the mad stunts he used to pull, or the trouble he used to get us into. He was a wild heart, and it cost him his life. It cost me a hell of a lot, too. Yet I can't blame Brad for that entirely, I could've said no—I played a part too.

It's an odd parallel. I'd pretty much done the same thing with Mac last weekend. I'd gotten drunk with him and made a bad decision. Just like I'd gotten drunk with Brad on my twentieth birthday, and gotten into a car with him. Why haven't I learned? Am I bound to relive that stupid decision over and over for the rest of my life? I've lost my career over it, my financial stability, my reputation, and my childhood sweetheart. Maybe one day, I'll be allowed to have something lasting. I try not to ask for much. I know I deserve the hell I'm in, but one day… I'd like to have my emotional debts paid off.

"I can't believe you're here!" Mike's excitement is contagious and now that I see him, I can relax.

"You told me to come whenever I wanted and, well, I wanted to surprise you."

"I'm certainly surprised and extremely happy. I wish you would have called though, I could have planned something fun for us."

"I don't need fun. I need… peace and quiet. I need a friend."

"What's happened now?" he asks and I'm wishing I hadn't been so honest. I don't want to talk about Mac or *what's happened now*.

I glance over at him. "What do you mean? I already told you everything… before."

"Yeah, hard to forget that call, but that was a full two weeks ago. I need an update." He closes the door behind me and I'm relieved I don't have to leave again. It's been a long ass week, and all I want to do is relax. Of course, I quickly see just how small this apartment is, and now I'm a little worried about where I'm going to sleep. It's literally one room with a small kitchenette and smaller bathroom.

My shoulders droop. "It's just hard… I don't have anyone there now. Megan…"

"I get it," he says and I'm so glad because I don't want to talk about it. I came here to get away from it. I only wish I could stop thinking about it. Thinking about Mac. I can still hear my phone buzz every once in a while, and it's taking everything I have to ignore it.

I finally pull it out of my purse and hold the off button down without looking at the screen. Then I drop it back in. There is nobody I need to talk to this weekend. This weekend is about hanging out with Mike, forgetting everyone else. Especially *him*.

I look around and realize, as small as his place is, it's heavenly because Megan isn't here and Eric isn't here, and I can get a break from all the crap I've been dealing with. A real break, with a person who really wants to hang out with me. Not someone who's pretending so he can spring some bad news on me later.

"Great place," I say. "Where are you sleeping?"

Mike laughs and says, "There's that sense of humor I missed."

"You know I'm kidding. I'm just so glad to be here."

"No worries, Kelley, you can have the bed. I'll take the couch." He lifts an eyebrow and says, "Unless... you know..." And he's wearing a sassy grin.

"Forget it, pervert." I toss my bag at him.

Of course, he catches it with no problem. Mike, unlike Brad, is pretty damn big. He's over six feet tall and wide, with broad shoulders and bulging muscles. I think he's actually gotten bigger since the last time I saw him. Brad was strong, but slender, not bulky like Mike. It's a relief since his size is the one difference that reminds me he's not Brad. His black hair is cut pretty short, but he wears it in messy spikes. Pretty stylish for someone who's never cared much for impressing the ladies.

"I'm just saying, you know, since you and Eric broke up and you're single now...."

The reminder pushes the smile from my face and stabs my heart. I'm not single, I'm married... or at least I was until I signed those papers this afternoon.

"I'm kidding. Don't freak out."

I fight for a calm expression. Mike thinks this is about Eric when really it has nothing to do with him. "I know. Sorry, I just remembered something."

"Okay, because you're practically my sister. I mean, you're not, but you almost were, right?"

Now I outright frown at the reminder of my abandoned wedding plans five years ago. "Yes. Almost."

Mike's shoulders drop, and he tosses my duffle on the bed. "I'm sorry."

"Mike, where do you think we'd be if it wasn't for the accident?"

He shrugs, his eyes dropping to the ground. "I don't know, Kell, but I'm not sure it's such a good idea to go there, if you know what I mean."

"You're probably right." I think about it and say, "I'd be married to your brother and probably fighting with him every day."

This makes him laugh. "You guys did love to fight."

"Yep. We were young and passionate… about absolutely everything."

He sits down across from me. "What are you now, Kelley, if not passionate about everything?"

I roll my eyes. "I can't afford to be passionate."

"Are you still trying to pay off all those medical bills?" he asks.

"Yeah, you could say that."

"Do you need help? I have some money put away."

"Thank you so much for offering. Really." I shake my head. "But, no, thank you."

"Brad would want me to make sure you're okay." He reaches out for my hand. "Will you let me do it for him?"

"No. Absolutely not." I shake my head again. "I'm doing fine, Mike. Really." The lie slips out all too easily.

"Would you tell me if you weren't fine?"

"You don't remember my call two weeks ago?" I say, tilting my head. "I was a mess and snotting all over my cell."

"Hard to forget. I felt so helpless." His expression hardens. "I wish you'd let me kick Eric's ass. He's due, ya know."

"Oh, I know it." I purse my lips and say, "But he's not worth the jail time."

"How about you move here, with me? You can be a trainer at CrossFit."

"I don't even have my degree yet."

"You can transfer to Cal State Hayward. I'm sure they have a kinesiology department." He points to his left and says, "It's not that far, and you can live with me. Maybe in a bigger place though." He nudges my shoulder. "With your background in dance and your kinesiology degree, you'd be a great personal trainer. You're what, only a year from finishing your degree? That makes this a great time to get started and build your client list."

I look down at my hands and pick a hangnail, but really, there's nothing to consider. I close my eyes and shake my head. "Thank you, Mike, but it's not dance." When I say this, it's nearly a whisper. I want to teach dance. If I can't be a dancer, then I'm going to teach dancers. It's the only trade-off I'll accept. I'm not going to stop until I reach that goal. Even if it means I'm sleeping in a tent somewhere on campus.

I glance up at him, and he has a big smile on his face.

"What are you grinning about?"

"The fire is still lit," he says.

I draw my eyebrows together, not sure what he's talking about.

"You are still passionate. You may have mellowed, but the fire is still lit, and I'm happy to see it."

It's true, I'm still passionate about dance. How can I not be when it's the only good thing I have left in my life?

CHAPTER SEVENTEEN

Mackensey

When I walk through the door, I smell female. It stops me in my tracks. How the hell does my house already smell like a girl? It's only been a couple of hours. I'm trying really hard to be annoyed about it, but I'm not—I kind of like it. I call out for Kelley, but she doesn't answer. Walking into the dining room, I see what's stinking up the house. The flowers I bought are arranged in a vase in the middle of my dining-room table. Man, are they strong.

"Kelley, where are you?" I call out.

Nothing.

I glance in the kitchen, and she's not there, but I can see the groceries have been put away. I walk back through the house with Luna following me the entire time, begging for my attention.

"Kelley?"

No answer.

I walk through the hall and glance in each room, but she's nowhere. Her bags are gone from the living room, so I know she unpacked. Maybe she's in the backyard. I head back through the house, checking outside. No Kelley.

I pull out my phone and text her.

Me: *You're not at the house? You okay?*

I wait. She doesn't answer. My message says it was delivered, but it doesn't say read. This scares me.

Me: *Kelley? You okay?*

But nothing.

Me: *Babe?*

I sit on the back steps. Ten minutes later, I haven't received a response. This is weird. Where the hell could she have gone?

As I'm walking back into the house, I get this sinking feeling like something's wrong. It's a weird pain in my chest, and it occurs to me to check where she put her things. I go into the office and tug on the closet door.

Her things aren't there. I stare into the empty closet for a full minute, trying to process. Then I send another text.

Me: *Did you leave? I don't understand.*

I turn and look around the room. That's when I notice the large framed photo propped up on my desk. It's the beautiful blowup of Kelley and her partner in a lift pose. I stare at it, trying to process, then I snatch the Post-it note and read.

You can keep this. Consider it a wedding/annulment gift.
~Kelley

What the…?

I pick up the framed photo and immediately see the rings. Our matching wedding bands from Reno are sitting there, glinting at me. I pick them up and stare at them for a long moment.

I get a flash of memory from the night we got married. Kelley was beaming and my cheeks hurt from smiling, too. Both of us laughing through the ceremony... at least for most of it. I also vaguely remember losing the smile when I said my vows.

I fist the rings, holding them to my chest as I try to rub away the ache. Jesus. I made a vow to this woman, she made a vow to me. That should mean something—it does mean something. What has she done... and why? I lean against the desk and that's when I notice a stack of folders I've never seen before. I pick up the first file. Inside are annulment papers and a bunch of other legal docs, including a summons and a waiver of service, and Kelley's signed everywhere indicated. I stare at them, heart hammering, and lower myself into the desk chair, not sure my legs are going to hold me much longer. I don't understand what I'm looking at and that agitates me to my core. When did she have the time to do this?

And that's when I see it.

My sister's business card is stapled to the inside of the file folder. *Emily... what have you done?*

I throw the paperwork across the room with as much force as I can muster. Of course, it's paper, so I get zero satisfaction out of it, which just pisses me off further. I fist the rings tighter in my hand, shifting to look back at my desk for something more substantial to throw, and that's when I see the other file. It's thicker and has photos sticking out of it. I flip the top open, and this time the stapled business card belongs to Richard Edwards, Private Investigator.

I stuff the rings in my front pocket and stare at the top photo. It's a picture of someone lying in a hospital bed. From the long, dark hair I can tell it's a girl, but her face is swollen. She's got some contraption around her head that looks like a brace people wear when they're recovering from a broken neck.

I pick the photo up and take a closer look. A headline catches my eye. Under the picture is a photocopy of an article from the *Portland Tribune.*

DANCER'S DREAMS SMASHED IN
POSSIBLE DRUNK DRIVING ACCIDENT

There's a photo of Kelley and some guy. He has his arm around her, and they're both smiling ear-to-ear.

I glance at the framed picture and realize the guy from the article looks like the same person from the blown-up photo. His face is partially hidden, but I can see just enough to tell it's him. A moment later I hear the front door open. Clicking heels on the hardwood floor follow.

"Kelley!" I nearly scream it. I'm so relieved, I can barely breathe.

"No, not Kelley," someone calls out.

"Emily!" I shout, and her footsteps stop in the hall. "What the hell have you done?"

I hear her treading toward me again and then she's standing by the door to my office. "I guess you found the paperwork." She leans against the doorframe and says, "I know you two haven't made a decision but I thought I'd get the paperwork ready, just to be prepared."

"You gave these to Kelley?"

"What? No, I left them here for you."

"Emily, you shouldn't have done that." I'm so angry, I can barely see straight. She's lucky she's a woman. She's lucky she's my sister. Anyone else would've been knocked flat by now.

"Mackensey, you can't sit on this. You need to take care of it." She lifts her hands, and says, "I feel awful. I didn't know about her troubles, and she seems like a really nice person, but she can potentially drag you down with her."

"This is none of your business."

"Have you looked at the file?" She points to it and says, "Have you read that?"

"I don't care about what's in this file." I drop it on my desk with a thud. "She found these, she thinks I did this!"

"Mac, you don't know anything about her. She's been to rehab too. She has debt that surpasses a hundred thousand dollars."

I stare at her, not sure I want to believe it. "How do you know she was in rehab?"

"It was court ordered. She was in a horrific drunk-driving accident, and as an underage drinker, the judge forced her into rehab." Emily walks over and picks up the file. "This poor woman's been through hell. Like I said, I feel bad. Some of it could've been avoided if she'd only had a good attorney."

I snatch the file from her hand and flip it open. I grab the first article and start to read.

One person dead, two injured in a late-night accident on the Ross Island Bridge last night. Up-and-coming favorites from the Mankas Dance Company, Kelley Kontos and Bradley Murphy, were out celebrating Kontos' twentieth birthday after a sold-out show last night at the Oregon Ballet Theater, when Murphy lost control and swerved his Chevy Camaro into oncoming traffic in the eastbound lanes, hitting a semi-truck driving in the opposite direction.

Bradley Murphy was killed. Kontos was admitted to Providence Hospital in critical condition. The driver of the semi-truck suffered minor injuries.

Bradley Murphy and Kelley Kontos were well celebrated for their pairing on stages from New York to Los Angeles. Engaged to be married, they had planned to wed in the fall at the end of their current U.S. dance tour. Murphy was twenty-one, and it's believed he was drinking when the accident happened. Toxicology reports are yet to confirm this.

Jesus… *my God, Kelley*. I'm speechless, but determined to know more. I flip through the file and come across the medical bills and school loans. I look back at the photo of the girl in the hospital and it sinks in. I feel sick. Seeing Kelley beat up like that, two broken vertebrae in her back… her partner dead. It's too much for one person. As I flip through, I catch glimpses of other eye-opening details, like her birthday. The day of the crash. May seventeenth. That was last week. Two days before we went to Reno together. There are other pictures of her recovery and more photos of her onstage before the accident. There's even a mention of false reporting and the possibility of leaked personal medical information.

I want to throw up.

"Goddammit, Emily! You went too far."

"I just asked for a basic background check from Richard. I didn't know there would be so much." She sits on the loveseat and takes the file from me. "She was kicked off the dance tour due to a morality clause in her contract. They were pissed about the underage drinking. She didn't have medical insurance. Murphy had just bought the car. It still had paper plates, and he didn't have insurance either. Everyone—his family, the Mankas Dance Company, the newspapers, they all vilified her for this."

I look up at Emily and say, "That's horrible." Closing my eyes, I imagine Kelley's face; what she must have thought when she found this file. "Emily, we made a promise we wouldn't Google each other. This… It's too much."

I rest my face in my hands, and the desire to drink right now is so strong my throat burns with the need. I just want to drown in it, stop thinking about how horrible Kelley must feel right now, how I've somehow managed to let her down.

But I can't. I need to keep my shit together so I can find her. I need to fix this. I grab my phone and text Jeff.

Me: *You available?*

Jeff: *Just got home from work. You okay?*

Me: *No. Not at all.*

Jeff: *Be right over.*

Then I text Kelley.

Me: *I'm so sorry. Emily did this. She prepared the paperwork and the background check. She was trying to help. I didn't know, Kelley. I wouldn't do that. You have to believe me, please.*

I wait... and wait... but she doesn't respond. I shake my head and look up at my sister. "I'll never be able to make this up to her."

"You haven't done anything wrong, Mackensey." She gets to her feet and drops the file back in front of me. Then she takes a closer look at the framed photo sitting on my desk. "Is that her?"

I nod, unable to look at it.

"She's so beautiful. I can't believe how terribly she was treated after the accident." Emily shakes her head and says, "She had very little support from the dance community. Bradley Murphy's family blamed her publicly. I couldn't imagine losing my fiancé and my career like that, much less on my birthday. Everything was taken from her."

I quickly look over at her. Emily knows exactly how it feels to lose the person you love. She's lived through it herself. I try to remember this. I have to. Otherwise, I'm not sure how I can forgive her. "How did he find all of this?"

"It's all public."

"Bullshit! Those medical records wouldn't be public."

She sits back down and reaches out to place her hand on my forearm. "I'm sorry. I wish I hadn't left them here. It didn't occur to me that she'd see them."

"Two weeks ago, she found her boyfriend in bed with her best friend. That day was the first time I laid eyes on her." I stand to pace the room. I'm ridiculously relieved I don't have alcohol in the house because I want a drink so bad it's causing me to sweat. I can barely stand it and I'm thankful for Jeff and his constant support. Who else would come to my rescue so quickly? "She was sitting at the bus stop in front of Starbucks, and she was crying her eyes out." I shake my head as I remember the look on her face that day. "Literally, hysterically crying, talking to someone on her cell phone."

"That's how you met her?"

I shake my head. "No. A week later, I walked into Starbucks after having brunch with you, and she was there. I hadn't been able to get her out of my head since the day I saw her crying. So, I sat next to her, and we started talking." I stop pacing and lean against the wall, crossing my arms over my chest. "Yesterday, I showed up at her apartment, unannounced. I didn't realize it, but she's been living there with her best friend and the ex-boyfriend. After she caught them together, the best friend moved the asshole in with them. Kelley's been trapped there with the two of them acting like they haven't done anything wrong. That's why she was crying… she didn't have anywhere else to go. She was stuck."

"Stuck how? I don't understand. Why didn't she move out?"

"She didn't have the money to move, Emily." I gesture toward the file of information. "Christ, you've seen the file. Moving isn't cheap, you know that."

"What did you do when you found out she was still living with them?"

I can tell by the look on her face that she's worried I did something that could get me in trouble. But as much as I wanted to beat Eric's ass, I managed to keep my cool. For Kelley. "I packed her up and moved her out of that apartment. We couldn't get everything, but we grabbed a bunch of her stuff, and I brought her here. That was early this afternoon. I told her to put what she could in this closet, and we'd work it out later, then I left for my meeting."

"And when you got back?" she asks with a pained expression on her face.

I point to the Post-it on the framed photo of her and Bradley Murphy. "She was gone."

"Do you know who she was talking on the phone with, the first time you saw her?"

"No, why?"

"That's probably who she's with. If she has someone in her life close enough to call during a time like that, that's where she'd run to."

I didn't think of that. "I don't know who she was talking to, I never thought to ask."

"I'm sorry, Mac. What can I do?"

I walk over to the desk and rip the private investigator's business card from the file and toss it at her. "You used this guy to dig up all this information, now use him to find her." I drop the file onto her lap and point to her. "You said she's in debt, you said she was mistreated, and you said she should have had a good attorney. Well, now she has one. Fix whatever you can in that file. Make it right, Emily."

She lowers her eyes. "Of course. I'll do what I can."

I turn and leave the room. I need to move, I need to do something. I need not to drink. When I walk through the living room, I can hear Jeff on the back deck, talking to Luna. I step out to greet him.

"What's up?" he asks. He's looking me up and down as if he suspects I've already had a drink.

"A lot… a lot of shit. Can you ride with me while I run an errand? I'll tell you everything on the way."

CHAPTER EIGHTEEN

Kelley

I wake up with a horrible headache. I crack open my eyes and glance around, but nothing looks familiar. I turn to the person lying next to me. It's Mike, fully dressed and knocked out. I quickly look down at myself. I'm wearing my t-shirt and jeans, thank God.

I survey the room and see the empty bottle of Jack Daniel's on the coffee table. That's why I don't remember last night. We ate Chinese food and drank... a lot. This instantly makes me heavy with guilt. I'm such an idiot. It's a proven fact that I'm incapable of making good decisions when I'm drinking. You'd think after all the crap I've been through, I would have stopped altogether and after Reno, I promised myself I would. Partly because of the stupid-ass thing I did in Reno, and partly because... well, I wanted to stop for Mac. It just seemed like the right thing to do.

I creep out of bed and walk to the bathroom, trying my hardest to be quiet. Mike's apartment is freezing, and it's the end of May. What the hell is up with this weird-ass weather in Oakland? I look outside and see an overcast sky covered with clouds. It's spring, it should be warm outside. I'm not even sure I brought a jacket with me. When I come out of the bathroom, I stumble around Mike's messy apartment and I can't help but compare it to Mac's place. This thought just dampens my mood further. I need to stop thinking about him since he's no longer going to be a part of my life. He's just another man who's let me down. Yet another person I shouldn't have trusted.

I snatch a blanket from the back of Mike's sofa to wrap around myself. Then I go into his kitchen, if you can call it that, and look for the fixings to make coffee. When I see Mike's Keurig, I sigh. It looks like I won't be having a caffeine fix until he wakes. This apartment is too small for me not to wake him up with the noise.

I walk over to the large window with the window seat and curl into it with my blanket. For Saturday morning, Oakland's pretty busy. I watch people below as they walk by, wondering where they're off to. It's Saturday morning, people, sleep-in already. Then I roll my eyes and scoff.

I know. It's me, not them.

I'm thoroughly annoyed at the world. There's nothing wrong with the weather in Oakland, there's nothing wrong with the early risers, there's nothing wrong with having a Keurig coffee machine.

I'm just completely over it.

Over life, over the hand I've been dealt. I know I'm feeling sorry for myself and I hate that. Moaning about my problems won't solve any of them. Getting drunk with Mike last night didn't either. I still have a broken heart, I still have a job that doesn't pay enough, I still don't have a place to live, I still have a friendship in tatters, and I still don't know what the hell I'm going to do about school next year. This makes me wonder about the price of rent in Oakland. I'm sure it's higher, but I also already have a potential roommate and a job offer. It's hard not to be tempted.

Do I even want another roommate after Megan? Can I pay rent without one? No, I can't.

Then I consider how much I'd lose by moving here. I'd lose the partnership Mary offered me. I'd miss the dance students I've already grown attached to. I'd have to transfer schools. And Mac... which shouldn't matter since I've already lost him, but it does.

I need to have my head examined. Why am I so broken-hearted over him? Why did I trust him so easily?

I've quite literally been through two breakups in two weeks. Three, if you count Megan. Losing Eric didn't hurt so much. I was mad, and that anger was directed at Megan for betraying me and our friendship. I guess it took losing Eric to recognize he wasn't that important to me.

And Mac. I lost Mac before I even really had him, and I guess it took losing him to understand how important he is to me. Why didn't I go with my gut and walk away when he asked me to lunch? I knew, when he flashed me that practiced smile in Starbucks. I knew right then he was trouble. I'm foolish for letting myself fall for him. I know better. I even went on the Reno trip with zero expectations. I wanted to walk away with no regrets. That was my plan. But then, Mackensey happened. He was more than I'd bargained for. More than I was expecting.

He was just so much more...

I lean my head against the cool glass of the window. Maybe I should consider moving home. Getting the hell out of California before it eats me alive. But home... that means running away from the life I've begun to build, disappointing my mom. She had high hopes for me even after I destroyed my career. I want to show her she was right for believing in me. Home also means facing all those people who didn't have faith in me, admitting they were right about me all along. I just can't bring myself to admit defeat. I will not return home with my tail between my legs. I won't force my mom to face her friends or the rest of her family and admit that her daughter couldn't manage on her own. It was bad enough that I lost my professional dance career; I won't go home until I can prove I'm capable of doing something productive with my life.

Twenty minutes later, Mike's awake, and we're having coffee. Once he's drained his cup, he slaps my leg and says, "Get up. You need some exercise, and I run around Lake Merritt every Saturday morning. It's a ritual that can't be broken."

I nearly snort at him. "Why would you do something stupid like that?"

He unzips my duffle and starts rifling through it. "Do you have sweats and running shoes in here? You can't run in flip-flops."

I grab the bag and jerk it out of his hands. "I have sneakers and yoga pants, will that do?"

"Perfect. Go change, you can shower after the run."

I drop my shoulders and give him my pathetic, puppy-dog eyes. "One more cup of coffee, please?"

"No! Get your ass up. We'll hit Starbucks later, now we must exercise."

"Ugh, fine." I drag my ass to his bathroom and change my clothes.

When I come out, he's already in his sweats, and he's jogging on the spot. "Ready?"

"I need a hoodie. It's cold in this godforsaken city."

That amuses him. He opens his closet and tosses me a hooded sweatshirt that's much too big, but I don't care because it's warm and I'm still freezing.

Mike only lives a few blocks from the lake. When we get there, I'm glad he forced me out. It's nice to be outside, and the fresh air has already dissolved my headache. We hit the trail at a steady pace, and I surprise myself by smiling. It feels good to run. It's been a couple of weeks since I've worked out. Between what happened with Megan and Eric and my finals and then Mac, I haven't had time to devote to myself. I need to remedy that. I can't let other people dictate my life. I can no longer let toxic people bring me down. I need to take control.

The lake is beautiful and calm, sitting serenely like a pane of glass. Even with the darkness of the clouds, it's still bright out. As we pass the Camron-Stanford House, I slow down to admire the beautiful, old building, tempted to make Mike take me inside. When he pushes me forward, I turn back toward the lake and I can't help but think of it as a little bit of paradise nestled in the middle of the city. People are everywhere, other joggers, walkers and lots of others stopping to snap photos and selfies by the lake.

I glance at Mike, and he's smiling too. "Thank you," I say and breathe out a laugh. My head feels like it's finally clearing, the fresh air shoving aside all my troubles.

"See, you feel better already, don't you?"

"I do." I pick up the pace and pass him, but not for long. He does a quick sprint and then slows it back down. "Don't throw off my pace, Kontos, or I'll throw *you* in the lake."

This makes me laugh again. When we're halfway around, the overcast sky starts to burn off, and the sun is peeking through. Mike stops and tells me we're going to do ten-second sprints. He's a diehard, and I'm starting to pity his clients.

"Ready," he says. Then he looks at his stopwatch. "Go!"

I sprint for what seems like a lot longer than ten seconds, but then he yells stop. "Oh, my God. I think you're trying to kill me. How long is this path around the lake?"

"It's a little over three miles." He grins. "Let's walk it off and then do another sprint."

I'm a little confused about where we are. The area looks familiar. "Hey, is the ballet company nearby?"

"It is. Do you recognize some old stomping ground?"

I scan the area as memories flood my mind. My first time seeing a live ballet was here in Oakland. My dad had brought me along on a business trip. I was in such awe of the dancers and their perfection. Even at eight years old, I immediately knew it was what I wanted to do with my life. When we returned to Portland, my dad asked my mom to enroll me in classes… he was as excited about it as I was.

Two years later my dad was gone and I focused all my energy on dance. It was an escape from the grief I felt at losing him.

That weekend and that trip had been one of the last happy times we had together. The weeks following the trip, my dad had been diagnosed with cancer and everything changed for our family. I close my eyes as the memories of being here with Brad collide with the memories of my dad. Brad and I had spent weeks here while on tour. I remember the first time we walked onstage in Oakland, the rush of feelings it brought on, the rush of grief, but also the rush of pride. I knew my dad was watching me. It was as if I could feel his pride as I danced on the same stage as the professional dancers we'd admired during our trip when I was a kid.

"You okay, Kelley?"

Hearing my name pulls me from the memories. I glance at Mike and the pang of grief hits me again. If only he didn't have Bradley's eyes. "Yeah, I definitely recognize the area. It looks a little different, but not different enough." I gesture toward the neighborhood to my left and say, "Isn't the CrossFit gym nearby?"

"Yep, right around the corner. I can walk there from my apartment."

"That's really cool, Mike," I say, as I turn my back on the neighborhood to face the lake. "Do you like being your own boss?"

"Well, I have two partners. All of the decisions are a majority vote so it's not like I can do what I want."

"But you're successful. The Oakland CrossFit is doing well, right? I know all of the Yelp reviews are excellent. I always look at them, and I'm so proud of you."

He grins, and it really makes me happy to see it. He worked hard to start his business and now that hard work is paying off. "We're doing well," he says. "We're talking about opening up another location, maybe two more." Then he gestures to the path and says, "More sprints."

We do three more until we reach the end of the trail and turn toward his apartment. I'm so warm now, I have his oversized sweater tied around my waist, and I'm begging for a shower... maybe even a nap.

"Let's hit the café for breakfast," Mike says. "I think it's time you tell me what else is going on."

CHAPTER NINETEEN

Mackensey

I finish telling Jeff the story as I park at the apartment complex where Megan and Kelley live. I think I've left him speechless. Hopping out of the car, I rush up the steps to the second floor with Jeff hot on my heels. I knock hard even though I'm sure Kelley's not here. I don't see her coming back here, but I have no idea where else she would've gone—I just know I need to find her.

Megan answers the door, and rolls her eyes when she sees me. "I guess you're here for the rest of Kelley's stuff."

"Does that mean you haven't seen her?"

"What? No. Not since you raced out of here with her earlier." She lifts her hand and lets it drop on her hip. "Have you lost her already?"

I stare hard at her. I don't have time for this, I need to find Kelley now. "Where would she go?"

"I don't know." She lifts her eyebrows in question. "Until two weeks ago, she would've come to me. Now, I don't know. What happened?"

"I left her at my house to go to a work meeting. When I came back, she was gone."

"What did you do to her? She wouldn't have left unless you did something horrible." She points at me and says, "I've heard stories about you. Kelley doesn't know, she doesn't listen to your show, but I do."

"I didn't do anything. It was a misunderstanding, and I just want to make sure Kelley's okay."

Megan opens the door farther and says, "Come in, I'll make some calls."

Jeff and I sit down and watch as she paces the living room, making calls and asking questions. It's killing me to sit still, and my knee is bouncing up and down so hard it's vibrating the entire room. Jeff gives me a look, and I know what he means; he's trying to tell me to calm down, but I can't.

As I watch Megan pace, I realize that I'm not the only one worried. I don't know this girl at all, but I know enough to recognize worry when I see it and the expression on her face makes me ache for Kelley's sake. She finally finishes the last call and looks over at me, then she plops down into an armchair and blows the bangs off her face. "Nothing."

"Nobody has seen her?"

"Either they haven't seen her, or they're not telling me if they have." She rests her elbow on the arm of the chair and lifts her thumb to her mouth to bite the nail. "I even called the Dance Studio, but Mary won't answer the phone if she's in the middle of a class." Her eyes drift to the floor. "I don't know who else to try."

I lean forward and say, "What about her parents? Do you think she would have gone home?"

"Her dad is dead. Her mom hasn't heard from her, and she's worried now too." She lightly pounds her forehead with her palm. "I shouldn't have called her. That was stupid, she wouldn't go home."

"Why not?" Jeff asks.

"Because she's in trouble." Megan waves a hand at us like it's obvious. "Well..." She rolls her eyes. "She's not literally in trouble, but she's out there thinking she has nowhere to live and zero friends to help. She wouldn't want her mom to know that. She wouldn't admit defeat to her mother." She rests her hand on her chest and says, "I'm just saying, I know Kelley, and she only calls home when things are going really well for her."

This only makes me feel worse about the entire situation. I had no idea Kelley had lost her father. I glance over at Jeff, and I'm sure he suspects this is what I'm thinking.

"This isn't your fault, Mac," he says.

"Ah, yeah it is," Megan says. "You shouldn't have dragged her out of here. She was fine, we were going to be fine."

"Bullshit!" I slam my fist down on the coffee table. "Don't sit there and act like you're innocent here." I stand up. My anger is getting the better of me—I need to leave before I put my fist through a wall. "She's pissed at me over a misunderstanding, but you're the one who actually betrayed her."

"We would have worked it out. You don't know Kelley like I do. She wasn't in love with Eric. She doesn't care about him and she's going to forgive me. She just needs some time." She scoffs and says, "But you had to swoop in and rescue her."

"You don't know shit about Kelley if you really believe that. You don't seem to have any idea how badly you've hurt her." When she starts to dispute this, I hold up my hand and say, "Forget it! It's not worth the argument." I storm out of the apartment, heart thumping in my chest, and pound down the stairs with Jeff on my heels. I don't want to get in the middle of their drama, I only want to find Kelley.

Before I hit the bottom step, I hear Megan say, "Wait! Take my number and call me when you find her."

I want to flip her the bird, but I don't. I know it would be childish and wouldn't make me feel better. I rush back up the stairs and grab the Post-it she hands me with her number on it. Then I pace around my car for the next few minutes, trying to figure out what else to do. Who else to ask. Where else to look. There are only two places I can think of, and they're pretty meek ideas. I don't have a choice though—I need to find her.

I decide the first stop should be the dance studio, but I only have a rough idea where it's located. If I can't find it, I'll call Megan for the address.

Jeff and I drive over to Fifty-Sixth Street and H. I circle the blocks and it only takes me a few minutes to find the place. It looks like a small dance school for kids. The sign on the building is in primary colors and a kid-like font, but when I peek through the windows, there are adults inside, and it looks like they're learning the tango or something similar.

I walk in and wait in the small vestibule as I watch the couples. Some are young, and some are seniors, but they all look like they're having a good time. I see an older woman, probably in her late sixties, and she makes eye contact before walking over to talk to me.

"May I help you?" she asks.

"I hope so," I say, and try putting on what I hope is a charming smile—I don't want to look like some kind of stalker creep. "I'm looking for Kelley... Kelley Kontos. I believe she works here as a dance instructor."

She smiles back at me. "And what's your name?"

I reach out my hand and say, "I'm Mackensey Thomas." I'm not sure whether to call myself a friend, boyfriend, or husband. I have no idea if Kelley's even mentioned me to her.

"So you're Mac." She's smiling big now. "I'm Mary."

I tilt my head in surprise. "It's lovely to meet you, Mary. Has Kelley told you about me?"

"Excuse me." She calls out some instructions to her students and then looks back at me. "Yes, when I insisted she take the weekend off. Of course, she was just thrilled about school being finished and being done with her exams." She narrows her eyes at me. "And she seemed pretty happy to be spending time with you this weekend."

"Yes, well, the day started out great, but then there was a misunderstanding." I lower my gaze because I have no idea what to tell her. I don't know how to convince her that I'm genuinely concerned without worrying her. "She won't answer my calls, and I was hoping to find her here."

"Oh, I am sorry to hear that." She stares at me for a moment and then says, "If she's not home, and she's not here, I don't know where she would go."

I nod and say, "Thank you. If you see her, will you please ask her to call me?"

"Of course. And I hope you'll do the same—I don't want to worry about her all weekend."

"Yes, I'll make sure." I give her a slight wave as I exit the building. I feel awful about Kelley's excitement over the weekend. She must have been crushed to find those files. I have to fix this.

I get back in the car and glance over at Jeff.

"Now what?" he asks.

"I only have one place left to look, and it's a long shot." I start the car and head toward Starbucks, praying the redhead is there.

When I walk in, the place is crowded as usual. I stuff my hands in my pockets to keep from fidgeting nervously. So much has happened since the last time I was here... so much has changed. Who would have guessed that after finally getting a chance to meet and talk to the green-eyed girl, I'd be scouring the city to find her a week later? Who would have guessed she'd become my wife?

I wait in line, and when it's my turn, I look down at the kid's name tag and say, "Hey, Brice, can you tell me the name of the redhead who usually works the morning shift?"

Brice nods quickly and says, "That has to be Lexi. She's not here."

"Do you happen to know where she lives?"

After asking this, we're interrupted by an older barista, who I assume is the manager. "Excuse me, Brice." She looks at me and says, "We cannot tell you where an employee lives. Why do you want to know about Lexi?"

"She's friends with my girlfriend, Kelley, and Kelley is missing. I was hoping she could help me."

"Oh, I know Kelley," Brice says, but the manager waves him away.

"We can't give out personal information about our employees or our customers. I'm sorry."

I sigh and drop my head back. "Can you tell me when she's due to work again?"

"No, we can't," she says, and I can tell she's getting annoyed with me, which is fine since I'm equally annoyed with her.

I walk out of Starbucks without ordering a drink because, well, screw them. I sit down at one of the patio tables, and Jeff joins me. "What's it going to be, Mac?"

"I have no damn idea. I guess I'm going to sit here until Lexi shows up."

"Listen, I know you're feeling really shitty about this, but you need to stop with the guilt. You haven't done anything wrong."

"I have, by not setting boundaries with my family." Just thinking about Emily makes me so angry I can barely think about anything else. "Emily never should have felt that it was okay to do what she did. To get involved like that."

"As your attorney, it's literally her job to protect you," he says. "I understand she's created a huge problem for you, but she meant well."

I know he's right, but that doesn't make me any less mad. "The road to hell is paved with good intentions."

"Speaking of the road to hell, how are you feeling? You must have called me to join you on this little fieldtrip for a reason."

I rest my head back and focus my eyes on the bright sky. How do I feel? I assess myself, not totally sure. But once I consider it, I realize I am sure. I shrug as I tilt my head toward Jeff. "Right now,

I'm fine. When I first found out what Emily did, I was freaking out. I had the strong urge to drink. I instantly wanted to wash away my problems and forget. But I don't feel that way now, I feel in control."

"What changed?"

"I'm not sure. Maybe it's having a goal, knowing that I need to find Kelley."

As Jeff's about to ask me another question, my phone rings. Speak of the Devil and the Devil shall appear. "Emily?"

"Hey, Mac, Richard just called."

I'm nearly jumping out of my chair when I hear this. "Has he found Kelley? Where is she?"

"He hasn't found her, but he knows where she went." I hear a rustle on the phone as if she's placed her hand over the speaker, then she's back on the line. "She bought an Amtrak train ticket to Oakland."

"What the hell is in Oakland?"

"I don't know, hon." She's quiet for a moment, then she says, "Can you ask her friend?"

Right! I have Megan's phone number. "Yes, I'll call you back." I hang up and search my pocket for the Post-it Megan gave me.

"Jeff, let me use your phone?"

"Why can't you call her with your own phone?"

"I don't trust that bitch with my phone number. She'll post it all over the internet or something."

"Of course. It's much better for her to post my number all over the internet," he says as he hands it over.

"Thank you."

I dial her number, and stand to pace. I have the urge to keep moving. Megan sounds angry when she answers. "Hello?"

"Megan, it's Mac."

"Oh," she says sounding surprised. "The unknown number threw me off. Glad I have it now though, so I can check in with you."

"It's not my number, it's Jeff's." I glance over at him to make sure he knows I've squashed any chance of her sharing the number.

"Oh… okay. Did you find Kelley?"

"She bought a train ticket to Oakland. Do you know who she'd visit there?"

"Oakland? That's weird. I don't think we know anyone…" She pauses for what seems like a lifetime, but then she says, "Damn… I didn't even think about him."

"Him who? Who lives in Oakland?"

"She's probably gone to see Mike."

My back stiffens when I hear the name. "Mike? Who's Mike?"

"He's an old friend of ours, from high school. Kelley used to be engaged to his brother."

"What's his last name?"

"Michael Murphy. He just moved to Oakland a few months ago. He went into a partnership with two other guys. The three of them opened a CrossFit gym near Lake Merritt."

"Great, thank you." I hang up before she has time to say anything else and hand the phone back to Jeff before pulling mine from my pocket. I dial Emily's number and when she answers, I say, "Michael Murphy. He lives in Oakland, and he's part owner of a CrossFit gym there."

"And…"

"And get his address!"

"Mac, she's with another guy. Do you really want to go there and see that?"

My chest hammers as I realize she's right: I really don't know what I might find. I pace in another circle and consider this, but then realize it doesn't matter. Whoever Mike is to Kelley doesn't matter in the end. What matters is who *I* am to Kelley, and I'm not going to be the next in a succession of people who have hurt her. "Emily, I don't care. Get the address."

I disconnect the call and shake my head as I look over at Jeff, who's staring at me. "What?"

Jeff shrugs as if he has nothing to say, but then changes his mind. "Are you going to this man's house to look for her?"

"Yes, of course."

"Mac, I don't think that's a good idea."

"Why not?" I'm thoroughly confused by his reaction. "Why wouldn't I go there?"

"I'm starting to believe this girl isn't healthy for you... or this relationship."

"Jeff, she's done nothing wrong. This is something Emily did to her. Something she thinks I did. I need to make it right."

"Why?"

"Are you kidding me?" I stare at him, wide-eyed. "You're asking me why I need to make this right with her?"

"Yes. Why?" He shakes his head and stares at me. Then he finally says, "Do you want to be married? Is that what you're doing? Are you tracking down your *wife*?"

His questions stop me in my tracks. I don't know. I only know that Kelley thinks I had annulment papers drawn up and she believes I paid someone to do a background check on her. The idea of Kelley believing this about me makes me insane. I would never betray her like that.

"You've got the wrong idea, Jeff. You don't understand. She thinks I did this to her. She's been through hell. You don't know, you haven't read the file. With Eric and Megan... and all the other crap that's happened to her, I can't let her believe that I'm just another asshole who doesn't give a shit. Because married or not, I *do* give a shit." I brush a hand at him. "If you can't understand, go home."

"I can see that you care, but I'm wondering if you care too much."

I nod and purse my lips. "You might be right. I might care too much, but that doesn't mean I shouldn't make it right."

"Mac, I'm going to ask you to tread carefully. If you go to that man's house with guns blazing to retrieve your wife, it's going to be too much."

"What are you suggesting?"

He thinks about it for a few minutes as he stares at me, then says, "I think you should wait until tomorrow."

When I start to protest, he holds up his hand and says, "Maybe even wait until she gets back. You could be there for her at the train station when she returns. Did Emily say when her return ticket is for?"

"No. She might not even have a return ticket."

"It wouldn't hurt to give you both some time before you show up there."

I rest back in my chair and lift my eyes to the sky. Is Jeff right? Rushing to Oakland this evening might be overkill. I don't want to make things worse.

I pull out my phone and retrieve her contact. All of my messages are sitting unread. I start typing.

Me: *Kelley, I'm so sorry about this. I hope you know it's a misunderstanding. I didn't ask Emily to do that. I wanted to talk to you about things. You wanted to wait until after your finals, and I wanted to wait too. I wanted time with you. I didn't know what to do, and I still don't, but I know I don't want to let you go. Please call me.*

I hit send, and the weight on my chest grows heavier. I don't like it. I don't like how this feels. The emptiness of Kelley being gone. The hurt of knowing she hates me. The worry over not knowing if she's okay or not. It all makes me want to drink... to drink until I forget.

CHAPTER TWENTY

Kelley

Mike's staring at me like I'm an idiot. I can't blame him: he's right. Someone who gets drunk and marries a stranger has to be an idiot. It's pretty much what I was expecting from him when I decided to tell him about Reno, not that he gave me a choice. He knew something was up with me besides what happened with Megan—he knows me pretty well.

We're sitting in a small café near his apartment, eating breakfast. I'm still in my sweaty yoga pants and sneakers, and I feel gross, but that's intensified by the expression on Mike's face.

"So," he says. "You just left?"

I drop my shoulders in defeat. "What else was I supposed to do?"

"Face him." he says, leaning across the table toward me. "Make him tell you to your face, Kelley."

"Why? So he can see me…" I close my eyes and fight the tears.

"Cry? Yes! Unless you really don't care about him."

I open my eyes and glare at him.

"So, you *do* care about him? Because if you don't, there's no point in having this conversation. You just need to walk away."

I shake my head and say, "How I feel doesn't matter. I've already walked away, that's why I'm here."

"But you're only here for the weekend. What happens when you go back, Kell? Where are you staying?"

"I have a friend I can stay with for a few days."

"And after that? You need a long-term plan."

"I'm working on it, Mike. I was supposed to look at an apartment today, but I'm here. I'll just have to figure it out when I get back on Monday."

"Did you call to reschedule? Can you look at it on Monday? The gym is closed for the holiday, so I have the day off. Do you want me to drive you back instead of taking the train, go with you to see the place?"

"Whoa, big fella, take a breath."

"I'm worried," he says, throwing a blueberry at me from his small bowl of fruit. "You're living on someone's couch. You won't take any money from me, and you're freaking married to some dude I don't know."

I reach out and squeeze his hand. "Thank you, really, for being such a great friend." I pull my hand away, and my eyes drop to the table, where my breakfast sits uneaten. "I haven't rescheduled. I've had my phone off since I left town yesterday to avoid seeing Mac's texts."

"Wait. He's texting you?" His eyebrows scrunch together. "That doesn't sound like a guy who's ready to end things with you."

"Oh, he's ready to end it, but he's not a monster. I'm sure he feels bad for letting me find out the way I did."

He snickers at me. "Kelley, I think you're missing some fundamental understanding of how a man's brain works." He waves a finger and says, "A clean break is a clean break. If he really didn't want to have something going with you, he'd consider this a clean break and be on his merry way."

I shake my head. "No, I think he's afraid I'll tell people we're married, ruin his playboy reputation… or maybe he's worried I'll ask for something in the annulment." Saying this and knowing how true it is makes my stomach hurt. "Not to mention his sobriety. I'm sure he feels he needs to make amends and apologize." Of course, he would.

"So, let me get this straight: Mac rescued you from Megan and Eric, he also moved your stuff into his own house even though he barely knows you, and even though he had annulment paperwork in his office, he's still trying to contact you. Does that about sum things up?"

"Yeah, and again, he's a high-profile person. He has to protect himself, right?"

Mike stares at me for a long time, shaking his head as if he's trying to figure out the situation. "If I'm being honest here, Kelley, it sounds more like he's trying to protect *you*, but…." He lifts his hands in question. "I don't know the guy so I'm just calling 'em as I see 'em."

Before I can stop it, a tear falls from my eye. My voice won't work, so I shake my head and quickly swipe my face. "No, I'm sorry. I can't continue to pretend he cares about me."

"Are you sure you don't want to talk to him about it? Make sure you're not reading this wrong? How many times has he texted you?"

"There's no point, Mike. There's no point in trying to talk to him. I can't continue doing this to myself. I have a limit, okay?" When my voice breaks, I lift my shaking hand to my forehead and say, "I'm up to here with it, okay? I've reached the limit, I can't take any more…" With these words, my face crumples.

"Okay." He reaches out for my hand and squeezes it. "It's okay, Kell. I get it."

I inhale deeply and then exhale a shaky breath. "I'm fine. Dammit."

He gives me a lopsided grin. "Sure you are."

"Shut up."

"Think about this, okay?" He holds up a finger to keep me from interrupting him. "Consider this for a moment, Kell. If he's really an alcoholic and he needs to make amends, you should let him. You may believe he doesn't care about you, but if you care about him, you need to let him end it the way he needs to. Your stubbornness isn't worth a man's sobriety."

I draw back when he says this… I never really thought about that, but he's right.

"You should at least let him know you're okay. Because he wouldn't be texting you if he wasn't concerned."

"You think so?"

"Yeah! Think about it. You took off without telling him. Did you leave a note? Let him know where you were going?"

"No."

"So, Kelley, he thinks you took off with nowhere to go and no one to help you. If he's any kind of a man, he's got to be worried about you."

"Mike…" I can't say anything, I can't argue with that. He's absolutely right. I lean forward and rest my head in my hands, overcome by a sinking feeling in my heart because I'm not sure I can face Mac, knowing he's read everything about me in that damn file.

"Come on," says Mike. "You'll feel better after a shower, then we'll turn your phone on and see what he has to say."

I look up at him. "Thank you."

He grabs my hand and pulls me out of the booth and into a hug. "You're going to be okay, Kelley."

Hearing this reminds me of the last words Mac said to me.

I've got you, Kelley.

Thinking about Mac—the way he held me, the way he spoke to me—I suddenly feel uncomfortable in Mike's arms. Like it's wrong, even though our relationship is platonic—even though Mac and I are over. I pull away and follow him out of the café.

When we get back to his apartment, he beats me to the shower, so I sit down and wait. I take in the space and notice the small family portrait next to Mike's bed. I walk over and pick it up. It's the five of them, both of his parents with Mike, Brad, and Diana.

Brad was the youngest and the smallest in the family. Mike's the middle child, yet the tallest. His sister Diana, the eldest of the three siblings, is sitting front and center between her brothers. She's beautiful, with her silky, dark hair. Staring at the photo, I take in how much I've lost.

They hate me. It pains me to know how much they despise me. I get it, though. As much as it hurts, I understand why. They blame me for everything, and maybe they're right: Brad would still be alive if I'd stopped him from driving that night.

I'd love to be able to say I tried to stop him, but I can't. The truth is, I don't remember anything. The entire night is a complete blur, most of the day too. I remember waking up that morning and being excited about opening the show to a sold-out crowd in my hometown. It was my birthday, and I was spending it with my new fiancé. A few friends had planned a party for me after the show and I knew Brad had something special planned as well. I was on top of the world that morning. I had everything I ever wanted in the palm of my hands. A wonderful man in love with me, a fulfilling career with infinite potential, and enough money in the bank to keep me worry-free for some time. I almost forget what it was like to not worry about money.

It was a happy time... until it wasn't.

I stare at the photo for a few minutes longer until I hear the bathroom door open. I turn slightly to find Mike with a towel wrapped around his waist. Jesus! I twist back to avoid staring at him. He's certainly... filled out. I have to fight the blush as it creeps into my cheeks.

"Sorry," he says. "I forgot to bring my clothes into the bathroom with me." When he walks to the dresser, he peeks over my shoulder to see the photo in my hand. "You okay?"

With a nod, I say, "How are they?"

He scoffs. "Why do you ask?"

"Just because they hate me doesn't mean I feel the same about them."

"You should hate them after what they did to you."

I place the framed photo back on his nightstand. "I can't. They were important to me once… and they lost their child. I understand why they feel the way they do."

"Yep. They lost a child. That happens, but that's no excuse for them blasting you to the media the way they did. It was totally unfair and uncalled for."

"Was it, though?"

Mike sits on the bed next to me. "Yes, it was. That accident was no more your fault than it was mine. They could just as easily have blamed me, but they didn't."

"You and Diana are all they have left."

"They had you too." He sighs and run his hands through wet hair. "When you and Brad got engaged, they went on and on about how happy they were to have another daughter. They called you their daughter, and then they completely abandoned you when you were hurt, when you needed them most. They loved you, and that's how they treat you? No, they were wrong. Don't make excuses for them."

"I doubt they'll ever forgive me."

"You're right, they probably won't, but that's on them, not you. You need to stop trying. You need to stop letting them make you feel guilty. Stop taking the blame and get on with your life. Brad, and only Brad, is responsible for his death. I was at the party too that night, Kelley. I could've stopped him from driving, but I didn't—I was too busy having my own good time." He grabs my arm to make me look at him. "If I'd stopped him, I could've saved his life and saved you from being hurt."

When he says this, the spot on my back tingles with remembered pain. "I still blame myself," I whisper. "I should have stopped him."

"So, then you think I should blame myself, just like you blame yourself?"

I glance over quickly. "No, I didn't say that."

He points to himself. "As his big brother, it was my job to watch out for him. But I didn't—I let him walk out of that party and get into his new car. I didn't even hesitate."

"It's not the same thing, Mike. You didn't get into the car with him… I did."

"That's a ridiculous comparison and you know it. I hugged you both goodbye, Kelley. I was standing there when you left. To be honest, I didn't think Brad had had much to drink. He seemed totally fine when you left otherwise I would have stopped him."

I think back to the few blurry moments I can remember from the day, but for the life of me, I can't remember the party. I only know what other people have told me about that night. Including Mike's parents. "Your mom and dad don't seem to have trouble believing it's my fault."

"My parents are self-righteous pricks. Do you really want to know what these wonderful people have done since losing Bradley?" he asks.

I shake my head because I don't want to hear it. "Don't, Mike. Don't do that."

"No, Kelley, you need to know."

"Mike, stop."

"No. You need to hear this. You would think losing Brad would drive them to want healthy relationships with the rest of their family, but they don't. They're so overwhelmed with grief they couldn't care less about my life, Diana… or even their granddaughter. Worse than not being able to get past their grief, they can't understand how Diana and I are able to go on with our lives. As if there's something wrong with us for moving forward. As if being successful is a disservice to Brad's memory. How warped is that?"

I don't know what to say. As much as Mike's trying to make me feel better, it's making me feel worse. This is what I've done to his parents. To his family. "I'm sorry, Mike."

"Stop doing that. This isn't your fault. It's been five years, Kelley. We all need to move on, including my parents. Brad wouldn't want this. Dammit, he'd be pissed to see them like this."

I think about that and I know it's true. Brad would hate what this is doing to his family.

"Olivia barely knows her grandparents."

My heart hurts when I remember Mike's beautiful little niece, Olivia. She was born a few months before the accident. I remember that full head of the curliest, black hair I've ever seen. She's five years old now, and that makes me feel really old. "How is Olivia?"

Mike snorts out a laugh, and I'm glad he's no longer yelling about his parents. "She's spunky, just like her mother."

"I'm sorry they can't move past what happened to appreciate what they have left."

"Me too, Kelley. Life is too short to be angry. You'd think they'd have learned that by now." He nudges my shoulder and says, "Life is too damn short to carry around undeserving guilt."

I stand up and turn toward the bathroom. "I'll be done with the shower in a few minutes."

As I close the door behind me, I think about how I don't need another thing to dwell on. Being a part of that family meant everything to me once. Now, it feels like trying to catch smoke with my bare hands.

CHAPTER TWENTY-ONE

Mackensey

It's 7 a.m., and I can see Lexi inside Starbucks. I got zero sleep last night, and had to sneak out this morning to avoid waking Jeff, who was sleeping on my couch. I didn't drink. I wanted to, but all I could think about was how that would affect Kelley. Jeff's already made it clear he thinks our relationship is a problem. It doesn't take a rocket scientist to see that everyone from my boss to my family would blame her if I fell off the wagon twice in one week. And yes, I get that's a sorry excuse to maintain my sobriety, but it works, so I'm going with it. I also promised Kelley I wouldn't let her be the person who drove me to drink and I'm planning to keep that promise.

I walk inside and get in line. Even on a Saturday morning, this place is busy. The rich smell of coffee brewing, usually one of my favorite scents, makes me jumpy. I wait in line and order my drink. I go pretty unnoticed until Lexi slides the Americano across the bar to me and looks up. Her entire face changes, but I can see she's trying to hide it.

"Where is she?" I ask quietly.

"Why would I tell you that after what you did?"

"I didn't do anything. My sister is a lawyer. She's the one who brought over the paperwork and ordered the background check. She left them on my desk without telling me."

She continues making the next drink, not responding, so I try again. "I'm worried. She didn't even leave a note. At least tell me she's okay. Is she at your place?" I know where she is, but I don't want Lexi to know it—I need all the sympathy I can get.

She glances over, and I can see she's wavering. "Is that true, about your sister?"

"I swear it's true. I would never do that to Kelley."

Her eyes lower to the coffee in her hand, and she mutters, "I had a feeling something was off. I tried to get her to slow down and talk to you, but she wouldn't."

"Will you help me?"

"There isn't much I can do. I think she turned her phone off. She's not responding to my texts."

"But you know where she is, right?" I dread the idea of telling Kelley that I found her through the same private investigator that gathered all the information on her. If I can get Lexi to tell me, it'll save me from having to use the information from Richard.

Lexi looks over her shoulder and says, "I need a quick break." She puts down the coffee she's just finished making and calls out the name, then walks around the counter and faces me. She stares me down for a good thirty seconds as if sizing me up. She's good. I can tell she's serious, but she's got nothing on Kelley—Kelley's eyes can bring me to my knees with one simple glance.

Lexi finally agrees and pulls her cell phone out of her back pocket. After a few swipes, she holds it up to show me the address. I quickly type it into the navigational system on my phone, and I'm so grateful, I could kiss her. "Lexi, this means the world to me. Thank you so much for your help. I promise I won't do anything purposefully to hurt Kelley."

She narrows her eyes at me. "Don't accidentally hurt Kelley, either. You got it?"

I give her a sincere smile. "I got it."

I make a stop on my way, and due to ridiculous traffic, it takes me a solid three hours just to get to Oakland. It's the longest three hours of my life. I feel like if I can just get Kelley to listen to me, force her to let me explain the situation, she'll understand. Of course, there's no forcing her to do anything she doesn't want to do. My gut is in knots and I'm so stuck in my own head, I finally turn the radio on for a distraction.

It takes another half hour of driving before I reach the apartment building. Parking is a bitch too. I finally find a spot two blocks away. When I reach the building, I tug on the door, and I'm thankful it's not a security building.

I climb three flights of stairs and make a right until I'm standing in front of the apartment door. I take a deep breath and then another... and then I knock.

The door opens, and this guy is standing there in a towel... in *only* a towel. He looks just like the guy in the photo from the article I read yesterday about Kelley's accident. I don't know which bothers me more, his lack of clothes or the fact that he looks so similar to Kelley's dead fiancé. I take another deep breath because I don't want to start trouble, I just want to find Kelley.

"Are you lost?" he asks when I don't say anything.

Before I can answer, a door inside the small apartment opens, and I hear Kelley say, "Who's here?" She comes into view, and my heart jumps in my chest. She's beautiful, and seeing her reminds me of how much I have to lose.

"Mac?"

I still can't talk, and I'm not sure what to say. The guy in the towel has me wondering what the hell is going on.

"This is Mac?" he asks.

"Maybe you should get dressed, Mike," I say, and I see Kelley's bright green eyes widen. I stare at her for a moment but finally say, "Can we talk?"

Mike scoffs at me and raises his eyebrows. We're staring each other down when Kelley steps between us. I'm still looking at Mike over her head, but she's what I want, so I look down at her.

She's glaring at me. "What are you doing here?"

"I'm here to talk to you," I say, trying to keep it simple.

Her arms cross over her chest and she says, "How did you find me?"

"Lexi gave me the address."

I watch her face as she calculates this and I can tell she's not sure whether to be mad or relieved.

"Can we talk?" I ask again because Mike is still watching me and I really want to send a flying punch to his face. The sooner I get Kelley alone, the better.

He takes a step back and says, "You don't have to, Kelley."

I want to grab her and throw her over my shoulder, and that urge is almost as strong as the one that wants to pull her to me and never let go, but I do neither of those things. Instead, I wait for her to answer.

"It's fine," she says. "Everything is fine." She reaches over and snatches up a grey hoodie sitting on the couch. "We can go for a walk."

Kelley walks out past me, and I reluctantly turn and follow her down the stairs and out the building. Once we're outside, she turns on me. "I don't think we have much left to talk about."

I stare at her, fighting to breathe… fighting not to scream at her for being in some half-naked man's apartment. "Do you want to sit in the car, or is there a place we can go so we're not standing on the street?"

"There's a coffee house around the corner." She turns, and as she's walking, she throws on the hoodie she's carrying. It's way too big and drops nearly to her knees.

I growl at the sight of her in some other man's clothes.

My restraint is evidence of how much I care about her since all I want to do is rip that sweatshirt off her and tear it to shreds. I want to rant at her and find out what the hell she did with that guy, and then a wave of grief crashes into me. I have to remind myself why I'm here and why I followed her. I'm the reason she ran.

We walk into Peet's Coffee, and I order. I know she likes mochas, so I don't even need to ask her what she wants. Our drinks are up quickly, so I grab both and walk over to the table where she's waiting for me. I set down her coffee, and she whispers a thank you as she glances up at me. Her green eyes are dark and hooded, her face sad. I hate that—I hate it almost as much as I hate the image in my head of her and Mike in that apartment together.

"Who's the guy?" I ask before I can stop myself.

She looks at me with one of those expressions. The one that says she wants me dead. I've known her a week, and I can already read her face. "You shouldn't ask questions when you already know the answer. You did just use his name, so you obviously know who he is. But, to simplify, I'll tell you that Mike is an old friend. I'm sure you know just how old a friend after receiving all that information from the extensive background check you had done on me."

"What are you doing here with him?"

She tilts her head and says, "I don't think that's any of your business."

"Really? Because I think it is." I lean forward. "You could have left me a note."

"You could have discussed an annulment with me first. You could have asked me about my background instead of having some stranger check into me like I'm some street criminal. You could have had that conversation with me instead of conveniently leaving the paperwork out for me to find." Her eyes harden as she watches me. "Was that really your move or were you planning to spring the news when you gave me the flowers and cooked dinner for me?"

"I'm sorry," I say since it seems like I started out on the wrong foot. "But I didn't do any of those things."

"Then how did those files end up on your desk?" she asks, and her voice is raised. I can see little pink spots pop out on her fair cheeks.

"My sister is an attorney," I explain. "Emily is *my* attorney. She brought that paperwork over to my house."

She shrugs and says, "I guess that was nice of her to take care of it for you. I wondered how you got it done so quickly."

"No, you don't understand—"

She raises her hand to stop me. "It's okay, Mac. You don't have to feel bad. It was inevitable anyway."

"Was it?" I ask, and I get a sinking feeling in my stomach that almost makes me dizzy.

"Apparently, it was. I just wish you'd told me outright instead of trying to soften the blow with a nice dinner and flowers. I don't need all that, I just need the truth."

"Kelley, the truth is, I had nothing to do with it. I didn't ask Emily to do that. I never even had a conversation with her about it. I had no idea. I'm mad as hell at her for it."

She looks up quickly, and her expression is questioning. "You didn't ask her to dig up all that information on me?"

"I wouldn't do that. I promised not to Google you. Remember? I wanted to take you at face value, and I wanted you to do the same with me."

"Yeah, *I* remember."

"Babe, you saw that paperwork before I did."

Her eyes well with tears. "Well, I didn't know that."

I almost want to laugh in relief. "That's why I'm here."

When tears slide down her face, I'm concerned. I don't know what she's thinking, but I don't want her to be upset. I reach out for her hand and say, "Are you okay?"

She drops her hand in mine. "I didn't know... I just assumed. Why would Emily do that?"

I shake my head and close my eyes. "She said she got the annulment paperwork together to be prepared for when we made the decision. As for the rest, I don't know. She said she wanted a basic background check and that's what she ended up with. I'm sorry. I can't excuse her, but I guess it's my fault for not having firm boundaries with my family."

Her bright eyes are startlingly green and I realize they're always brighter when she cries. I reach out to wipe the tear streaks from her face. "Don't cry, beautiful."

"I'm sorry," she says.

"Tell me about Mike," I say because I need to know… I need the reassurance.

"He's an old friend from high school." She lowers her eyes and says, "I was engaged to his brother Brad until he was killed in an accident on my twentieth birthday."

"I'm sorry about Brad and I'm so sorry it happened on your birthday. That must have been a terrible time for you."

"It was a horrible time. Mike's one of the few people who stood by me and supported me."

"I'm glad you have someone like him in your life, especially now that you can't rely on Megan. But you two looked pretty cozy when I arrived. Are you sure there's not more to it than just friends?"

"No, Mike's just a friend… actually more like a brother. It's not anything like that, Mac. I didn't come here for that, I just needed to get away."

Since she doesn't look in the least bit happy or relaxed, I have to ask, "Did it help?"

She shakes her head and says, "No, not really. It was nice to see Mike and spend some time with him, but it didn't take away the crappiness of my life."

"I'm sorry for what Emily did. Believe it or not, she is too."

"Good!" she says, and the volume has returned to her voice. "She should be sorry." She's silent for a moment but I get the feeling she has more to say. "Mac, we still need to talk about it. Just because you didn't ask for the annulment papers doesn't mean you don't want an annulment."

"I know it doesn't." I drop my gaze to our linked hands. "Did you get any of my texts or voicemails?"

"No, I've had my phone off since I left Sacramento."

When our eyes meet, I take this moment to confess something to her. "I've never done this before... it's strange, you know. Married before a relationship." I chuckle in disbelief. "I don't know what to do, but I know I want you out of Megan's apartment and I certainly don't want you here with Mike."

"I guess I can understand that. Mike offered me a job at the CrossFit gym. I can transfer my credits to Cal State Hayward and finish my degree there."

"I know you're in limbo right now because of Megan and work and school. I don't know what to do, Kelley, but I don't want you to leave."

"You've told me what you don't want. Maybe you should tell me what you do want," she says, and her eyes are intense. I can feel her scrutiny as she watches me.

"I want a lot of things. I just don't know how realistic they are... but mostly, I want you in my life... every day."

"You do?" she asks, and her cheeks grow pink again.

"I do, but that doesn't mean anything if it's not what you want."

"I want to be with you," she says. "We don't need to be married, but I don't think what's happening between us is a bad thing."

This makes me laugh. "I don't think it's a bad thing either. Just the opposite, I think it's a good thing. An amazing thing. At least, it is when we're communicating."

She shakes her head and says, "You have no idea how horrible it was to find those files on your desk."

"I can imagine. The last twenty-four hours haven't been nice for me either. At first I actually thought you had left the annulment paperwork, but after looking at everything, I realized what happened."

"I'm so sorry for taking off the way I did."

"Before I left for my meeting, I told you to trust me. You didn't. And just like in Reno, you took off before we could work things out."

"I know I did… I was so hurt… and scared." Her face crumples and she covers it with the sleeves of the large hoodie she's wearing and mutters, "I'm sorry."

I reach out and take her wrist to pull her hands away from her face. When she opens those bright green eyes and focuses them on me, I say, "I'm sorry too. I'll keep my family in check from now on." I lift out of my chair and lean in to plant a gentle kiss on her forehead. When I return to my seat, I give her a sheepish smile. "Can we move on now?"

"Yes," she whispers.

I reach into my pocket and pull out the little black box I've been holding onto. When Kelley sees it, her eyes widen. "Don't panic, it's not what you think it is." I flip open the top of the box and pull out a long gold necklace. Looped through the chain are the gold bands we purchased in Reno together. "We might not have been of sound mind when we bought these, but that doesn't mean the thought behind the act was completely careless. So, I think they should be kept together until we figure out what this is."

She comes around the table to wrap her arms around me. I pull her into my lap and embrace her with a heavy sigh. "I missed you."

Her lips meet mine in a kiss so heated, my dick grows hard underneath her.

She pulls back with a slight grin. "You did miss me." Her hands rest on my shoulders, and she says, "I missed you, too. Terribly."

"Will you wear these and keep them safe?"

Kelley agrees and lets me drape the chain around her neck until the rings rest between her breasts. I pull her in for another kiss and mumble, "Can we go home now?"

CHAPTER TWENTY-TWO

Kelley

The relief I feel… the sheer joy of having that weight off my shoulders is overwhelming. Mac walks me back to Mike's apartment, but before leaving Peet's, he insists I take off Mike's oversized sweater. Well… he actually takes it off me himself and drapes his jacket over my shoulders. I get it. I'm sure I wouldn't like walking in on him with some girl dressed in a towel. I plan to make sure he's convinced of my feelings later when we're alone. I can't wait for that—I really did miss him.

When I knock on Mike's door, I'm relieved when he answers fully dressed. We step in, and I see Mac trying to maintain his neutral expression. First, the apartment is a mess, and I'm sure that bothers him. Second, Mike's not exactly friendly to him, but he doesn't know the whole story yet—he still thinks Mac did this.

"Everything okay?" Mike asks.

I have trouble fighting the grin as it spreads across my face. "Misunderstanding," I say.

"Really? Seems like a pretty blunt understanding to me."

"My sister's a lawyer, she left the paperwork. I didn't know about it," Mac says, and if I didn't know any better, I'd think he was trying to make his voice deeper. Men are so dumb like that.

"So…" Mike points between us. "You're staying married?"

"Um…" Mac says. "We're staying dating, we'll decide the rest later."

"But you are married."

"Yes, we're aware of that," Mac replies.

"So…" Mike says.

"So, Kelley and I will figure it out as we go. We don't need other people forcing us into doing something we're not ready for. Be it getting annulled or being married."

"But you *are* married," Mike repeats, and this time he's looking in my direction.

"What's your point, Mike?" I finally say.

"My point!" His voice is raised, and that makes me nervous. Mac is already on edge with Mike, and I don't want them to fight. "My point is that you've been miserable all night and morning, and now you're suddenly happy… but what happens when he changes his mind in a few months?"

"You're assuming I will?" Mac says.

"Human nature says you will." Mike leans forward aggressively. "Am I wrong?"

"I don't know." Mac takes a step closer. "But whatever happens, it will be between Kelley and me."

"You mean like it's been between you and Kelley for the last twenty-four hours?"

"That's my fault," I say. "Will you stop? Mike, I get where you're coming from, but Mac and I don't have all the answers yet."

Mac lifts a hand in defense. "I'm not going to do anything to hurt Kelley. If we don't make it past the next couple of months, it'll be a mutual decision."

"I'm holding you to that," says Mike, pointing to Mac. "If she shows up on my doorstep crying again, I'll be looking for you."

Mac looks over at me. "You were crying?"

"I wasn't crying. He's exaggerating."

"What the hell…?" Mike says.

This makes Mac smile. Here I am expecting a fight, and this asshole is smiling.

"You know what, Mike? You're not the first person to threaten me over hurting Kelley. You're not even the first person today. I get it, she's important to you. You know how I get it? Because she's important to me too."

Mike gives Mac a long, calculating look, then says, "You know, she said good things about you, so I feel like I need to believe that."

"You said good things about me even after what happened?"

I glance up from my duffle bag. "Now he really is exaggerating. I said crappy things about you and he tried to give you the benefit of the doubt."

"And see, I was right," says Mike. "Maybe you should listen to me more often, Kelley."

Once my duffle is packed, I approach the door. Mike gives me a big hug, lifting me off my feet. When he puts me down, he reaches a hand out for Mac. "Hey, Mac, will you do me a favor?"

"I can certainly try."

"Will you smack that little bitch Eric for me? You can do that, right? Since your sister's a lawyer, she can keep you from going to jail."

Mac grins again, and he's about to agree when I stop him.

"Absolutely not!" I say. "Nobody is getting smacked."

When we're strapped into the car and on our way, I turn my phone back on. I can't believe the number of messages and voicemails I have.

Mac glances over at me and says, "You need to call your mother, Mary, Lexi, and Megan."

"Did you call out the National Guard too?" I ask when I see the voicemails from my mom. "Geez! How am I going to explain this to her?"

I start with Lexi, since she's the one who gave away my location. I send her a stern message and then thank her for having my back.

She was right in the first place when she said I shouldn't run away. I text my mom and Mary to let them know I'm okay and not to worry about me. I actually lie and say I'm "home", even though I don't technically have a home. Then I look at the messages from Megan and put my phone down in my lap.

As if he knows what I'm thinking, Mac says, "Megan was pretty worried about you."

"Good. She deserves to worry."

He grunts at that, but doesn't say anything else. I pick my phone back up and start reading through his thirty-plus text messages. They're confused at first, then scared, and then pleading. When they grow apologetic, I want to put the phone down because it's like an outline of his pain and hurt. I reach out for his hand and hold it while I'm reading. When I get to the end, I'm fighting tears. I shouldn't have jumped to conclusions. I should have asked him about it… but how was I supposed to know Emily was a lawyer?

I shift in my seat so that I'm facing him. "I'm sorry."

He shakes his head. "It's okay. I'm just glad you're here." He lifts our entwined hands to his lips and kisses mine.

I watch him, thinking about the fact that he is way too good for me. Much too kind and considerate for someone as selfish as me. Then I remember that he has a file full of personal information about me on his desk at home. "So… you read that file, and you still came looking for me?"

"Of course I did."

"Why?" I ask, and I'm dead serious. "Why would you still be interested in me after finding out all that stuff?"

"Kelley, don't do that. Okay?" He squeezes my hand. "You shouldn't be so hard on yourself."

"Shouldn't I, though?" I gaze out the window and say, "Did you look in the file?"

"I flipped through it a little. I didn't examine it, Emily gave me a breakdown."

I scoff at that. "Oh, I bet she did."

He looks over at me. "It's not like that. Emily's concerned, she said you were mistreated."

"Really? Because she would be the only one who thinks that."

Mac lifts his eyebrow and says, "Mike obviously thinks so too."

"What do you mean by that?"

"Mike's a Murphy. Emily told me the Murphys didn't support you after the accident. I'm assuming he didn't share his parents' feelings about what happened."

"Things haven't been the same in their family since Brad's death. Mike has been very supportive whereas they've blamed me for everything."

"It sounds like he's fair-minded. I'm not sure what information in that file you feel is justified. Are you talking about the accident?"

"Yeah, well… I did let my fiancé drink and drive. His parents think he was killed because of me and so do I." I'm fighting for levity because it's the only way to explain what happened without getting emotional.

"Kelley, he was a grown man who made a poor decision. That's not your fault. Could you have even stopped him if you wanted to?"

I shrug because I'm not sure. "I guess we'll never know."

"Do you even remember what happened that night?"

"No, I don't. I barely remember that entire year. I spent months in the hospital and I scarcely remember any of it. I distinctly remember waking up and my mom telling me Bradley was dead… but that's it really." I hold my breath to fight the rush of emotions that always hit me when I remember that moment. Without fail, pain shoots through me as if I'm reliving it all over again. I give myself a minute to make sure my voice won't falter, then I say, "The next thing I remember is being put in a rehab center for alcoholism."

"I'm so sorry, Kelley." He glances over at me with the saddest expression and I know he's sincere. His hand tightens around mine and he says, "I'm sorry you had to go through that. All of it. You should have had more support."

We sit in silence for a few minutes but then he says, "And what's up with putting you in rehab? You're not an alcoholic."

"They thought it would be an appropriate punishment since they couldn't legally charge me for the accident."

"It's such bullshit. You were a victim."

"I wouldn't go that far."

"Why do you do that? Why do you take responsibility for things that are not your fault? You did the same thing last weekend when I broke my sobriety."

I shrug because I don't really have an answer to that. "I guess I'm just primed for being the bad guy. Years of scrutiny over the accident has trained me to take on the guilt instead of questioning what the truth is."

"Well, stop that. Okay? You're not the bad guy. You're a beautiful person who deserves so much more than you've been given."

We both go quiet until he turns his head slightly and asks, "Will you tell me more about your injuries? About why you're not still dancing?"

"Oh, um… the worst of them was two fractured vertebrae in my upper back. I also broke my left wrist."

"So you can't dance because of the back injury?"

"No, I can dance, Mac—I just can't dance like I used to. It took over a year for me to recover from the accident and get through rehab. A lot of things can happen to your body in a year."

"Yeah, but if your injuries weren't severe enough to keep you from dancing professionally, why didn't you try to get back into it?"

I'm not sure how to answer that because I'm not sure he's going to like the answer.

"I'm sorry," he says. "If you don't want to talk about it, I won't push."

It takes me a moment to gather the courage. "Um… honestly," I say, pushing ahead. It's going to come up again someday, so there's no point in avoiding the conversation. "In the beginning, I didn't want to dance without Brad. Besides mourning him, I was depressed and just generally unhappy. I'd been ostracized by the dancing community to the point where I didn't want it any longer. I had zero drive to be in the business and lost the desire to be in the spotlight."

"After the way they treated you, I can totally understand that."

"I'm sure you know something about this, Mac. You're in the spotlight all the time. It's not always easy. People think they can say anything to you. They act like they know you. You become an open target for whatever abuse they want to lay on you."

"Yes," he nods in agreement.

"I was just over it. I didn't want it any more." I tuck loose strands of hair behind my ear and say, "Now I can dance for pleasure. Of course, I'm broke, but now I can enjoy it without the judgment and the constant scrutiny. Now I can spend my time teaching kids how to love dancing, just like I once did."

"I want you to know that Emily is looking over all the financial stuff to see if she can help. You shouldn't have been held accountable for all those medical bills—Brad's insurance should have covered most of it."

"Brad didn't have insurance."

"Emily thinks he should have been on his parents' insurance. That would cover the accident."

I consider this for a moment and realize he's right, of course. At twenty, I didn't even think to argue—I accepted my licks without a fight because I was so upset over losing Brad and being kicked off the tour. Not to mention the months and months of depression and displacement over giving up my dance career. Five years later, I'm a little more clear-headed and savvier about… well, about everything. Brad should have been under his parents' insurance. I believe they even helped him buy the car. I haven't thought about the details in years. Maybe it's time I did.

When Mac glances over at me, I say, "I'm sorry I didn't tell you about it."

His brows draw together. "You mean, tell me about the accident?"

"Yes. I should have told you about everything."

"What are you talking about? It's not like you had time to sit me down and tell me your life story." He shakes his head in frustration. "Jesus! Kelley, I'm an alcoholic, and I didn't tell you."

I stare at him, and I know he's right. But I've already forgiven him for not telling me about his addiction. "I don't get a pass just because you kept a secret too."

"Megan and Eric, the apartment, you should have told me about that, but this is different. I'm not worried about the past, Kelley. I'm worried about the now. What's happening *now*. That's important to me." He lifts his eyebrows, and says, "But I'm kind of pissed you didn't tell me about your birthday."

The expression on his face relaxes and the atmosphere in the car eases. "Sorry. I don't do a lot of birthday celebrating since my twentieth."

"I figured as much. I guess I can't blame you for that." He squeezes my hand and says, "But I'm going to have to find a way to make it up to you."

I lean over and plant a wet kiss on his cheek. "Thank you," I whisper in his ear before snuggling back into my seat.

He grins and side-eyes me. "What are you thanking me for?"

"Just for being you."

"Give it a couple more weeks, and you'll be singing a different tune," he teases.

*

When we arrive at Mac's house, all I can think about is how badly I want to wash. I never got my chance since he showed up minutes before I was planning to get in the shower.

Mac has the best shower in his master bathroom. Double shower heads like in a fancy hotel, amazing water pressure, and the water stays hot for what feels like days. It's just what I need after the day I've had. While enjoying the spray, I start thinking ahead. What next? I still don't have a place to live. Mac hasn't technically invited me to stay with him. He only said he didn't want me at Megan's or Mike's.

This makes me wish I'd called to reschedule the viewing I'd set up for that attic apartment. I'll have to bump that to the top of my list and hope it's affordable. I'll need to talk to Mary about taking on more classes too, or I'll have to look for another part-time job. Maybe I should try to get certified as a yoga or Pilates instructor. Although that training takes money and I can't spare any right now.

When I get out of the shower, I wrap myself up in a fluffy towel and head into Mac's bedroom. When I hear him talking, I freeze because I'm not sure if someone is in the house with us or if he's talking on the phone. And I'm not ready to face anyone yet. A few minutes later, he walks into the bedroom.

I'm not dressed yet, and I can tell he was hoping to find me in this position. He has a seductive smile on his face, and he's staring at me like the cat that got the cream.

"Everything okay?" I ask.

"Perfect now," he says, and his voice is husky and full of yearning. "I just had to check in with Jeff."

He approaches me and carefully pushes a strand of wet hair off my face. "I was thinking about interrupting your shower, but I decided that might be too presumptuous."

"I wouldn't have minded if you'd joined me..." I tug on the edge of the towel until it drops to the floor, leaving me totally naked. "I wouldn't have minded at all."

"Have I mentioned how much I like it when you're naked?" he asks.

I nod with a grin. "Yeah, every time."

"At least I'm consistent," he says as he lifts my chin so he can kiss me. And damn, the man can kiss. My belly erupts in nervous fluttering and my core instantly heats. Every worry I have fades away… All I want is this moment, his lips on mine, his hands on my body… but he's not touching me beyond this luscious kiss.

I'm reminded of our first time in Reno when he tortured me with slow, deep kisses long before he laid his hands on me, until I was practically begging for it. Playing strip poker like a cat and mouse game. It had felt dangerous, like nothing I'd done before. Like nothing I'd ever felt before. The reminder heats my blood, not that his heart-stopping kiss hadn't already set me on fire. I reach down and grab both of his hands and lay them on my breasts. I need him to touch me. I can feel his breathing hitch as he kisses me. I'm awake. My body is singing in sensations and emotions. I want all of him and that desire is so strong, I could cry.

His mouth moves to my breast, his tongue caressing my nipples, and his hand is between my legs. It feels good… better than good, it's fantastic. I start groaning with pleasure, I can't contain it. He's incredible, and I'm wondering what happened to turn my luck around. One day I'm crying over Megan and Eric and the next, I'm fighting against feelings for a man I just met. When he grips my nipple between his teeth, I lurch forward, trying to get closer. I want more. More hands, more lips, more teeth, and a lot more touching. More everything.

Mac's got two fingers inside me now and I'm moving in rhythm with his probing, trying to stay upright. My knees want to buckle, but I'm holding on, afraid he's going to pull away if he knows I'm struggling to hold out.

Before I understand what's happening, he's got me off my feet and on the bed. I'm in awe of his strength, his confidence. His clothes hit the floor in record time, and then he's there, above me, his weight resting against me, and my senses are full of him.

His eyes are bright, the pale blue standing out in the darkness, and I could look into those eyes forever. His musky scent is filling me with longing, and his lips... they're full and soft, and I love when they graze my lips. I love the erotic bite of his teeth. I want him so badly, and I know at this moment, I'll do anything for him. Anything to keep his hands on me.

His head lowers to my breasts again and then to my belly. He lingers, and I can feel his breath as it brushes against me. Goosebumps rise on my skin, and it makes him chuckle.

"You're so beautiful, Kelley. Everything about you is everything I could ever want."

"Mac..." I say as his head dips between my legs and he slides his hands under my hips to lift me closer to his mouth. "Oh God." His tongue swipes and dips, and it breaks me, sending me into a frenzy I can't control. "Oh God, Mackensey... I can't... I can't wait."

He swipes again and adds more pressure, and then his finger joins his tongue. I'm sure my heart's going to explode, but then he wraps his lips around my clit and sucks. It's as if he pulls the orgasm from me. I shudder, and my entire body stiffens before I succumb to the tide of ecstatic pleasure.

My body lays limp, and as I try to get my wits about me, he's kissing the inside of my thighs, behind my knees and a moment later, I'm on my belly. Mac's rubbing up and down my back and then around my hips. I feel a flutter of his lips on my lower back and then up my spine. He stops when he skims the scar on my upper back, then his kiss rests there for a long moment. I pause because no one has ever touched me there and the sensation takes me off guard. I feel even closer to him. My stomach swoops in surprise but he's achingly gentle.

He's leaning on the bed to my left now, and I reach up to move my long hair off my back and out of his way. As I turn my face, he kisses my lips hard, then my shoulder softly. When his hand rolls up my spine to the scar, he whispers, "Does it hurt?" His voice... his touch... is so tender, I feel the swell of tears again.

I shake my head because I don't want to give away any emotion in my voice.

He hands travel down my back, adding just enough pressure to make me want to purr like a kitten. My eyes are closed, and when I hear his voice in my ear, it surprises me.

"You're still on the pill?" he asks, and I feel a nip of his teeth on my shoulder, sending a shiver down my spine. When I nod, he says, "I'm not using a condom." My eyes pop open, and I can see that he's staring down the line of my body with a look of pure decadence on his face. "Is that OK, babe?" he asks and his gaze follows the movement of his hand as it skims over my back and around my ass cheeks. "I want to feel you completely."

When I whisper my permission, his eyes lift to my face. He leans in and kisses me hungrily, his tongue exploring me properly before nipping my bottom lip as he pulls away. Then he slowly travels back down my body, one kiss, one nip at a time. The contrast of his soft lips to his sharp teeth, from tender to sensual, is hypnotic and incredibly arousing. I'm so relaxed yet so on edge at the same time. Is this his plan... to make me burn for him, to make me beg?

When he spreads my legs and kneels between them, it's hard not to gasp in surprise. His hands travel over my ass, taking in every inch of me, and down between my legs, where he hooks his thumb inside me and massages my clit with his finger. This new sensation feels amazing and robs my focus from everything else. His voice breaks the silence and that's another shock that pulls my attention. "Lift your hips for me."

I do as he says and then his fingers are there again, entering me and rubbing until I'm moving along with the motion of his hands. Before I realize it, he's resting his cock at my entrance and then… then he's inside. It's the most incredible feeling. He's slow at first but then his hands grip my hips, and he's lifting me higher and moving inside me faster, and harder. I can't stop the cries and moans escaping my lips. It's intense, and oh God, I'm going to come again. I lift higher for him because I'm so close and I'm afraid he's going to stop.

"Do you like that?"

When I hear his voice, a tingling shoots up my body, and I've got to bite my lip to keep from crying out louder.

"Tell me what you like, Kelley. Tell me what you want." He's panting, and the words come out like grunts. It's sexy as hell.

"Just like that," I cry. "Don't stop… please, Mac."

"What's that, baby?"

"Mackensey, please don't stop."

He's pumping fast then slow, then he speeds up again, driving me to heights I've never reached with another man. It's too much, but I don't want it to stop. It's too much, but I still want more. Before I grasp what's happening, I'm on my back, and Mackensey is over me again.

"I want to watch you come this time. I want to see it in your eyes."

He's sitting back on his knees, and he's lifting me by the hips again until my ass is resting on his lap. He grabs my ankles and spreads my legs. I'm totally open to him and exposed, and it's more erotic than anything I've done before. I love it. I love when he watches me. I love to see the fire in his eyes when he looks at me. Knowing I light that fire is powerful, and it makes me want nothing more than to let it burn.

He moves rhythmically inside me, harder and deeper than he's ever been, and I'm glad he's holding onto me because all I can do is brace myself against the headboard for leverage. When he hooks my legs over his shoulders and leans forward, I'm so thankful because I want to touch him. I firmly grip his shoulders and pull him in for a kiss. I greedily explore his mouth with my tongue, losing myself in it.

I'm doubled over with my knees near my head, and when Mac pulls back from my lips, his expression is serious but he's also smiling. "Are you okay, sweetheart?"

I close my eyes for a moment because the sound of his voice sends another wave of pleasure radiating through me. With a smile, I nod quickly as my body starts vibrating and tightening, getting ready for the release. "Yes. God, Mac… just don't stop." I'm fighting to keep my eyes on his as I grow closer, my body tingling in anticipation. When I feel him grow even harder, even bigger inside me, and see the glow in his eyes, I finally let go.

CHAPTER TWENTY-THREE

Mackensey

I'm in awe of her. She's the most perfect creature I've ever touched. I know I'm gushing like an idiot, but I don't care. The more she lets go, the less control she maintains, the more beautiful she becomes. I love watching her. I love her undone. It's the sexiest thing I've ever seen, I—

I freeze mid-thought. *Love?*

I glance over at her, and she's smiling, which instantly relaxes me. I chuckle and say, "What are you thinking?"

She turns to face me. "Nothing. That's the beauty of this moment—a clear mind."

"I can't believe how much better it gets every time," I say. "I can't believe how flexible you are. I was afraid I was hurting you, but the smile never left your face."

She leans in and plants a kiss on my shoulder. "Dancer's body. You didn't hurt me at all."

"Promise you'll tell me if I ever do," I say, my tone turning serious.

She nods and snuggles against me, burying her face in my chest, and now I feel like she's trying to hide from me. Like now she's being shy. I wrap my arms around her and slide her up, which is easy since we're both covered in a sweaty dew. I nuzzle her ear and drag my lips across her cheek until she lifts to me. I brush all that beautiful dark hair off her face until I can see her again. I feel rocked. Rocked to my core and looking at her like this just intensifies the feeling.

A moment later she closes her eyes and whispers, "I'm happy."

No other words could have hit me like those two. My heart starts racing because I'm not sure what to say. What to do… what to think.

It's been my goal since the first time I laid eyes on her. I want her to be happy. I want to see Kelley smile. Her closed eyes tell me what she doesn't—the intimacy of sex doesn't scare her. But handing over that little bit of her soul is a big thing. Allowing someone control over her happiness, over her heart. That's huge. I'm so damn thrilled to be here with her it scares me.

The realization strikes me hard. I'm holding the key to what Kelley needs in her life. I'm holding her heart in my hands, and that's the biggest thing I've ever done. I don't want to mess this up, I don't want to hurt her. I'm reminded of Sammie and that kills me. I don't want this to turn into something she regrets. I don't want her to hate me one day… the way Sammie hates me now. I look around my room as it grows darker, contemplating what I've done.

Sex, in my house with a woman, *my wife*, who… who has her things here. Kelley's stuff is here… with her.

This isn't a one-night stand.

I seldom bring women here. It's not what I do. Usually, when I'm with a woman, I spend time with them at their place. Things are more comfortable for me that way. I can get out as quickly as I need to, I'm in control of the situation.

Kelley and I had sex without a condom. Twice. The fact that it was an accident the first time is crazy by itself. I never do that. The second time… the second time I outright decided I didn't want to wear one.

What the hell is going on with me? I feel the cold sweat as it breaks out on my skin. My heart is manic now, and I try to take a deep breath. I glance down at Kelley again, and she's almost asleep.

I need to get out of here and get a grip on myself—I don't want to have an anxiety attack in bed with this woman. I lean forward and kiss her temple and whisper, "I'm going to run out and grab us some dinner. I'll be back, okay?"

When her eyes pop open, my heart lurches at her expression, and my dick hardens involuntarily. Even in the dark, I can see the intense green in them. My reaction is one of immediate attraction and intense desire, but I push it back.

"Do you want me to come with you?"

"No, stay in bed, get some rest. I'll wake you when I get back."

She lays her hand on my cheek and pulls me closer for another kiss. I rest my lips on hers and wait as I take a deep breath. It's as if I want to set the moment to memory—I don't want to forget this time with her. I can't screw this up.

No. I will not screw this up.

I want this woman, and I'll do what I need to do to make it happen. I'll do whatever I need to do to hear those whispered words of happiness from her again.

I gently slide my arm out from under her and get out of bed.

Once I'm dressed, I grab my keys and make my way to the front door. Luna is watching me, and I can see her confusion—I don't think she's ever seen a woman here. I pat her head and say, "Take care of her, girl, I'll be back in less than an hour."

Once I get my truck started, I lock my phone into the hands-free device and pull away from the curb, tapping Mimi's contact.

"Why are you calling me on a Saturday?" she says as she answers the phone.

"You busy?" I ask. I'm trying to maintain a normal breathing pace because I instantly want to freak out now that I have her on the line.

"What's wrong? Has something happened?"

"Nobody is dead," I say to calm her down. "Just… girl trouble."

"What are you talking about? You're the smoothest guy I know, you don't have girl trouble."

"See… that's what I thought too, but here I am, fighting an anxiety attack with the hottest woman on the planet in my bed."

"You have Beyoncé in your bed? Score, Mac!"

"Shut the hell up and help me."

"Oh, okay, this *is* serious. Okay. So, what's your problem? Why are you freaking out? What were you doing when you started to feel anxious?"

"I was in bed… afterglow moment," I say.

"Oh." I hear her shuffle the phone and then she asks, "Were you in your bed or her bed?"

"Mine. She doesn't have a house, remember? I picked her up before the meeting yesterday and moved some of her stuff to my house." As I'm talking, I realize she doesn't know what happened next. "Lots of shit happened after the meeting yesterday." I take a deep breath and give her a quick rundown.

When I finish telling her, the line is silent, and for a moment I think we got disconnected.

"Wow!" she finally says. "Are you super pissed at Emily?"

"Yeah, you bet. She owes me big time. Anyway, I brought Kelley home from Oakland today and, you know, we did our thing." I close my eyes for a moment, remembering the way she tastes and the hot little noises she makes when she comes. Jesus. I can still smell her on my skin. Damn, and I left her naked in my bed. I grunt and say, "I'm an idiot. Who leaves a naked goddess alone in their bed to go get food?"

"So, your excuse to get away for this anxiety attack was to go get takeout?"

"Yep. I don't know what happened. We were lying in bed, cuddling, of all things, and I just got spooked."

"Did she say something… like, I love you?"

I inhale deeply, then exhale. "No, not exactly. She said she was happy."

"Oh. That's almost the same thing. I mean, I wasn't there, so it's hard to interpret, but that's heavy."

"I know. I feel like with everything Kelley's been through, that's a huge thing for her. I don't want to hurt her… I don't want to damage that."

"Then don't, you asshole."

"I don't know what I'm doing, Mimi. I've never done this before… she has stuff at my house. I don't know if I'm ready for this shit. I'm not relationship material, you know that. And Jesus, I've already made a commitment to this woman! I don't know if I can go straight, Meems. You know what I mean? Live with a woman? One woman?"

"Okay, stop freaking out, Mac. Take a breath. Let's break this down. Baby steps, okay?" She's silent for a moment and I'm sure it's to give me a second to calm down. "Honestly, Mac, I don't get you. You barely blinked when you woke up married but now she's in your bed and you're freaking out. Why now? What took you so long?"

I think about that and everything that's passed since we woke up married. "Then it was just a piece of paper. It was funny, you know." I stop and think about how I felt that day. "I was too busy being hungover to worry about it. Besides that, I knew Emily could get me out of it."

"That's still true. Right?"

"You mean, about Emily getting me out of it?"

"Yeah… and it's still just a piece of paper."

That stops me cold. It was just a piece of paper when I didn't know Kelley. But now that I've gotten to know her… now that I know what she's been through, it's different. I stop short of telling Mimi this. "Pretty much," I answer vaguely.

"All right then, yes, you've already made a commitment to her, but that commitment is a false ideal at this point and Kelley knows that. Right?"

"Yes, well, I told her I couldn't make any promises."

"So, it's not like you're leading her on or making her believe you want to be married."

"Not on purpose." Jesus! Have I? I don't know. "But that doesn't mean she's not reading more into it. I did race out to Oakland and bring her home."

"Dammit, Mac. Do you even know what you want? You need to figure that out before you do anything else."

I run my fingers through my hair several times and try to relax so I can think. "I don't know."

"So, let's evaluate here. How do you feel about having her things in your house? Her shampoo in your shower? Her feminine products in your cabinet? Is it bothering you? What's your first reaction to her stuff? I feel like knowing your gut reaction is the best way to get down to your real feelings here."

I think about this for a minute, and I remember the scent of the flowers on the dining-room table. I liked it. "When we returned from Oakland, the first thing Kelley did was take a shower," I say. "When she got out of the shower, she was rifling through her duffle bag to get clothes, and my first thought was that she needed a drawer."

"Mac," she says, and I can hear the smile in her voice. "Honey, the fact that you didn't freak out over that is a good sign. The fact that you freaked out after making love to her is also very telling."

"What does that mean?" I say, feeling a little frantic because I don't understand what's happening. "If that's so telling, what the hell is it telling you?"

"God, you're so pathetic. You really don't get it, do you?" And it's as if I can hear Mimi rolling her eyes. "You're really dense about this."

"Fine, call me whatever you want. Just tell me what to do, because I'm clueless."

"You're freaking out now because you're invested in this relationship. You're both invested in each other now and that scares you." She hums for a moment, then blurts out, "Mac, I think you're in love with her."

I pull my truck over and put it in park. I can feel my pulse pick up and I'm starting to sweat again. I can't talk, it's as if my brain has seized. I snatch my phone from the hands-free device and open the door to get some air. I circle my truck, taking deep breaths. I can hear Mimi's voice calling out from the phone.

"Are you there?"

"Yeah," I breathe, unable to do anything else but lean against my truck.

"You really have never been in love before, have you?" she asks.

When I don't respond, she says, "You know, it doesn't have to be a bad thing. You might actually like it." She hesitates for a moment, and I think I know what's coming next. "Mac, you need to stop thinking about what happened with Sammie. You need to put that out of your mind before it kills any chance you have with Kelley."

Hearing Sammie's name does nothing to calm my nerves. If anything, it forces my heart to hammer faster. "That's a lot easier said than done."

"I know that. I know what you went through, but all the shit that happened with her, none of that was your fault. You know it wasn't, so... just stop, okay? Sammie was an addict before you came into her life."

"What do I do?" I mutter.

"Go slow, Mac. Take your time because you don't want to hurt Kelley, and you don't want to get hurt yourself. The stronger your feelings for this girl are, the more painful it's going to be if she walks away."

"Okay… go slow. Should I give her a drawer?"

"I think you might need to because you're not the type of person who's going to like her shit lying all over the place." She chuckles and says, "We don't want to set her up for failure right off the bat."

"Okay, yeah. You're right, Kelley needs a place to put her things." I think about that for a moment, and it makes me pause because she's going to want to get her own place. "What if she wants to go? She talked about looking for a place. She even talked about moving to Oakland."

"You should be asking yourself that. I can't answer for you. How do you feel when you think about Kelley moving?"

It occurs to me at that moment that I don't need Mimi, I just need to trust my gut. That's where she's leading me… to figure out my feelings. I rest my head back and stare up at the darkening sky and think about it… really think about how I would feel if Kelley found her own place, or another roommate. I feel sad. I feel like *I* can be her roommate. I have enough space for both of us. "I think I'm going to ask her to stay."

Mimi sighs and then says in a tearful voice, "My boy is growing up."

"Okay, I gotta go. Thank you for talking me off the ledge, Mimi, and please don't share this with anyone at work. I don't need that grief."

"You know I won't, but I think you need to let everyone meet her. If they get to know her, they'll be more respectful of her when we're on air."

She's absolutely right… but that's *huge*. That's exposing her to the assholes who think I don't have a soul. Something I've never done before. "I'll think about it."

"Okay. I hope you do, though, I'd like to meet her. She must be some girl."

"She is."

"Okay, well, call me anytime you need me, Mac." She waits a moment then says, "Try to enjoy your weekend with Kelley and don't freak out every time something feels good. Feeling good is what you want out of life and relationships. Okay?"

"Okay. Thanks again."

I disconnect the call and I'm still staring up at the sky. I take a moment to consider the last day or so and everything I've learned about Kelley. She's been hurt over and over… in the worst way. If I'm going to ask her to stay, I know I need to own it. No half-ass shit here. No hesitation. If I'm inviting her to stay, I'm in this. I'm committed to a relationship with her and I can't change my mind tomorrow. I inhale, filling my lungs with the warm evening air, and in my heart, I know I want this. I know I'm not going to change my mind tomorrow.

CHAPTER TWENTY-FOUR

Kelley

The gentle kiss wakes me up. I don't know how long I've been sleeping, but I can see that it's totally dark outside. Mackensey is leaning over me, and Luna's nose is nudging my hand. I reach up and pat her head as I glance up at Mac.

"Did you have a nice nap?" he asks.

"Mm-hm... I did. Especially since I didn't get much sleep last night." I sit up, gripping the blanket to my chest. I'm a little sore, and I know it's a mixture of running ache from this morning and acrobatic sex ache. The reminder increases my grin.

"Why didn't you sleep last night?" he asks, and I hear a little strain in his voice.

"I drank too much and stayed up too late." When I meet his eyes, I can see it. The question he doesn't want to ask. "No, I didn't sleep with Mike."

"I didn't ask," he says.

"You didn't have to."

He sits on the edge of the bed, and his stare relaxes. "I'm sorry."

"Don't be. I understand. If I found you with a woman dressed just in a towel, I'd worry about the same." I watch him for a moment and say, "I woke up this morning still fully dressed. All we did last night was talk... I had a lot to get off my chest. And we drank. A lot. I'm sorry about that. I promised myself I'd stop drinking after Reno."

He gives me a sad smile. "That much regret, huh?"

"No, I just don't think it's fair. If you can't drink, then I don't want to."

"Thank you, but you don't have to do that. I don't mind. It's usually not a problem when people drink around me. Last weekend... well, that was different."

"Did you get food?" I ask.

"Yeah, it's on the table." He nudges his head in the direction of the dining room when he says it.

"Go get it," I say. "Let's have a bed picnic."

His eyes widen, and for a moment I'm not sure I understand his hesitation, but then he says, "You want to..." He points down and says, "Eat in bed?"

"Yeah, haven't you ever had a bed picnic?"

He laughs, and I can tell he's a little embarrassed. "No, but there's a first time for everything. Sit tight."

He leaves the room and then returns a few minutes later with a bag that holds two enormous salads. Mac has drinks tucked under his arm and forks between his teeth.

He sets everything down on the dresser, then grabs the edge of the blankets and yanks them down to the end of the bed, leaving me completely naked and exposed. I don't think he meant to be so aggressive about it, but from the tilt of his head, and from the look on his face, I sense he's starting to like the idea of a bed picnic. He points a finger at me as if to say *one moment*, then pulls his t-shirt over his head. A second later, he's tugging that same t-shirt over my head.

"Thank you," I say. "But... I may need bottoms too."

He turns and pulls open a drawer. After tossing me a pair of his boxer briefs, he says, "Will that do?"

I chuckle as I hold them up. "I think these will work." I struggle to get them on, and then I sit cross-legged on his bed. He kicks off his shoes and sits across from me.

He hands me an incredible-looking salad. "Where did you get this?"

"That's Pop's Hearty Grain Salad with tri-tip, and it's amazing." He digs into the bag and says, "Would you prefer the blue cheese vinaigrette or the house vinaigrette?"

I stare at him in silence. How does he already know what I love? "Blue cheese vinaigrette with a tri-tip salad, is there any other way to eat it?" I reach my hand out, and he grins at me.

"You're a woman after my own heart." He pulls another container of blue cheese dressing out of the bag and says, "I wasn't sure, so I got both, but I love the blue cheese too."

Before he starts eating, he leans over and grabs his phone. After a few swipes, I hear music playing from his office. It's James Morrison. I have to smile because I love James Morrison too.

It's not until I take my first bite that I realize how hungry I am. I dig into my salad, and as I do, I think about how much better I feel after my nap… and how much better I feel after being well serviced by Mac. The thought brings heat to my face, and I'm afraid to look up at him. When I hear him chuckle, I can't help myself. I look up, and he's got a mouthful of salad, and he's wearing the most childish and sincere smile I've ever seen. It's funny because when I first met him at Starbucks, I couldn't help but think of him as arrogant. I got the impression he was affected… or purposeful. As if his smiles were practiced. Looking at him now, I see none of that. I only see a man who's genuinely having a good time. He's out of his shell, and it's like watching a kid in a candy store for the first time.

It causes a little flutter in my chest, and then my heart sinks as I'm reminded of Brad. Brad was always like this. He always looked for the joy, the fun or the extraordinary in life. In the end, it killed him.

Mac isn't like that, though. He's thoughtful, and he's careful. Looking at his space now, it's a glaring clue to his personality. The hesitation to eat on his bed, and his obvious discomfort that's now sheer joy. Is this a result of his sobriety? Or something else?

I think about earlier and how he decided not to wear a condom. That seems so out of character for him, and I wonder why he did it. I glance up at him again, and he's watching me.

"You're blushing," he says. "Why?"

"Um…" I say, and even more heat rushes to my cheeks. I put my salad down and say, "I… ah… was thinking about the… um… no condom thing. What made you decide not to use one? It seems very unlike you."

He stares at me, and I can see the fire behind his eyes. "You got checked after Eric, and I was also checked a few weeks ago, so we're both clean, and you're on the pill. I figured if we're exclusive, why not?" He tilts his head and says, "I hope that's okay?"

I nod and try to hide my embarrassed smile. I like exclusive. Exclusive makes me happy. I was already exclusive with Mac, but I wasn't sure what he was thinking about our relationship. A second later, he's leaning forward, and we're nose to nose.

"I like the way you feel," he says. "If I can have all of you without a barrier, I'm going to take all of you." Jesus Christ, he's sexy. Our lips meet, and now I'm hungry for something else. Before I can stop myself, I'm on my knees, and we're making out over the food. I pull away and take a deep breath. I need it, he leaves me breathless and too hot.

"I think we should stop or we're going to completely destroy your bed. Dirty sheets are one thing, but I can't get vinaigrette out of the mattress."

He nods at me with a huge grin. I love his smile. His *real* smile… the one that doesn't show itself very often. I wonder if anyone else gets to see it or if it's reserved just for me. But surely that can't be. I know Mac's been with lots and lots of women. He's a typical playboy. I'm sure I'm just another number.

This thought hurts. I don't want that. I glance back up, and he's devouring his salad and still smiling. I can't be just another number, can I? His expression when he looks at me. The tenderness in his eyes when he talks to me. The way he touches me. He can't be like that with every woman, can he?

"What's wrong?" he asks, taking in my expression.

"Nothing." I shake my head and try to let it pass. I don't want to ruin the moment with him—I like him this way.

He lowers his fork and says, "I don't believe you."

"If I wasn't here, what would you be doing today?" I ask to change the subject.

"I don't know." His eyes drift to the ceiling, and he says, "I'd probably be…" He looks around and whispers, "At the river with Luna."

A second later, I hear her nails click on the floor as she enters the bedroom.

"I take it she knows what that means."

He nods, wide-eyed, as if to tell me not to say the words. "She loves the water."

He glances over at me and says, "What would you be doing?"

My eyes drift back to my salad, and my appetite is diminished at the thought. "I'd be moving," I say with a sigh. "Somewhere. I was supposed to go look at that apartment today, but I missed the appointment."

Mac suddenly looks uncomfortable. He starts to sweat a little, and the color drains from his face.

"Are you okay?" I ask. "You suddenly look sick."

He clears his throat and says, "Yeah, um… fine."

I watch him as he takes a couple of deep breaths. A moment later he says, "Don't do that."

Confusion ripples through me. "Don't do what?"

He lifts a finger and says, "I'll be right back."

I watch him go into the master bathroom. He's gone for a few minutes, so I try to eat a little more, even though I really don't want to. I hear the water run, and a moment later he's back on the bed, staring at me.

"You okay?" I ask.

He nods quickly and says, "I want you to stay here… with me." As soon as the words are out of his mouth, his shoulders relax and he looks relieved.

"You want me to stay here?" I ask, still not sure I understand. "And live with you?"

"Yes, exactly. Exactly that. I want you to move in here with me." He takes a deep breath and then another. Color is starting to return to his cheeks, and he mutters, "That wasn't so hard."

"What the hell is going on with you?"

His eyes grow wide again and he stares at me for a moment; I can see he's trying to make a decision. "I'm sorry." The air rushes from him, and he says, "I've never done this before, and I'm not sure how."

"Done what, Mac?"

"I've never had a relationship with anyone… like this."

I straighten my back and stare at him. "Never?" I'm struck by just how incredibly nervous he is. He was cocky as hell a moment ago when he was talking about being exclusive and not wearing condoms, but now he's totally falling apart at the idea of being in a *relationship*. This leaves me totally confused.

"Nope. Never." He shakes his head and says, "I've had sexual relationships but never emotional relationships… not really."

I'm shocked. I have no idea what to say, mostly because I'm not absolutely sure, but I think Mac might be telling me he loves me… without actually saying it. I think about it for a moment and consider how literal he is. A sexual relationship equals a relationship where you're sexually exclusive to one person. Did that mean an emotional relationship would equal a relationship where you're emotionally exclusive too?

"In your mind, how is a sexual relationship different from an emotional relationship?" I ask finally.

He pales again, and I'm starting to feel bad, like I'm teasing him, but I'm not: I'm just trying to understand. He starts rubbing his hands together nervously. I'm humbled... I'm humbled that this hot, sexy, thoughtful person who seems to always have the right words is having trouble communicating how he feels *about me*.

"W... Well..." he stutters. "The thing is, I have feelings for you. So, I guess it means that I want more than a sexual relationship with you, but like I said, I've never done that before."

I want to eat him alive right now, but I don't move for fear that I'll scare him away. I fight the huge smile that breaks out on my face. I can see it's hard for him to navigate this and he obviously doesn't know what to do. Asking me to move in, that's huge. I want to be calm... normal, so he doesn't freak out, but it's damn hard. I take a deep breath. "Mac... I have feelings for you too."

"You do? Does that mean you're willing to try living with me? Because I would just rather be your roommate than see you live with someone else and I definitely don't want you to move to Oakland." Once he gets all the words out, he looks relieved again, but then he says, "I mean, I thought we could try it to see if you like it."

"Mac, babe, I would love to wake up next to you every single morning. But what if *you* don't like it?" I ask. Especially since he's so rigid with his space.

"Oh, I'm going to like it."

This makes me giggle and I feel... full. Happy. It's been a long time since anything or anyone has meant so much to me. "Mac, have you ever lived with anyone before?"

"I had roommates in college, but I've never lived with a woman I was in a relationship with." As if sensing my hesitation, he says, "Let's just try it. If you're not happy here or if for some reason I lose my mind and decide I don't like having you in my bed every night, we'll reconsider."

My smile falters a bit. "I would love to live with you."

"But..." His gaze locks on mine. "Why do you look hesitant?"

"I'm not hesitant because I don't want to be here. I just... if it doesn't work out, I'm going to need time to find another place." Saying this out loud weighs heavy on me because I so badly want it to work out. It hasn't hit me until just now how much I want this relationship with him to work. Maybe it's because he's trying so hard to open himself up to me even though it goes against his nature... or maybe it's just because I love him.

He nods quickly and says, "Of course! I certainly don't want to put you in another bad situation. I wouldn't do that. I'm probably not the easiest person to live with, though. I do recognize that about myself, and I'm willing to be open-minded. Just have patience with me."

"I can do that," I say, as the smile transforms my face again.

He lifts up and reaches out for me and our smiling faces lock together in a hard kiss. His hand cups my face and I'm so happy I could cry but I don't want to put more pressure on him since this is clearly such a hard conversation for him to have.

When he pulls away, he's grinning like a kid again and digs into his salad with renewed interest.

I watch him for a moment and then blurt out the question I know I shouldn't ask. The question I probably don't want an answer to, but I can't help myself. "Mac, how is it you've lived thirty years without having a relationship with a woman?"

"Um..." His eyebrows lift as his gaze drops. "Well, I used to drink a lot and party quite a bit. That kind of lifestyle doesn't lend itself to healthy relationships." He shrugs and says, "I've never been interested in committing to any of the girls I've been with. I've never been interested in committing... period. I used to laugh at my married friends."

It's obvious he's holding something back and I'm about to push him for more when he says, "I probably should have told you this before." He waits a beat before looking back up at me, then says, "About four years ago, I was hanging out with this woman. We'd gotten close, but I guess I didn't consider how close until after things ended. I wasn't trying to be in a relationship with her, I thought we were just having some fun. Of course, most of the time we spent together we were drinking, so I don't remember much."

Mac shrugs again, and I suspect it's not a careless shrug. His features have grown heavy, and his expression guilty.

"What happened when things ended?"

His foot starts bouncing. Another sign of how nervous he is. "She overdosed... and almost died."

"Oh my God, Mac."

"Yeah, she took a bunch of pills and chased them down with a bottle of vodka. Her roommate found her and called an ambulance." His mouth forms into a frown when he says this, and I reach out for his hand, wanting to offer comfort. I understand his guilt all too well.

"I'm sorry." I wasn't expecting something like this. I don't know what I was expecting, but it wasn't this.

"She blamed me. Blamed our relationship." When he says "relationship", he uses air quotes. "I didn't even realize we were in a relationship." He throws his hands out and says, "I was seeing other women and having a goddamn good time enjoying life. I never meant to make her think we were serious—or even exclusive." He pauses for a moment and I can tell by the look on his face that he's having a hard time talking about this. "That's when I stopped drinking, Kelley. I realized my behavior contributed to what happened. I basically encouraged her to destroy herself."

"Is she okay now?"

"Yeah, well, you met her at the Comedy Fest. It's Sammie Collins."

"Oh my God. I guess that explains her behavior." I rest back against the headboard, a little stunned. "How long were you with her?"

"We were only seeing each other for a few weeks." His eyes drift to the ceiling as if he's trying to remember. "She was touring with James Foster, and their final tour date was here in Sacramento. I went to the show to hang out with James. That's how I met her. Sammie and I hit it off immediately. So, she decided to stay in town for a while since the tour was over. We partied... a lot."

"Were you just drinking or was there more?" I ask, trying to get the full picture.

"Sammie was a pill popper. She was always popping Vicodin and Percocet. I don't know where she got it, but she always had it."

"Did you use too?"

"Yeah, you know. Sammie offered so, yeah, I wanted to have a good time."

I suck air through my teeth when he admits this. I've heard too many horrible stories about people who suffer from prescription pill addictions. "That's a bad combination, Mac."

"I know, but hell, I was just a kid having fun. I wasn't thinking about anything else."

"A kid?" I lift an eyebrow. "Four years ago you were only a year older than I am now."

He shakes his head and says, "Yes, but I was a full-blown alcoholic. I wasn't doing anything smart like you are. You're doing shit to improve your life, you're working your ass off to get shit done. I was making loads of money from the show and spending it almost as fast. There was no value to my life at the time."

"You were already working with Mimi on the show?"

"Yes... and I almost blew it." He runs his hand through his hair and says, "The third week Sammie was here, I missed several days of work and things got bad. I got caught up with her in this bubble, forgot all my responsibilities. When they threatened to fire me, I told Sammie to go home."

"And… I guess she didn't take it well?"

"No, she didn't, but she left like I asked her to. I didn't realize just how bad my own drinking was until I got a call from her roommate, telling me what happened." He runs both hands through his hair. "Her roommate told me how upset Sammie was about our breakup." His eyes widen as he repeats the words. "Breakup!" He laughs sardonically and says, "Honestly, I couldn't even remember half of the conversations I'd had with Sammie because I was wasted the entire time we were together. I could have said something that made her believe I wanted more than I did and maybe I just don't remember."

"Do you think she did it on purpose? Was she trying to kill herself?"

"No, I don't think so. She says she wasn't, and she was always popping pills. But she was just depressed and trying to numb herself. Honestly, I'm not sure it matters. I drove her to the edge of the cliff and pushed her over. Whether she overdosed on purpose or not, it almost resulted in her death."

"Mac, babe, that doesn't mean you're responsible. I hope you know that."

"Yeah, after rehab and months of therapy. James helped, too. He told me Sammie had been a mess through most of the tour. She'd had a problem long before I met her, but so did I. It just took her overdose to snap me out of it."

"Probably saved your life."

"Yeah, it also made me realize I needed to be more careful with people. I needed to be clearer about my intentions with women."

His words sink in and reveal a sick truth that hurts my heart. "You carry yourself so carefully with women to keep from giving them the wrong idea about your intentions, and you're flayed for it every day at work, but in reality, what's portrayed on your show isn't really who you are."

He purses his lips and nods, but then his eyes lift to mine. "Unfortunately, it's who I am. Or at least, who I was. If you think about it, they're not entirely wrong. I don't commit to women. Before rehab, I was all over the place. A different woman every night. I'm not quite as bad now, but I do avoid getting close to them. I try to date women who aren't interested in a relationship. It's not like there's a shortage of women who are looking for the same good time I'm usually looking for." He fists his hands and says, "What bothers me is they portray me as a heartbreaker, as if I use and abuse women. I don't do that. I try to always make my intentions clear."

I rest my hand on my chest and say, "You made your intentions clear with me in the beginning... except for that whole drunk wedding thing."

"This is different." He reaches for my hand and says, "I like having you here. I like who I am when I'm with you."

I stare into his eyes and say, "I like who you are with me too, and I'm willing to try living together if you are."

He smiles and whispers, "Good."

I glance around the room and wonder what the mortgage is on this place, absolutely sure I can't afford half of it. "Okay, so, how much is the rent, roomie?"

"Rent?" He lifts his hand in question. "I own the house, there's no rent."

"No, what will *my* rent be?"

He scrunches his eyebrows. "There is no rent, Kelley. You're not paying me to live here."

"Yeah, I am. I can't live here for free. I'm not taking advantage of you like that."

He leans over and grabs the rings dangling from the chain around my neck and holds them up. "You are my wife. I don't have to charge you rent if I don't want to."

This statement hits me hard. We are married. He's my husband. I don't know how this fact keeps slipping my mind. It's just so crazy to think about, especially after the story he just told me. "You know, Mac, if I'm here and we live together, you will lose your ability to file for an annulment later. If we don't work out, you'll have to file for a divorce."

He stares at me for a long time, and I can see he's thinking about this. His expression is warm and affectionate, and that makes me feel a lot better about what I just said to him. It's comforting to know he takes this relationship seriously. That means a lot to me.

He shakes his head slowly. "That's the last thing on my mind. I'm not worried about it."

Butterflies flutter in my belly, and I have to fight for breath. After giving myself a moment to let this sink in, I say, "I'll pay what I've been paying for the apartment with Megan." I push back against the emotions and give him a final nod. "Is that fair?"

"No," he says, "I'm not taking money from you. Use it to pay for school. Take a full load of classes and finish. Nothing would make me happier than to see you walk the stage and get your degree."

I press my lips together to stop the tears that instantly form in my eyes. The visual that came with his words struck me where it hurts because that's all I've wanted for so long. I just want to finish. I just want to show all the naysayers that they couldn't keep me down, and show myself that I can persevere. That I can be a success.

Mac reaches out, cups my cheek with his hand, and swipes away a tear with his thumb. "You'll get there, Kelley. I promise."

I don't know how he knows, but he does. He gets me without even trying, sees right through to my soul, and that makes me love him more. I fight to keep my face steady when all I want is to crumple into his arms.

CHAPTER TWENTY-FIVE

Mackensey

We show up at Megan's apartment unannounced. That's how Kelley wanted it. She didn't want to give them any warning, she just wanted to get there, pack up, and get the hell out. I can see how hard this is for her. She's lived with Megan for years, and they've been best friends for most of their lives. She's putting on a brave face, but I can feel it… I can feel the anxiety roll off her in waves. I don't say anything, I'm just trying to be there for her. I know that's what she needs, silent strength… someone to have her back. That's me. Now that I can admit that to myself, I feel much better about this entire thing… and by "thing", I mean *relationship*.

What can I say? I'm a work in progress.

While Kelley packs, I carry the boxes down to the truck. She's not saying much, and I think that's because Megan is having a complete meltdown. But she brought this on herself when she slept with her best friend's boyfriend. Why she thought Kelley wouldn't move out is beyond me. I can't figure out why she's taking it so hard when she's the one who betrayed the friendship. As for Eric, I have no idea where he is. I haven't seen him at all, and that's fine with me.

When I return to the apartment for another box, I hear Megan shouting at Kelley.

"How am I going to pay the rent now? I can't afford it by myself and Eric doesn't have the money yet."

"Megan, that's not my problem." Kelley stares at her for a moment and says, "Seriously, what were you expecting? Did you think I'd want to stay here with the two of you after what you did?"

"If it weren't for *him* you wouldn't be moving!" Meg points at me when she says this. I keep my mouth shut because it's really none of my business. I already know I'm the winner in this situation. Thanks to Megan and Eric's lack of loyalty, I get the girl. I almost want to smile at her.

"No!" Kelley finally shouts back. "If it wasn't for *you*! If it wasn't for *Eric*! Stop blaming other people for your bullshit. You did this, Megan. You've crossed a line that can't be uncrossed. You've burned a bridge that can't be unburned." She points at her and says, "And you're completely clueless about it. You don't even know what you've done by letting that jerk move in here."

"What are you talking about? You act like I don't know who Eric is. I've known him as long as you have."

"You don't know shit… and maybe that's my fault. Maybe I should have shared more with you."

"Shared what, Kelley?" Megan looks doubtful now, and I'm a little confused myself. "Tell me."

"You were a revenge fuck for Eric," she finally says.

Megan draws back and says, "What are you talking about?"

"He's been asking for months to move in with me—with us. He wanted to share our apartment, but I wouldn't let him. I kept putting him off. I told him we had an agreement to not let guys move in, no matter what." She sighs and says, "Remember when I told you I was planning to end things with him weeks ago?"

"Yes. And you did. Which is exactly my point. Why are you mad—and moving out? You didn't even want to be with him."

"That doesn't make what you did okay, Megan. But that's not my point. My point is, when I finally broke up with him, he threatened me. Promised to get back at me… promised to make me regret it."

Megan plops down into the armchair. "So you think I'm the revenge?"

"I know you are. He planned for me to walk in and find you guys. Ultimately, it was the perfect revenge, especially since you actually let him move in here."

This entire story is making me nauseous. I really wish Kelley had told me all of this. It's yet another thing she held back, probably because of sheer embarrassment. I'm wondering if I should leave the room, but no, I don't want to. I need to stay and continue to be a source of strength for Kelley. As I'm watching her, she looks like she's withering.

"Kelley," Megan says, "that's not really how things went down."

Kelley lifts the box she's filling and stares at Megan for a long time before she finally says, "Let me guess, you two have been screwing around for months, right?"

She nods and says, "First of all, I never planned for this to happen. It was an accident."

"You *accidentally* slept with my boyfriend and lied about it for months?"

At least Megan has the decency to look guilty. "Remember that night I went out with those girls from work, when I called you at Eric's apartment because I was too drunk to drive?"

I didn't think it was possible but Kelley's face loses even more color. "Yeah, and I sent Eric to pick you up?"

Megan nods, her eyes focused on the floor. "When he brought me home, I was really drunk… he helped me up the stairs and into the apartment."

"And you fucked him?" Kelley asks, dropping the box and crossing her arms over her chest.

Megan nods. "I don't remember much, but yeah." She shrugs with her eyes still on the ground.

Kelley draws back and says, "You're lying, Megan."

Her head shakes slowly. "No, I'm not lying. It's true I don't remember much about that night, but I remember enough. When Eric was done with me, he left to return to you at his apartment."

"If that were true, you would have told me." Kelley points to Megan. "If Eric took advantage of you that way, you would have said something to me. You wouldn't let me keep sleeping with the bastard."

"I didn't say he took advantage of me. I was drunk, but I wanted it. I remember that much. I was aware enough to do it."

"Why, Megan? What could possibly motivate you into doing that?"

She shrugs again. "I don't know, but I'm sorry. I was drunk and I regretted it the moment I sobered up."

"More lies, Megan. If that were true, you would have told me instead of lying about it for months. You would have stopped instead of carrying on like that for so long."

"I wanted to stop. I felt really bad for betraying you, but Eric threatened to tell you I hit on him, that it was my idea. He said he'd poison you against me... I guess he really did."

"Bullshit, Megan. *You* shouldn't have done what you did. He didn't poison me against you, *you* poisoned me against you." Kelley throws her hand out and says, "Besides, if you really were being blackmailed, why did you let him move in here? Why is he still in your life? Doesn't sound like coercion to me."

Megan leans forward and says, "That's not what this is. Not now." She glances at me and then back to Kelley. "Honestly, letting Eric move in has nothing to do with you. I let Eric move in because I'm pregnant."

Kelley's face is completely blank, and it's the first time I've seen her without expression. She doesn't speak for a long time, staring at Megan with glazed eyes. When she finally breaks her silence, she says, "Well, isn't that wonderful? Now you're stuck with the bastard... I guess karma does exist."

"You don't mean that," Megan says. "This friendship means something to you, Kelley, I know it does, and now you're going to be an auntie."

"Don't do that! Don't you dare try to manipulate me, Megan," Kelley says. "I refuse to continue in this toxic relationship, and if I didn't believe it was toxic before, I certainly do now." She throws her hands up and says, "I concede. You win, Eric wins. You both got what you wanted. He got his revenge by tearing our friendship apart and you've finally got the perfect little family you've always wanted—and apparently with the guy you wanted."

"How do you think I feel? I have to choose between my baby's father and my best friend. I don't want our friendship to end. Can't we just work past this?"

"You don't have to choose. I'm choosing for you, Megan," Kelley says. "It's too late to salvage this."

"You're my best friend and I need you."

"Yeah, I know, because once Eric finds out you're pregnant, he's out. I hope you realize that."

Megan crosses her arms over her chest. "You don't know that."

"I know Eric." Kelley releases a heavy exhalation, then she reaches down for a box and hikes it up on her hip. "I'll return for the rest of my stuff when nobody is here. Goodbye, Megan, and good luck—you're going to need it."

Kelley turns, exits out the front door, and bounces down the stairs. When we reach the truck, it's apparent how upset she is. She's not speaking, but I can see it on her face. I want to comfort her, but I'm not sure how so I keep moving. I just keep moving forward. I feel like that's the best I can do for her. She turns to me with the saddest expression.

"I'm sorry, babe. I know this is hard for you." I reach out and try to pull her into a hug, but she pushes against me. Her entire body stiffens as she fights against her emotions.

"I need to get away from here. Can we get the rest another time?"

"Of course. Do you have what you need to get through the week?"

She nods abruptly, and I can tell she's avoiding my eyes. I'm not okay with that. I reach out and tug her chin so she looks at me. I can see that she's embarrassed, but I don't care. I lean down and kiss her slowly. After a moment I feel her relax.

When I pull away, I'm met with a fiery stare. "I'm sorry," I say. "But I wish you'd told me all that stuff about Eric."

"I told you, Kelley."

We both turn to find Eric standing near the front of my truck. He's smiling at Kelley. I'm three strides away from wrapping my hands around his neck when she grabs me by the waist and pulls me back.

He chuckles and says, "I told you this would happen."

"Go to hell, Eric!" she says. "You got your wish, I'm leaving. You can have the apartment."

"It's messed up," he says. "I didn't want the apartment, I wanted to live with you. Too bad I'm stuck with the wrong roommate."

I take another long step toward him, but Kelley has a strong grip on me. "Back off, Eric," I say, and it comes out as a growl. "You've fucking done enough here. You don't get to talk to her."

Kelley catapults herself between us. "You're so full of yourself. What you actually mean is that you wanted both roommates, right?" She cocks her head. "Too bad you're not man enough to handle it. You thought you'd work your magic and get both of us in bed, but I blew that plan when I dumped you. You just couldn't make the sale. Couldn't quite close the deal, could you?"

Eric sneers and says, "I can't believe you. It's barely two weeks, and you're already screwing someone else like I didn't exist."

I take a solid step forward, but Kelley turns to face me. "Don't, please don't," she says. "He's not worth the trouble."

I place my hands on her shoulders and look back up at Eric. "You *don't* exist, you little shit! Run along home before I turn you into a eunuch."

Kelley turns and puts her back against me, facing Eric: "Just to be clear, walking in on you and Megan was the best thing that ever happened to me." She smirks and says, "Thank you, Eric. If it wasn't for you, I wouldn't know the truth about my best friend... and I wouldn't have met Mac."

As happy as I am to hear this, I can see the anger burning in Eric's eyes. I make the split-second decision to grab Kelley and turn her away, curling my body around her and removing her from Eric's reach. My timing is almost perfect... almost. Eric's punch misses Kelley, and I feel the blow behind my left ear. My temper explodes, and I want to kill him. Not for hitting me but for taking a swing at her.

My vision goes red, and before I can stop myself, I've landed two solid punches to the center of Eric's face. He's on the ground holding his nose and I think Kelley's screaming, but I can't actually hear her because my ears are ringing.

I lean down and grab him by the shirt. "If I find out that you've ever raised a hand to a woman again, I promise you'll walk funny for the rest of your life. And that includes Megan, you fucking asshole!" I throw him back down.

My pulse is pounding in my head, and I still can't hear properly. I pace in a circle and try to walk it off, fighting to lower my adrenaline and calm my heart. I know I've screwed up, but I don't care. I can't deal with abusive assholes like him. He should be neutered, he should be in jail.

Kelley's staring at me, and when I can think clearly, I ask, "Has he ever hit you before?"

I watch her eyes, but I'm not sure what she's thinking. I'm too hyped-up to read her. When she doesn't answer, I ask again: "Kelley, has he ever laid hands on you before?"

She shakes her head. "No, Mac. Eric's never hit me. Do you think I'd stick around for that?"

I take a deep breath and then exhale slowly. I shake my head, but I hardly know what I'm agreeing to. Megan's outside now, tending to Eric, and there's a crowd gathering. Kelley looks around and then grabs my arm and leads me to the passenger side of the truck. "We need to get the hell out of here." She opens the door and pushes me toward it. "Get in, I'll drive."

I do as she says because I'm not in the right frame of mind to argue. When she pulls out of the parking lot, I say, "I thought you didn't know how to drive."

"I know *how* to drive, I just don't like to drive. Nearly dying in a car made me a little skittish. Head-on collisions with big rigs do that to a person." Her snarky tone tells me right away that she's not as calm as she's pretending to be.

"How long has it been since you were behind the wheel of a car?"

"Five years," she says, completely straight-faced.

"Jesus! Really? You haven't driven since before your accident?" Now I feel like a huge ass for putting her in this position. Dammit! I need to get my shit together. She shouldn't have to drive me around because I can't control my temper. "I'm sorry. I'm sorry you have to drive. I'm sorry about Megan… and I'm sorry about Eric," I say. "I just reacted, I couldn't stop myself. I can't believe he was going to hit you."

She reaches over and grabs my hand. She's shaking, and I'm not sure if it's because of what just happened or because she's driving. "Thank you."

This surprises the hell out of me. *She's thanking me.* I turn to stare out the window as East Sacramento turns into Midtown and the busy, tree-lined streets zip by. I squeeze her hand, relieved things weren't worse. I know how much trouble this could cause, but I don't care. Eric can sue me if he wants. He can do whatever he wants. I don't care because I got the girl, that's all that matters.

I lift our intertwined hands and hold them to my chest. I got the girl and I'll be damned if I'm going to stand by while some asshole takes a swing at her. When she glances over at me, I say, "I love you, Kelley."

Her head whips toward me. "What?" she says, and it's nearly a shout.

I'm not sure if she didn't hear me or if she's shocked at what I said, but her hand really starts shaking now. I squeeze it for reassurance. It's crazy, and I know that, but watching Eric take a swing at her made everything clear for me. It's as if the blow to my head, the one meant for her, and the push of blood frantically rushing through me put my entire world into focus. I love her, I want her. And God forbid anyone ever try to hurt her. Ever.

Kelley pulls the truck over in front of my house and pops the curb. Then she turns in her seat to stare at me. "Are you okay?" she asks. "Eric hit you pretty hard. Did it affect your brain? Are you going into shock?"

I turn to face her. "Did he?"

She throws her hands out in question, and then I realize what she's talking about. "Oh, yeah, you mean the punch that was meant for you. No, he didn't hurt me. I barely felt it."

"I have a feeling when you come down from the adrenaline rush, you're going to feel it… you're going to feel a lot of things you regret."

CHAPTER TWENTY-SIX

Kelley

I start unloading my stuff, trying hard not to think about what he said. I'm sure I misunderstood. I'm sure he has some sort of concussion. When he grabs a box, I point inside the house. "Stop, you need to go sit for a while. Have some water and take a break."

"What are you talking about? I'm fine," he says, lifting the box.

I grab his hand and look over his knuckles. They're already bruising and the skin is broken. I prod his hand and say, "Does this hurt?"

"No." He tries to pull away. "It's completely fine." I glance up and look at his face, turning to see the side of his head where Eric hit him. He looks okay, but I don't believe it, and I can't help but look over my shoulder, expecting the police to show up. When he walks away with the box, I pull out my phone and text Megan.

Me: *How's Eric?*

Megan: *I'm sure his nose is broken. I'm taking him to the ER now.*

Me: *Good.*

And I mean about the broken nose, not that she's taking him into the ER. I don't care if he sees a doctor.

Megan: *WTF was that about? Why did Mac attack him?*

Me: *Are you kidding me? Mac didn't attack Eric. Eric attacked ME! Mac was defending me.*

Megan: *What? Are you serious?*

Me: *Dead.*

Megan: *How?*

Me: *He tried to hit me. When Mac pushed me out of the way, Eric hit him instead.*

Megan: *Seriously? Eric tried to hit you?*

Me: *Dead serious, Megan*

Am I speaking a foreign language right now?

Me: *He better not even think about pressing charges against Mac, or I'll press charges against him. Actually, WE will, since Mac's the one who was assaulted first and Mac's sister is a lawyer.*

Megan: *I'm sorry. Didn't get the whole story from Eric. I'll make sure he doesn't press charges.*

Me: *Thank you.*

When Mac steps back outside, he's texting someone too. I'm sure it's his sister. At least, I hope it is. I don't know how much pull Megan has with Eric and I'm worried this will affect Mac's job.

Mac looks up from his phone and says, "How's Eric?"

"How did you know I was texting Megan?"

He shrugs with a crooked grin. "I've got you figured out, I guess."

"I guess you do." I shake my head and say, "Megan says his nose is broken. She's taking him to the emergency room, but she says he won't press charges."

His eyebrows lift in question.

"At least, she says she'll talk him out of it, if he considers it."

"And you think…?"

"I think he'll try, or he'll at least threaten to. I don't think Megan has any real pull with him." I purse my lips and then say, "But who knows? I thought I knew them both—I was obviously wrong."

Mac approaches me. We're standing on his front porch, and Luna is circling us, fighting for our attention. I'm feeling a little shy after what he said in the car, also emotionally exhausted from my fight with Megan.

He wraps his arms around me and holds me against his chest for a long time. "I know you're worried about Megan and after everything I've heard and seen today, I am too."

His words drag feelings from me that I thought were dead. I don't know how, but he gets me. A little too well. With my face buried in his chest, I inhale the scent of clean laundry and sweat from loading and unloading boxes. The combination is intoxicating. I fight the emotions rising in me and make an effort to focus on him and not on people who don't deserve my attention. I don't want to care about Megan. I don't want to be worried, and God, more than anything, I don't want to cry on his shoulder about her, but I can't help myself.

She's having a baby without me.

These are the words that keep repeating in my head.

Megan knew exactly what to say to me. We've been talking about it for years. I wanted to be Auntie Kelley to her children. I'm an only child and she was the closest thing I've had to a sister. Especially since the Murphys cast me out.

I can't hold it in any longer. Mac's comfort shatters me, and before I can stop myself, I'm sobbing on his chest. I can't help it. He doesn't say anything, and I'm thankful.

After a couple of deep breaths, I try to wipe my face, but he beats me to it. His big hands brush the tears and then his soft, warm lips land on my forehead. Before I can say anything, a car pulls up behind his truck. He sighs and drops his forehead to mine.

"I'm sorry, I asked her not to come," Mac whispers.

I turn into the house. I don't want Emily to see me cry—anyone but her.

I go into Mac's bedroom and close the door behind me. I drop down onto the bed and sit there for a full minute before I start to feel stupid. How dumb of me to hide like a child. I force myself to stand and walk into the bathroom, checking out my puffy eyes. I take a deep breath and give myself a pep talk, then turn and walk back outside.

To my surprise, Emily is carrying a box into the house. She stops for a moment, then leans to set it down on top of another box. "Hi," she mutters nervously.

I nod hello to her and say, "Thank you, but you don't have to."

Mac snorts as he enters behind her with another box. "Yeah, she does."

Emily waves a dismissive hand at him and says, "I don't mind." She heads back out of the house. She's wearing jeans and a tank top, and she looks relaxed. More relaxed then I thought she could look.

"You okay?" Mac asks.

"Oh, yeah. Fine. Sorry," I say, fighting to keep my embarrassment from showing.

"No need to apologize, Kelley."

I look around at all my stuff sitting in Mac's beautiful home, and that only increases my discomfort. Compared to him and Emily, I'm a white trash, homeless girl. What made me think I could fit in here? Why did I think I could ever be good enough for him?

"Geez, Mac. Where are we going to put all this stupid stuff?" I ask. "Maybe I should have gotten a storage unit."

"What?" His brows draw together. "There's plenty of room, we just need to do some rearranging." He points to the truck and says, "Once your dresser is in the bedroom, you can put some clothes away. Then we'll put your bookcase in the office." He walks toward the hall. "Unless… unless you want your own? I can turn the guest room into an office for you. That'll give you a place to study and do schoolwork."

I brush off his idea and say, "You don't have to do that. I can work at Starbucks… that's usually where I work anyway."

"Don't do that, Kelley."

"Do what?"

"Act like this is temporary. Don't act like you don't belong here. I want this to be your home… I'm trying here, babe. Will you meet me halfway?"

I drop my head and close my eyes. "I'm sorry, I don't mean to seem ungrateful. I just feel… I feel like I'm intruding."

"Why? Because I haven't done or said anything to make you think I don't want you here."

"I know. You've been perfect. I'm sorry."

Emily bangs through the door with another box and says, "I offered to help, not to do all the work myself."

"Oh, sorry!" I say and rush outside to grab another box.

Two more trips and everything is in the house. It's a mess, and I'm trying not to show how guilty I feel about this. Mac and Emily carry my dresser into the bedroom, and I'm so glad when I see that it fits fine and actually complements his bedroom furniture.

"See," says Mac, and he has the biggest grin on his face, and that makes me smile. "You fit right in." His enthusiasm is starting to make me feel better, and I'm even starting to feel more comfortable around Emily.

When I refuse to let him convert his guest room into my study space, Mac makes room in his office for the bookcase, and as he's trying to fit it in, he's mumbling about the basement. I'm not paying much attention until I hear Emily say, "Oh, that's a great idea. It's large enough to be a studio."

This gets my attention. I slide the box of books in front of the bookcase and say, "What are you talking about?"

"The basement," Mac says. "I can hang some mirrors, add some lights. It's nice and cool down there all the time so… I don't know, but I thought I could turn it into a dance studio for you."

I stare at him, trying not to show how this makes me feel. I'm not sure I'm pulling it off until he asks, "Would you like that, Kelley?"

"Well, really," Emily says. "It's large enough to be a studio with some workspace or even a home gym. Put some exercise equipment down there too. Why didn't we think about that before? I mean, the space is just being wasted now. You don't have anything down there."

I blink several times, taking in what they're saying. Finally, I smile. I can't help myself. "You'd really do that?"

"Yeah." He shrugs. "Of course. If it's something you'd like…"

I place a hand on my chest and say, "I'd… I'd love that."

"Good, we'll do it. How about pizza?"

I lunge for him, flinging my arms around his neck. Mac squeezes me, keeping his arms tight for a moment, and I'm trying really hard not to cry. "Thank you for working so hard to make me feel at home."

He rubs his hand up and down my back before setting me on my feet. "I'm going to grab dinner, I'll be right back." His voice is soft and I wonder if he's also trying to hold back emotions.

Going out in search of dinner, Mac leaves Emily and me alone. I'm uncomfortable at first, but I'm trying to work through it. I know living here with Mac means I'm going to see a lot of his sister and I want to get along with her—I have to.

Once he's gone, Emily says, "Can we talk? Do you mind?"

I nod, but on the inside, I'm cursing at Mac for leaving me in this situation. I don't need the big sister talk again—I've already been through that with her.

Emily grabs us both a water bottle out of the fridge and sits at the table. She leans over toward me with her hand on her chest and says, "Kelley, I'm so sorry for what I did."

"For what you did?" I ask because I'm not exactly sure what she's referring to. I mean, it could be the background check, it could be the ambush at Starbucks, or it could be the annulment papers.

She chuckles uncomfortably, and it makes me a little pleased to see her off balance. "For leaving those files out like I did—actually, no." She shakes her head vigorously and says, "Not just that. I shouldn't have interfered at all. I'm sorry for requesting the background check. I'm sorry for getting those annulment papers ready... all of it." She takes a deep breath and blurts out, "I'm even sorry for cornering you at Starbucks. It was never my intention to make you uncomfortable. I should have just minded my own business."

By the time she's done listing all of the things she's sorry for, I'm frowning in discomfort. Getting used to people admitting when they're wrong is hard. "Thank you for apologizing. I know Mac is important to you, I understand your concern."

She reaches over and places her hand on mine. "Mac and my mom are all I have. He and I are very close, and I may be a little overprotective, but he's been through so much I feel it's my job to watch out for him."

"I understand. Having someone like that must be nice. Someone who cares enough to step out on a limb for you."

She smiles at me, and I see a hint of her brother in her expression. "You have that now too, Kelley."

My frown deepens because I'm not sure what she means.

"You have Mackensey. He cares deeply for you. I can see it in the way he looks at you. In the way he speaks about you. You're important to him, and because of that, you're important to me."

I'm speechless. This isn't what I was expecting. Mac said he loves me in the truck earlier but with everything else that's happened throughout the day I haven't even had time to process it. My brain is cloudy and I'm tired. Emily must recognize this because she holds her hands up and says, "I'm sorry. I don't mean to overwhelm you, but I wanted you to know I'm sorry. I hope we can get past it and be friends."

When I find my voice, I say, "I want that too."

Her grin spreads, and I return it. "Can I talk to you about something else?" Her eyebrows draw together, and she says, "Something in that file?"

Is this where the evil sister returns?

"If you don't want to talk about it, I'll drop it. It's up to you."

I relax a little. "Go ahead."

"I believe the Mankas Dance Company was in the wrong for canceling your contract."

I tilt my head in confusion because I was expecting this to be about the accident and the Murphys' car insurance. I wasn't expecting to talk about losing my contract. I don't remember much about it, the details are a little fuzzy. "I'm not sure what you mean."

"Okay." She shakes her head and squeezes her eyes closed as if trying to bring up a memory. "If I remember what I read correctly, they kicked you off the tour and ended your contract because of the morality clause. Does this sound familiar?"

"Yes," I say. "I don't have solid memories of that period, but I have a fairly good grasp of the facts as they were told to me."

"Right." she says. "Of course. It must be such a blur to you——I'm sorry."

"It's fine. I've had a long time to get past it."

"Well, from what I've read, I think we can dispute their claims. Did you know that your blood alcohol level was under the legal limit?"

My back straightens and shock surges through me. "No, that can't be right."

"It's right, Kelley. It's funny too because my investigator was able to access that part of your medical records. It's as if someone published your blood alcohol level on purpose. I think someone from your medical team recognized you were unfairly targeted, so they anonymously released the information."

"A fat lot of good that did me," I say.

"It's going to do you some good now." She narrows her eyes at me and says, "I'd like your permission to file a suit against Mankas."

I shake my head. "I don't think that's a good idea—I really don't want to go down that road again." I can't bear all the bad memories and the pain it'll drag up.

"Kelley, it could mean getting enough money to pay off your student loans. I can get them to pay all of the wages you should have received from that tour, plus interest."

"How can you do that?"

"The amount of alcohol in your system didn't even amount to a glass of wine. Did you know that?"

"No, I don't remember that night, but they acted like we were both falling down drunk when we got into that car."

"You weren't. Bradley's BAC also wasn't over the legal limit. It was higher than yours but he was point zero zero five under the limit. Of course, since the accident was his fault, it doesn't matter if he was legally drunk. He's responsible regardless. But it's entirely possible that no one, including Bradley, recognized that he was too impaired to drive." She leans over and pulls a notepad and pen from her purse. "Can you tell me, did the Mankas Dance Company ever have celebrations with alcohol?"

I stare at her, completely stunned. I let what she said sink in: Bradley wasn't drunk, I wasn't drunk. That changes everything… everything. Why didn't anyone tell me? "Are you sure about this?"

She looks at me with sympathetic eyes and again, I get a glimpse of her brother. "Yes, Kelley, it's all true. From what I gather, you had a drink, Bradley probably had two drinks, and probably a meal over the span of a couple of hours. Neither of you were legally drunk… but still, he didn't have to be. He was still the cause of the accident. Sometimes you don't need to be legally drunk to have impaired judgment."

I nod vigorously. "Of course. You're right." I take a minute to get my thoughts together. Then I say, "I'm sorry. What was your question?"

When she repeats herself, I respond and say, "Yes, all the time."

"Did they ever serve you or Bradley? Maybe even just a glass of champagne?"

"Many, many times. Anytime we had something to celebrate, they had champagne. Good reviews, when we wrapped up in a city and moving on to the next… any excuse."

"So, they allowed you to drink? You didn't have to sneak it when they weren't looking?"

"No, it's not like they carded us. They pretty much treated us all equally. Anyone over eighteen was considered an adult. They were only careful with the underage dancers… I mean, under eighteen."

"That's what I needed to know." She looks at me thoughtfully and says, "Can you come into my office one day this week so I can interview you?"

I can't believe she's offering to help, just like that. "Sure."

"We also need to talk about the Murphys," she says. "I believe their insurance should have covered your medical bills. At least a portion."

I think about the last five years of guilt I've been carrying around because of the accident. How I blamed myself. Beat myself up because I let Bradley drive his new car while he was drunk… and now I find out he wasn't really drunk. He was careless… *He* was careless. Not me. I'm reminded of the conversation I had with Mike about his parents and his comment about Bradley not being drunk. He's right. This *wasn't* my fault, and it wasn't Mike's fault either.

I stand up and pace the room, absolutely horrified that the Murphys let me struggle for all those years when I didn't have to. I can't believe what I'm hearing. How could they?

"I'm so sorry, Kelley. I'm sure this is hard for you to hear. I just wish you had had an attorney or at least an agent."

"I don't understand how they were able to get away with this." I lift my hand in question and say, "The Murphys and Mankas. How was this even possible?"

"They got away with it because it wasn't contested. Nobody argued in your defense. Who was handling your affairs back then, professionally?"

"My mother was my manager."

"I wish she had sought help for you—you should have been better protected."

I can't even defend my mom because I don't remember anything. The whole thing is a haze. "I didn't know. I was so devastated and broken over what happened that I did what they told me to do. I just faded away without a fight because they'd convinced me that I was negligent." I walk back over and sit down across from Emily, remembering how horrible I felt and how much I hated myself for what happened. "The guilt tore me apart. I believed it was my fault. I've been blaming myself for the last five years." I think about my mom and how much the accident changed her too. "I'm sure my mom felt the same way. As a parent, it must be hard to watch other people lose a child. It's a different kind of survivor's guilt."

I lean forward on the table, bracing my face in my hands, overwhelmed.

"Kelley, when I lost my husband, I fell into a void too. It's like the world continues to turn and you're stuck in one place, watching life go on without you."

I look up and meet her eyes because she's spot on. That's exactly how I felt for a very long time. I stopped caring about my life and just let things happen to me. "I'm sorry, Emily… about your husband."

Her mouth forms into a frown and she says, "Moving on is hard, isn't it?"

I nod. "Especially when it's so easy to just be numb and stop feeling."

She pats my hand and says, "I think you're further on in the process than I am… and thank God for that because my brother is in deep with you, honey."

"You think so?"

"Yes, I do." She lifts her hand and jots down another note before saying, "I've never seen him like this."

"Why do I feel like I'm waiting for the other shoe to drop?"

"Oh, hon, I can't blame you. I've seen the stuff in that file. You've had a rough go of it, of course you're afraid to trust the good when it comes your way. But you can't stay numb forever, Kelley. You can't stay living in a safe little cocoon for your whole life. You need to take a chance sooner or later… Why not take that chance with Mackensey?" Her eyes drop to the table, and her cheeks pink a little before she says, "I've watched you dance… on YouTube."

"Really?"

"Yes, and I have to say, you were fantastic. But do you know what made you so good? What made you so fun to watch? What entranced your audience?"

I laugh and say, "Bradley's ass?"

She laughs too, and I'm glad we're sharing this moment. It makes me feel closer to Mac to be close to his sister.

"I do not deny Bradley had a nice ass," she says, but then she gets serious again. "What was so amazing about your dancing was that you were fearless when you were up onstage. You owned the performance without regret. You were incredible with Bradley, but alone, you were completely fearless and free."

I think about that, and I know she's right. I don't ever remember having doubts when I danced—I just did it, I just lived it. Decisions weren't made on the dance floor, everything came from instinct. Dance is a part of me even now, it's something that never goes.

"My point is," Emily says, "you should live your life like that. Love Mackensey like that."

I look up at her quickly because I wasn't expecting that.

"Be fearless about your life, like you were fearless about dancing."

CHAPTER TWENTY-SEVEN

Mackensey

When I enter the house with the pizza, the girls are sitting at the table, their gazes locked. This makes me curious about what I just walked in on. They don't look angry, but they do look very intense.

"Everything okay, ladies?"

They both nod… at the same time. That makes me nervous. I lay the pizza down in front of them, and this seems to break the spell.

"I'm starving," Emily says. "I hope it's the veggie."

"Prepare yourself for disappointment," I say, trying for a sweet smile.

Kelley leans forward and inhales, then gives me a questioning look. "What kind of pizza is this?"

I stop midway between placing a paper plate down in front of her. "It's chicken and bacon with garlic white sauce and roasted red peppers."

"No way!" she says. "I don't believe you."

Emily lifts the box lid to show the chicken and bacon pizza with garlic white sauce and roasted red peppers.

"Get out!" Kelley says, slapping her hand down on the table. "I don't believe this."

"It's my favorite," I say, thoroughly confused.

"It's *my* favorite." she says. "How is it that we always pick the same food?"

Her cheerfulness brightens my mood. I give her a heated look and say, "Great minds, babe."

I look over at Emily, and she's smiling too. A real smile even, not one of those fake ones she flashes when she's trying to be polite.

"So, what did I miss?" I ask.

Emily waves away my question and says, "Nothing much. Just discussing some of Kelley's options for dealing with… some old stuff. I'll let her tell you."

"Oh, okay." I get it. Emily can't share it with me if Kelley's going to be her client, so if I want to know, Kelley will have to tell me. Which is fine. I hope we're at the point where we'll share everything with each other. This party needs a boost anyway and I'm sure talking about Kelley's past will not improve the atmosphere.

When we've stuffed our bellies with pizza, we spend a little more time organizing Kelley's things. Or at least moving the boxes out of the way so she can work on it later. I get the feeling she's not comfortable with us helping her unpack. That, or she's still not comfortable with us living together. This thought makes me a little nervous. Especially since I'm all in. I'm one hundred percent into her and this relationship. The more I think about it, and the more time I spend with her, the more I want to be with her. It's no joke either, it's intense. Scary intense—the pounding I gave Eric is proof of that. As much as I want to kill the bastard, I'm a little thankful for the knock to my head. Seeing him go after her woke something inside of me. It's strong, primal.

I walk Emily out and spend a few minutes talking to her on the curb next to her car. It hasn't escaped my attention that while I have an amazing person inside the house waiting for me, my sister is going home alone. Emily spends far too much time alone, and that kills me.

"Thank you for your help today."

"It's the least I can do," she says, lifting on tiptoes to hug me. "Are you two going to be okay?"

"Why do you ask?"

"It seems a bit intense... I can't quite put my finger on it, but something seems... unsaid."

I chuckle at her because if Emily can do anything, it's read a room. She's spot on, too. "I blurted out an *I love you* on the way back from her old apartment. After breaking Eric's nose."

Her eyes widen. "Oh, I see. Wow, you picked your timing." She glances at the house, then back at me. "Did you mean it?"

I sigh and nod as a lump forms in my throat. I understand what I've been missing in my life, the Kelley-shaped hole she's filled, but Emily's already had that and lost it. I guess I don't want to rub it in.

She brushes her hand up and down my arm. "You okay, Mackensey?"

I nod again and say, "I'm perfect. Really. I said the words and I meant them. I know it's crazy, Em, but I feel so sure about this and about her. My only hesitation is whether or not I can make her happy."

"All you have to do is love her, Mac. That's all she needs. Your love and support. Make her the most important thing in your life, and everything will work out."

I brush her off and try for a smug grin. "That's easy." I pretend to crack my knuckles and say, "I got this."

She laughs, eyes crinkling at the corners. "Okay, smartass. Get in there and help her get settled."

I wait for Emily to pull away from the curb before I close the door. Once I'm back inside, I find Kelley in the bedroom, putting her clothes away. When I enter, she says, "I heard from Megan. She said not to worry about Eric, he's too embarrassed to press charges against you."

"Embarrassed? Why? Because he got his ass handed to him?"

She laughs with a wide, open-mouthed smile and says, "And he knows it'll be all over the radio if he pursues it."

"Smart guy," I say as she stands upright and stretches her back.

"It's going to be so nice not having to live out of a duffle bag."

I reach out and take the bag from her and toss it aside. She gives me a concerned look as I turn to face her. "Are you okay? Any headaches or anything?"

"I'm perfect—more than perfect."

My smile must make her nervous because her gaze drops to the floor. I sit down on the bed so that I can look up at her. I reach out and touch her chin until her eyes meet mine. "I meant what I said, Kelley. I know you think it was some concussion-induced mania, but it wasn't: I love you."

Now her eyes are unmoving as they're locked on mine, and it's as if she's trying to detect a lie. As if she's staring through me, but I don't care. I want her to see what's inside—she'll know how I feel.

She finally blinks and says, "Why, Mac?"

"Because you're exceptional. Because you have a kind soul. Because I've never felt complete until now. My entire life I've been missing something, and now I know it's you." I snicker and say, "Do you know that I never understood why people would legally tie themselves to someone else for life? It's such a huge commitment. The entire concept of marriage scared the crap out of me… and confused me, but now, now I get it."

She cups my face with her hands and says, "But I'm a mess. How can someone as perfect as you love someone who's such a mess?"

"You're a beautiful mess." I pull her closer so that we're nose to nose. "I'm not perfect, just perfect for you and you're *my* beautiful mess."

She straddles my lap and wraps her arms around my neck. Our eyes are locked again, and hers are heating as she stares. I can almost feel her body grow molten in my hands. "Mac, I want you to know something."

I kiss her lips and run my hands under her shirt as she's talking. Before she can finish, I tug the t-shirt over her head and reach between her breasts to unsnap her bra. When her breasts bounce free, it's like Christmas in May. "I'm listening," I moan, as I pull her nipple between my lips.

"I… I love you too, but I want you to know that I'm…" When her voice pitches higher, it almost sounds like a whine. I stop and look up into her eyes. "I've been fighting against these feelings since we were in Reno," she says, and the words rush out. "I'm so relieved to say it. When I was in Oakland, I was so miserable without you. I was so unhappy… I couldn't believe I'd lost you so quickly… and I—"

"Baby," I say, and my stomach flutters as I look into her sincere, green eyes. "Baby, you need to get those damn clothes off before I rip them from your body."

She jumps off my lap, and I'm glad she's taking this seriously because I'm about to burst through my jeans. She drops her pants as I do the same.

I reach out to run my hand down her sinuous midsection and I know I'm the epitome of a man in love with his wife. *Wife.*

If I've ever done anything right in my life, it was getting drunk with this woman and making her mine. I have no regrets. None.

I grab her hand and pull her closer. She straddles my lap smoothly then gradually lowers herself down on my cock. Her heat is intense and all-consuming. As she settles and leans in for a kiss, I want to growl in satisfaction, but all I can do is mutter the word, "Mine."

EPILOGUE

Kelley

One year later

I'm a little early, but I don't think he'll mind. It's our first anniversary... kind of. It's the first anniversary of our drunken wedding in Reno, and Mackensey wants to celebrate. If anything, we should be celebrating a year of sobriety for him. No matter though, I'm just happy to have him to myself for the evening. Between preparing for my finals, and planning for graduation, I haven't had much time to devote to Mac. He's always so patient and understanding though and that makes me grateful for everything that's happened over the previous year.

I haven't just gained an amazing man, but I've also gained a sister in Emily.

Emily has fought relentlessly for me. The Mankas Dance Company finally, finally agreed to settle and I'm so glad we didn't have to go to court. It was hanging over me and thank goodness I didn't have to go through with it. Thanks to Emily, I also received a smaller settlement from the Murphys' insurance. We didn't push for much. Knowing the Murphys let me suffer for years paying off the medical debt, and hid the fact that Bradley was covered under their insurance, made it easy to petition for money I should have been paid years ago. Not wanting to sit in court and relive everything, we only asked for enough to cover the remaining balance on my medical bills.

But I have come to terms with my own feelings for Bradley's parents. I no longer care to mend my relationship with them. They're not the people I thought they were. Between what they did to me and the way they've treated their surviving children, I decided I don't want to have them in my life. I'm not responsible for Bradley's death, and I'm coming to grips with that fact. After years, I am starting to accept it. I was a victim. A victim of theirs and a victim of the Mankas Dance Company, who were trying to deflect attention away from them by pointing fingers at me.

So, due to Emily and her persistence, I'm expecting to receive a check any day now. A check I desperately need to pay off the rest of my tuition. Thanks to Mac, I've caught up on most of my debt. Having a year of no rent and minimal expenses has made a huge difference. I wish there were a way to repay him, but being here with him, showing him respect, and loving him is the best that I have.

When I slip into the private dining room Mac reserved, I see that he's already there. Of course he is. What made me think I could beat him to the restaurant? He stands and leans in for a kiss, and has a familiar smile on his face. I'm wearing a black halter dress that exposes my back. Mac pulls out my chair and lays his hands on my shoulders before running them down my arms and whispering, "You look amazing. Did you wear that dress to torture me?"

I wink up at him because it was his birthday gift to me. "Yes, of course I did, and thank you. You look pretty scrumptious yourself."

He returns to his chair, still wearing the same knowing smile. It's the one he has when he wants to share a secret.

"What are you hiding right now?" I ask.

"Hiding? What do you mean?" he says, and the smile tips up on one side.

"I think you know exactly what I mean."

The waiter walks up and takes our drink orders, and I find it funny when they're always disappointed that we don't order expensive alcoholic drinks. It amazes me that Mac is never tempted. Except, of course, that one time. It makes me wonder where we'd be today if it weren't for that one time.

"Did you see Megan today?" he asks.

"Yeah, we had lunch at El Placer."

"And… how'd it go?" He leans forward and says, "Did she bring the baby?"

I can't hide the grin that breaks out across my face. "Yes, and my God, he's adorable."

"I guess by this stage they've lost the alien, newborn look."

"Little Brandon is absolutely perfect," I say. "She's doing well. I think she's actually thriving as a single parent."

"She didn't have much choice. When Eric left her, she just had to decide to get through it and then keep moving forward. I'm proud of her."

I roll my eyes and reluctantly admit, "Yeah, I guess I am too."

"She made a lot of bad decisions… a lot of mistakes, but she's trying."

"I know." I wave a hand of surrender. "Forgiving and forgetting isn't easy, but I'm trying. Baby steps."

"I'm proud of you too, babe. I know it's hard to move forward with someone who hurt you the way she did, but I think you're a better person for it."

I think about what he says and that familiar little spike of pain radiates through me when I think about what Megan did. Mac's one of the few people who really understands the damage done. The trust lost. Megan is realizing it too. It's not about Eric, it never was about him. It's about having the one person you trust the most betray you. The one person who's always in your corner, the one person you wholeheartedly relied on and leaned on for support, that person conniving behind your back, lying to your face, breaking your heart in the process.

After months of talking with Megan, I've grown to believe she's not at fault for sleeping with Eric that first time. He took advantage of her that night. Megan had to have been too drunk to give consent. She's tried to convince herself that she went along with it because that's easier to accept than admitting that Eric took advantage of her, but in truth, she doesn't remember anything. I know that if she'd been sober, she would have made a different choice.

Eric's proven over and over that he's not beyond taking advantage of people. He has no scruples. She never should have been too embarrassed or ashamed to tell me the truth. As her best friend, she should have been able to come to me, and that's what she and I are working through together. We have to, especially now that Eric's out of the picture. He took off as soon as he found out she was pregnant.

"I have something for you," Mac says and it brings me out of my thoughts.

"You do? I thought we weren't exchanging gifts for this odd occasion."

He lifts a shoulder and says, "This is different."

I grin at him because I have something for him too. "Well, it's a good thing I didn't come empty-handed."

"Oh, you little cheater! You brought me a gift?"

"Well, sort of. Do you want to go first?"

"Indeed, I do." He reaches into his pocket and pulls out a white jewelry box. It's larger than a ring box, but smaller than a bracelet.

I gasp, and wish he hadn't spent money on me. I already have everything I could possibly want. "What have you done?"

He hands it over and says, "It's not that huge so don't get excited."

I take the box from him and lift the lid. It's a beautiful pendant... actually, it's a locket. "Oh, wow, it's beautiful, babe."

I pull it from the box and realize it's not on a chain.

"Open it," he says.

I click the latch and snap open the top of the locket. On the right side is a tiny mirror, on the left an inscription.

My beautiful mess

"Oh, my God, baby, I love it!" I hold it up and stare at my tearful expression in the tiny mirror.

"It's for your chain," he says and leans over to tug at the heavy gold necklace I've been wearing for the last year, the chain that holds our wedding rings. "I don't want it to look bare when I take my ring back."

My head snaps up to look at him. "What?"

Before I have time to react, Mac is on his knees next to me and he's holding another white jewelry box. This one is smaller...

"Kelley, thank you for the last year of wonder and perfection. Now that you're finished with school, I would love the honor of being your husband, and I would love for you to be my wife." His eyes are glassy and his hands are shaking, and I'm so humbled by this man I can barely speak. Before I have a chance to respond, he says, "I know this is weird, but I want you to have the wedding you've always dreamed of... the life you've dreamed of and the family you've always wanted. I will give you all of that." He lifts the lid, and I'm almost blinded by the sparkle.

"Oh my God, Mackensey..." My eyes tear up, and I reach out to cup his face.

"Is that a yes?"

I nod frantically. "Of course it's a yes. It's always been a yes. You've already given me everything I've ever wanted—I don't need another ring."

He lifts to his feet and brings me with him. When his arms come around me, I lay my head on his chest and know that I couldn't have dreamed of anything better... of anyone better.

He pulls away and tugs the ring from the box. "I had this made especially for you," he says.

I look down and examine the ring as he slips it on my finger— it's an infinity band of diamonds. Mac points to the ring and says, "There's a diamond for every hour we knew each other before we were married in Reno."

I gasp, and I turn the ring on my finger. "Oh, babe. I love it."

"It seemed weird to get an engagement ring at this stage so I went straight for the anniversary band. You can wear it alone or with the gold band."

I remove the chain from around my neck and pull off the rings. Mac helps me add the locket to the chain, and he drapes it back around my neck. I take the larger gold ring and hold it out. "Does that mean you're ready to wear this?"

He grins so widely, it makes me smile too. "I'm more than ready."

I slip the ring on his left hand, and it's still a perfect fit. He takes my left hand, kisses my ring finger, and slips my gold band on with the diamond one. "Start thinking about what kind of wedding you want, okay?" he says.

I take a moment to think about that, then I chuckle. "Reno?"

He laughs too and says, "I think we can do better than that this time around. Maybe even think about inviting our mothers."

When our dinners arrive, we try to settle into our food but we're both so distracted. On my third bite, Mac says, "Oh, I almost forgot." He pulls an envelope from the inside pocket of his jacket and says, "This is for you too."

"What's this?" I ask, eyeing the envelope.

"It's from Emily, she asked me to deliver it for her."

I tear the flap and peek inside. "It's a check... holy crap!" I throw a hand over my mouth and mumble, "A very large check." Stunned, I pull it from the envelope and stare at it for a moment before handing it to Mac. "It's more than I thought. A lot more."

"Nice!" He looks it over and says, "Now you can buy the dance school outright from Mary."

My eyes widen, and I say, "You think so?"

"Oh, yeah," he says. "I'm sure… and if that's not enough, I can contribute some."

"Mac, no, you've already done so much for me."

He gives me a challenging look and says, "Try to stop me."

I lift an eyebrow and say, "Well, Mackensey, are you done handing out the gifts? Because I have one for you."

"We agreed no gifts today," he says, frowning.

"And you went against that agreement, so now I am," I say smugly. I reach into my purse and pull out an envelope and hand it to him.

He opens it and pulls out my new driver's license and Social Security card. "Why are you giving me— Oh, my God, shit just got real!" he says.

I wiggle my ring finger at him and say, "What are you talking about? It got real when you gave me diamonds. That's nothing compared to this."

He lifts his eyes to me, and they're glassy again. I can see that he's touched. I knew he'd like it if I took his name, but I guess I didn't understand how much it really meant to him. A lump forms in my throat, and I try to clear it before saying, "Are you happy?"

"Are *you* happy?" he asks, his voice thick.

"I've never been happier in my life," I say. "Thank you for that."

He reaches over and takes my hand before kissing it. "Mrs. Kelley Thomas, your happiness is all I've wanted since the moment I laid eyes on you."

A LETTER FROM DANA

I want to say a huge thank you for choosing to read *Accidental Groom*. As a reader, I understand how many options we have for great stories in today's market, and that's why I'm so glad you decided to choose mine. I can't thank you enough for your support. If you enjoyed it, and want to keep up-to-date with all my latest releases, including the second installment of the Accidental Love Series, just sign up at the following link. I promise I won't fill your inbox, but I'll keep you updated on what's happening with my books. Your email address will never be shared, and you can unsubscribe at any time.

www.bookouture.com/dana-mason

I hope you loved reading *Accidental Groom* as much as I enjoyed writing it and if you did, I'd be very grateful if you could write a review. Even just a few words and a star rating go a long way toward helping new readers discover my books for the first time, and I can't wait to hear what you think.

I love hearing from my readers and encourage you to connect with me on my Facebook page, through Twitter, Goodreads or my website.

Thanks,
Dana Mason

 danamason06

 @danamason06

 danamasonromance.com

ACKNOWLEDGEMENTS

I have an amazing husband. He picks up everything I drop. He brings me chocolate when I need a fix. He makes me move when I sit too long staring at a blank page. He's always there for me, and because of him, I get to fulfill my dreams. Jim, thank you. I love you more than you know and I'm so glad I get to grow old with you.

I want to thank my family for their constant support and understanding, including my extended family and friends who have sent countless tweets and shared countless posts on Facebook.

Nancy G. and Linda, thank you so much for your support and feedback. You've both been here from the beginning, and that means everything to me. Katie, Nancy T., Paige, thank you so much for your valuable feedback and for always dealing with my obsessive questions. Thank you all for reading every word I send you. I'm forever grateful for having you ladies in my life. You always have my back, even when I'm wrong. Thank you for never playing the devil's advocate, because sometimes a gal just needs to commiserate with people who understand. Lisa, you are a rock star! Ditto on all of the above and thank you for pushing me, and pushing me, and not giving up on me even when I wanted to give up on myself.

Christina Demosthenous, thanks for seeing a story through my hazy, haphazard, and vague list of ideas and thank you for offering me a place in this amazing publishing family. I'm so happy to be here.